Clerical Union

Catholic papers written by different persons and read at several times before the meetings of the Clerical Union in New York and Philadelphia, U.S.A

Clerical Union

Catholic papers written by different persons and read at several times before the meetings of the Clerical Union in New York and Philadelphia, U.S.A

ISBN/EAN: 9783741189791

Manufactured in Europe, USA, Canada, Australia, Japa

Cover: Foto ©Andreas Hilbeck / pixelio.de

Manufactured and distributed by brebook publishing software (www.brebook.com)

Clerical Union

Catholic papers written by different persons and read at several times before the meetings of the Clerical Union in New York and Philadelphia, U.S.A

Table of Contents.

CATHOLIC PAPERS.

Isaac Lea Nicholson,

BY DIVINE PERMISSION BISHOP

OF MILWAUKEE,

To the Reader Health and Benediction.

I COUNT it an honour, that I am asked by my brethren to write a few lines, as a Commendatory Preface, to this helpful book, which they are about to issue. . As one of the members, since its first inception in 1887, of the Society of Priests, in our American Church, known as "The Clerical Union, for the Maintenance and Defence of Catholic Principles," I have fully realized the large benefits resulting from that association— composed strictly of brethren who are all of

one mind, theologically speaking—in God's Great
House. It aided me in many a moment of
doubt, it comforted me in many an hour of
depression, amidst the large cares of a busy
parochial life; when infidelity, unbelief, cunning
and unscrupulous criticism, in so many of our
pulpits, seemed at times to unsettle one's faith
in the Church's solid position; and disturb that
quiet serenity which should steadily prevail
within the priest's mind, while going daily about
"the Father's business," here in the very Body
of Christ, the Church of the Living God, the
Pillar and Ground of His Truth.

I am grateful, therefore, that a few of the
essays, read at first only for our mutual edification, are now to appear in book form and be
given to the reading public, within and without
the Church. May Almighty God be pleased to
bless these pages, and make them the means

of helping others who are weak, lifting up some who are down, and making straight paths for their feet, as daily they "walk about Sion," and try to tell the beauty thereof.

To me, it seems that at no time in the chequered history of our Anglican Communion has there been more need than now, of a clear and distinct statement of the real faith, belief, and position of this Church wherein our lot is forever cast. At no time has there been a more imperative demand for the definite shewing of the real basis and meaning of our Prayer-Book doctrine and teaching, told in a genuine, historic, and undiluted way, than now. The Church, under the bewitchment of the hour, is even being miserably misled, and egregiously fooled, as to what that simple term "Catholic" means. No one word, in ecclesiastical language, is just now · being more abused, defiled, mutilated in its real

meaning, and juggled with, than is this venerable and historic word—Catholic. We think
these pages are most useful in shewing what
"Catholic" teaching really is (and always has been)
on some important questions of theology and
morals,—"Catholic" in its real and true sense ;
which is the only ancient and historical sense,
the sense it has held in the Apostles', the
Nicene, and the Athanasian Creeds, from the
beginning and ever shall continue to hold. Of
course, in these pages no regard is paid to that
modern notion concerning this noble word "Catholic," which makes it mean anything and everything, *except* definite belief ;—indeed, some hopeless jumble of indefinite *unbelief.* And while
on all sides to-day we hear it said (even in
some caricatures of Christian pulpits), that the
more hazy, uncertain, intangible, "liberal," one's
faith and belief may be, the more truly "Catholic" he is, we answer, 'God forbid!'

"There are, it may be, so many kinds of voices in the world, and none of them is without signification." As of old in St. Paul's day, so now;— many are these voices heard in the Church, and far too many of them with a very bad signification. We have this half-mad craze after a so-called "Church Unity," which looks to some like an attempt to unite Christ and Belial. We have the popular craze of a so-called "Liberalism," and undenominationalism. We have the craze of "Universalism," in the awfully important matter of the eternal state of men, after death. We have the conceited craze of a sort of "literary vivisection" over the words, and meaning of Holy Scripture—so painfully unsettling to the faith of some. Many, indeed, are these voices going out to day; and their din and confusion, to those who long for a stable faith, and fixed convictions in religious belief, verily is only as the discordant cry from another huge Tower of Babel, rising before our eyes! Amidst them all, may the Holy Ghost shew us what is the Catholic Faith, "whole and entire; what *is* "the Voice of the Lord," that glorious voice, so mighty in operation, which we can confidently follow, till at last we reach—

> " Those eternal bowers,
> Man hath never trod!"

And before that voice, as it passes by, let us "stand still, and *see* the Salvation of God."

Is it altogether a vain hope, or a wasted prayer, that these pages, all written by loyal and loving brethren, in our common priesthood, may enable some anxious souls the better to discern the sound of that voice, and to understand His will, so that hereafter they may be more "valiant for the truth upon the earth"? Perhaps, too, this book, and what it aims to teach, may draw others of the brethren to cast in their lot with our "Clerical Union;" and all the more strongly to preach the everlasting Gospel of Jesus Christ and His Church, after the determined manner of those who can confidently say with the Psalmist, "I *believed*, and therefore have I spoken."

✠ I. L. NICHOLSON.

President of the Clerical Union.

MILWAUKEE,

Nat. S. John Bap: 1893.

Introduction.

THERE is abroad a spirit of unrest, a spirit of rebellion against restraint, a spirit of compromise with the object of gaining an apparent peace. We are told that old truths must be presented in new ways, that the old formulas of orthodox belief must be given a new meaning, fitted to the spirit of the age in which we live, if they are to be retained at all; that the controversies of the sixteenth century interest nobody any more and that the literature of that period, its articles, confessions, synodal definitions—all must be tossed aside as worthless rubbish; that the race is moving onward, and has attained a deeper grasp of truth, which after all is only relative at best, and that the Incarnation is being more and more realized not in one person, the Son of God made man, the Saviour and Redeemer of the world, but in the divine human race, following in the steps of that noblest incarnation, the Christ of Nazareth. Only lately the assembled bishops of the whole Anglican Church issued a declaration which to the popular understanding said that they were willing to admit into Catholic communion any body of schismatics or heretics who accepted Holy Scripture, would receive the episcopate, administer two of the sacraments and believe the creeds! They might be Pelagians, or Adoptionists, or Eutychians, or Nestorians, or Monothelites, or Zwinglians, or Lutherans, or Calvinists, or Baptists, or Universalists, or the believers of any other blasphemy, and yet—so the world misunderstood our bishops—they could be received at our altars.

This spirit is spreading, and spreading not by honest, open declarations, but by dishonest, underhand methods, and the faith is being sapped away by those who are its sworn defenders, and who are reaping the wages paid them for building up that which, so far as they are able, they are plucking down. Of all those thus attacking the everlasting Gospel, the most dangerous are not they who openly come out and profess the "higher criticism" so-called; it is not the Cheynes, and Drivers, and Ryles; it is not those who flout the church's doctrines and the ecclesiastical spirit, such as Farrar, and Blakeney, and Freemantle; it is not these that are the most dangerous: it is they who pretend to be themselves sound in the faith, devoted to the Church, firm believers in the sacraments and in supernatural grace, and who coquette with rationalists with the hope (so they tell us) of winning them by concessions; who wish to make all things smooth and easy in Christianity; who minimize its mysteries and its demands upon faith, until the faith is gone altogether; who say they are trying to allay anxiety and remove uncertainty, while all the time they are grieving the hearts of the faithful and casting the weak and the wavering into the pit of unbelief. These are the Church's most dangerous foes, and because they may be outwardly holy in their lives, we must not allow that to close our eyes to their deadly heresy. Eutyches, the heretic, was of most holy life, and such has been the case with many another.

No advice of the ancients was wiser than *ab hoste doceri*, and I quote here the words of one who was as bitter a foe of our holy religion (though educated within its very walls) as can be found, the famous Ernest Rénan. In his *Recollections of My Youth* he makes these weighty remarks :

"One of the worst kinds of intellectual dishonesty is to play upon words, to represent Christianity as imposing scarcely any sacrifice upon reason, and in this way to inveigle people into it without letting them know to what they have committed themselves. This is where Catholic laymen, who dub themselves liberals, are under such a delusion. Ignorant of theology and exegesis, they treat accession to Christianity as if it were a mere adhesion to a coterie. They pick and choose, admitting one dogma and rejecting another, and then they are very indignant if anyone tells them that they are not true Catholics. *No one who has studied theology can be guilty of such inconsistency, as in his eyes everything rests upon the* INFALLIBLE AUTHORITY OF THE SCRIPTURE AND THE CHURCH ; he has no choice to make. To abandon a single dogma or reject a single tenet in the teaching of the Church is equivalent to the rejection of the Church and of Revelation. In a church founded upon divine authority, it is as much an act of heresy to deny a single point as to deny the whole. If a single stone is pulled out of the building, the whole edifice must come to the ground. Nor is there any good to be gained by saying the Church will, perhaps, some day make concessions which will avert the necessity of ruptures. . . . I am perfectly well aware how far the Church can go in the way of concession, and I know what are the points upon which it is useless to ask her for any. . . . For the Catholic Church to admit that Daniel was an apocryphal person of the time of the Maccabees would be to admit that she had made a mistake; if she was mistaken in that, she may have been mistaken in others, and she is no longer divinely inspired."

It would seem that the great trouble with us is that our writers have not " studied theology," and therefore they have no appreciation of the awful havoc they are working, nor of the nonsense they are talking. Each man thinks he has some new light to throw upon the subject, and the Incarnation, the Atonement, the Inspiration of the Divine Scriptures, etc., etc., are treated of as if no thought had ever been bestowed upon them before; and the result of these original nineteenth-century efforts is usually to revive some exploded heresy of a thousand years standing, all of which the author would have known had he first " studied theology," and the Church would have been saved the scandal of having one of its clergy write, and many in its priesthood, both bishops and presbyters, approve, that which is in reality most ignorant heresy and blasphemy. What must be the effect upon the man of the world of this emasculated, non-vertebrate Christianity? It can be nothing but to produce a feeling of contempt.

It was to oppose such a destruction of our Holy Faith that " the Clerical Union for the maintenance and defence of Catholic Principles" was organized. The Christianity which we profess is undiluted with German water, unseasoned with luxury's spices—it is the robust, uncompromising Christianity of the ages past, the Christianity (minus the innovations) of which Rénan speaks when he says:

" The Catholicism which was taught me is not the insipid compromise, suitable only for laymen, which has led to so many misunderstandings in the present day. My Catholicism was that of Scripture, of the councils, and of the theologians. This Catholicism I loved, and I still respect it; having found it inadmissible, I separated myself from it." This is honest. To the demand of God, "And let all the angels of God worship him," there came once again the answer, *Non serviam.* Rénan weighed the Revelation of the Infinite in the scales of his finite reason and found it wanting! In what pleasant contrast is the honesty of the French rationalist to much that we see about us to-day! So deeply must this be the feeling of every devout churchman, that I feel the reader will be glad to know these words of the same brilliant author : " But with my notions at once precise and respectful of Catholicism, I could not succeed in conceiving any honourable way of remaining a Catholic priest while retaining my opinions. I was Christian after the fashion of a professor of theology at Halle or Tubingen. An inward voice told me, ' Thou art no longer a Catholic ; thy robe is a lie ; cast it off.' " If our clergy had the same honesty, and would for " Catholic " substitute " Episcopal," what a blessed purification there would be! But loss of faith usually brings with it loss of morals, and we need not look for much of " honour " or " honesty " in those who have made shipwreck of the faith.

With these words of general introduction to shew the spirit of our Union, I proceed to the matters which we considered the principal errors of the day. For convenience we have divided them into four heads. First, All those opinions which, directly or indirectly, deny the consubstantial Godhead of the Eternal Word, or else shew their adherents to have an imperfect grasp of the Incarnation. Second, All those opinions which are subversive of due order and precedence, of the rights of prop-

erty and of the powers of the State, and would overthrow
those distinctions and grades of life which have been
established by Almighty God for the good of mankind,
and of which the Catechism so plainly speaks in teaching the young their duty to their neighbour : " to submit myself to all my governors, teachers, spiritual pastors
and masters ; to order myself lowly and reverently to all
my betters." Third, All those opinions which tend to
lessen the sense of the enormity of sin, whether original
or actual, if not to deny its very existence ; all such
opinions of God as would teach that he could not or
would not punish everlastingly ; all such opinions as
would so consider the mercy of the Father as to forget
or deny the justice of that God who is revealed to us as
" a consuming fire." And fourth, All those opinions
which exalt the human intelligence and make it, in practice at least, the judge of divine revelation ; all such
opinions as would shake the traditional acceptance which
the Divine Scriptures have received as the written Word
of God ; all such opinions as would take from the pleni-
tude of our Lord's knowledge as a teacher, and would
throw doubt upon the truth of his words, either because
of a supposed self-inflicted ignorance or because of lack
of illumination.

We feel that the principal and most dangerous attacks
which are being made upon Christ and his Church fall
under one or other of these heads, and therefore we have
Four Credenda which we require to be accepted by all
those becoming members of our " Union."

We consider the safest and most perfect remedy to
Arianism and kindred errors of the first class, to be a
sound faith in the Mystery of the Holy Eucharist, and
therefore our first doctrinal statement is as follows :

1. I believe that our Lord, really and objectively present in the Eucharist under the forms of bread and wine, is to be adored.

We consider that the full acceptance of the Ecclesiastical Hierarchy, possessed of absolute and exclusive power in the spiritual domain, is the surest remedy for the errors of Socialism, Communism, Anarchism, etc., etc., and therefore our second statement is as follows:

2. I believe the Priesthood received from Bishops in Apostolical Succession to be necessary to the valid administration of all the sacraments except Baptism and Matrimony.

We consider that the only effectual check which can be given to sensuality and luxury, sins which we believe to be intimately connected with errors of the third class, is that provided by our Blessed Lord himself, when he told us of "the worm that dieth not and of the fire that is not quenched," and that the denial of the doctrine of Christianity that the unending life hereafter depends upon the works done in the body, whether good or evil, can only result in bringing in a flood of immorality and crime. Therefore we have framed our third declaration as follows:

3. I believe that to every human soul God gives during the time of this life sufficient grace to escape damnation; I believe that as Probation consists in the struggle of the soul against sin and Satan, it is limited to this life; and that at the hour of death every soul passes into "an endless and unchangeable state."

We consider that the affirmation of the plenary inspiration of the Holy Scriptures and of their immunity from error is the only remedy for the poison of Rationalism, Latitudinarianism and other errors of the fourth class, and therefore our fourth credendum reads as follows:

    4. I believe the Holy Scriptures of the Old and New Testaments to be inspired by God in a manner wholly different from all other writings, and so that they are "the infallible and undeceivable Word of God," and whatever is contained in them is true.

In the following pages we propose to treat of each one of these points theologically, and to shew their importance, if Christ is to be followed and sin to be overcome.

The First Declaration.

OF THE HOLY EUCHARIST.

A S our Lord Jesus Christ is both God and man, it would seem to be impossible that anyone pretending to accept this great truth should affirm a presence of the Son of God which should not be adored, and yet we find that such is the case and that there are among us some who declare that they believe "The Real Presence," but at the same time consider all adoration of the Christ present under the sacramental veils as idolatry or idolatrous. Now it requires but little thought to see that such persons are really unsound in their faith as touching the Incarnation of our Lord Jesus Christ, and that they are either Arians or Nestorians, or else that they entertain one of the numerous modifications of these two deadly heresies.

Of course, a man may be perfectly sound upon the question of the incarnation and deny the worship of the sacrament altogether, but this is only the case when he denies that under the sacramental forms is the presence of his God. To affirm a presence of God the Son and to deny divine worship to that Presence is nothing but Arianism, veil the unbelief in what language you will. Some have affirmed the awful doctrine that what is present is dead Christ, and therefore, they say, there is no place for adoration. But this only shews their failure to believe aright the incarnation of the Son of God, for the Divine Person of the Son was united, not only to the soul, but also

and equally to the body of the Child of Mary, and therefore (as has ever been held and as they should have learned
long ago from our own Pearson *On the Creed*) each separately is the object of divine worship; the dead body of
the Lord in the sepulchre being as truly the body of God
as the soul in the place of departed spirits was the soul of
God.   Even, then, if the presence in the sacrament were
that of dead Christ, *i. e.*, of the body and blood separately, severed in death the one from the other and each
from the human soul, yet that divine body and that
divine blood on account of the hypostatic union must be
adored with the same supreme worship as is due to the
Triune God.

Others have taught that no adoration must be given
to the Lord in the sacrament because " he is not there
for the purpose of worship."   But besides the evident
fact that they have no possible reason for affirming that
such is the case, and further, that the whole Church, led
by the Divine Spirit, has always held an opposite opinion,
it is a matter of no importance whether the purpose of the
presence is for worship or no.   Wherever Christ is present
he must be adored because he is God, whether he vouch-
safes his presence for that purpose or no ; and to deny
that such worship is the duty of the creature or (worse
still) to condemn such worship as idolatrous, can but
spring from a failure to believe in the Godhead of him
that is present, and so resolves itself into Arianism.

There are others who say that Christ is present, but
that the presence is not "personal."   Now a non-personal
presence of the body and blood of Christ is an absurdity.   A person cannot be present except personally,
and the sacred humanity has no existence except as
united to the Person of God the Son,   To affirm, then, a

presence of Christ which is not a personal presence, is a curious and as yet unheard-of misbelief which shews conclusively another failure to grasp the Catholic doctrine of the incarnation.

As opposed to these and to several other similar doctrines, all of which in their last analysis are but Arianism, we make our first declaration.

" I believe that our Lord, really and objectively present in the Eucharist under the forms of bread and wine, is to be adored."

From this it is evident in the first place that we reject any doctrine of Transubstantiation which " overthroweth the nature of a sacrament"[1] by denying the real existence of any outward part after consecration. We affirm, in the words of the Council of Trent, that "the Holy Eucharist hath this in common with the other sacraments, that it is the sign of a sacred thing, the visible form of an invisible grace."[2] We keep sharply distinguished the two parts of the sacrament as set forth in the Catechism, viz : "the outward visible sign " and "the inward part or thing signified,"[3] and while accepting the truth of the famous sequence of St. Thomas for Corpus Christi Day:

"Sub diversis speciebus
Signis tantum et non rebus
Latent res eximiæ,"[4]

" Here beneath these signs are hidden
Priceless things, to sense forbidden ;
Signs, not things, are all we see."

We yet affirm in the words of the famous theologian, Cardinal Franzelin : " That that which in the Most Holy

---

[1] Art. XXVIII. [2] Sess. XIII. *De Euch :* Cap: iii. [3] Catechism in Bk: of Common Prayer. [4] Vide *Missale Romanum, in Festo Corp. Christi.*

Sacrament is the immediate object of the senses is something objectively real (*objective reale*) is demonstrated as well from the reason of the sacrament as from the clear teachings of the Fathers," " the declaration by the Fathers of the physical reality of the sensible species is frequent and most distinct." [5]

It will be noticed that upon the question of "the conversion of the whole substance of bread into the substance of the body of Christ our Lord, and of the whole substance of wine into the substance of his blood" [6] we, like the Book of Common Prayer, like the book called *Articles of Religion*, like the Divine Scriptures themselves, are silent. We neither affirm it nor deny it, God having, so far as we are aware, made no revelation upon the subject, and we would not be wise above that is written.

We are ready now to consider the "inward part or thing signified," [7] and this we declare to be " our Lord," in the words of technical theology "whole Christ," that is to say his body, soul, and divinity. Our Saviour says not only " Except ye eat the flesh of the Son of Man and drink his blood," [8] but he also says, " he that eateth me, even he shall live by me," [9] from which it is evident that the food we receive in the Holy Sacrament is not only that earthly body with its blood which he took " of the substance of the Virgin Mary his mother," [10] nor even that body animated with the spirit, as he said " the flesh profiteth nothing, it is the spirit that giveth life ;" [11] but also his Godhead, so that he said with perfect truth " The bread of God is he that cometh down from heaven," [12]

---

[5] *Tract. de SS. Euch. Sac. et Sac.* Thesis XVI. ij. 1, pp. 273, 274. [6] Conc. Trid. Sess. XIII. *De Euch.* Cap. iv. [7] Catechism. [8] John vi. 53. [9] John vi. 57. [10] Proper Preface for Christmas Day. [11] Jno. vi. 63. [12] Jno. vi. 33.

and again (as we have already quoted), "He that eateth me even he shall live by me." [13]   But even were not this truth with regard to the Blessed Sacrament so plainly set forth in Holy Writ, yet it would be a necessary article of belief arising from a full appreciation of the mystery of the incarnation which consists in this, viz: that "two whole and perfect natures, that is to say, the Godhead and manhood, were joined together in one Person, never to be divided, whereof is one Christ, very God and very man." [14]   From the hypostatic union therefore it follows that the sacred humanity cannot be separated from the divinity of God the Son, and since "Christ being raised from the dead dieth no more," [15] his human soul cannot be separated from his human body.   It is therefore of divine faith, that under the form of bread is present by virtue of the words of consecration the body of Christ, and his sacred blood and soul by concomitance, and that under the form of wine is present by virtue of the words of consecration the blood of Christ, and his body and soul by concomitance; and that by virtue of the hypostatic union the Godhead is united to each of the three, so that whole Christ is present under each form separately.   This is the great truth which, following the ancient Fathers, we have expressed in the words, 'We believe that our Lord is present under the forms of bread and wine.'

Our declaration still further defines that the presence of our Lord is both "real" and "objective."   As the reality of the presence has been but little questioned and never denied, except by Zwinglians (having been accepted, at least in name, even by Calvinists), we need say little

---

[13] Jno. vi. 57.   [14] Art. II.   [15] Rom. vi. 9.

upon this point, especially since almost all the theological writers of the Anglican Church have professed to believe "the Real Presence."[16] The objectivity of the presence, however, is quite a different thing, and while, perhaps, some may take exception to the expression as being one of German philosophy rather than of scholastic theology, yet it has been so freely used in the controversy on this doctrine in the present century, and so conveniently expresses the truth in the matter, that we think we do not need further apology for having introduced it into our credenda. That the body of Christ is "verily and indeed taken and received by the faithful in the Lord's supper" is not disputed by Calvinists, nor by any who hold "the virtual presence," *i. e.*, an absence as effectual for good as a presence. The great question is not whether the Lord is present but, Where is he present? Is it in the heart of the faithful recipient alone, or is it also "under the forms of bread and wine"? Now this matter is settled for us by Article XXVII., which asserts that "the body of Christ is given," as well as "taken and eaten in the supper." This is what we intend to declare by saying that the Lord is "objectively present." He is present, not because of the presence of any other person, nor because of the worthiness of any other person, whether minister or recipient, but simply by virtue of the words of consecration given by himself,

---

[16] Hallam says: "This question [of the doctrine of Anglican theologians upon the Holy Eucharist] is rendered intricate at first sight, partly by the strong figurative language which the early reformers employed in order to avoid shocking the prejudices of the people, and partly by the incautious and even absurd use of the word *'real presence'* to mean *real absence*, which is common with modern theologians." Hallam, *Const. Hist. of Eng.* Chapter VIII. *Foot-note on Bp. Andrews.*

spoken by a valid minister over valid matter and with sufficient intention, for "the sacraments be effectual because of Christ's institution and promise." [17] While, then, we affirm, as does the Anglican Church, the reality and objectivity of the presence under the form of bread and wine, we add nothing concerning the manner of that presence which, as we learn from other sources, is altogether supernatural, supersensual, sacramental, non-local, and spiritual; nor can we do better in this connexion than make our own the words of the famous Jesuit theologian Perrone: "The glorious and spiritual body of Christ, as the apostle calls it, is present in the Eucharist under the symbols only after a spiritual or sacramental manner, and in the manner of a spirit." [18]

We are now ready to consider the statement made in the First Declaration, for while, indeed, the real and objective presence of our Lord Jesus Christ, under the forms of bread and wine, is indirectly asserted by being taken for granted, yet formally no such assertion is made. All the declaration asserts directly and formally is this: "Our Lord is to be adored." The main object of our declaration is not to affirm the doctrine of the Real Presence, but to affirm the consubstantial Godhead of the Son, and thus to oppose Arianism in whatever form it may shew itself. Jesus is God; and wherever, however he is present, he must be worshipped as God. We make our own the words of good Bishop Andrewes: "Christ himself, the thing signified of the sacrament, in and with the sacrament, is to be worshipped." The spectacle of the Christian world bowing down in adoration before

---

[17] Art. XXVI. [18] *Prælectiones. Tract. de Euch.* § 150. *Cf.* with this the wording of Art. XXVII.: "Only after a heavenly and spiritual manner."

what Protestants blasphemously call the "Wafer God,"
is the most perfect setting forth of the divine worship
and equal adoration which is due to the Incarnate Son.
Here we see in the sacramental presentation of the Incarnation the true "kenosis" of the Eternal Word, the glory,
the power, the wisdom of the Incarnate Son, in whom
are hid all the treasures of wisdom and knowledge,[19]
veiled by the sacramental forms of bread and wine.
How beautifully St. Thomas sets forth this wondrous
truth in his hymn, "Adoro te devote, latens Deitas!"

> "God only on the cross lay hid from view,
> But here lies hid at once the manhood, too,
> And I, in both professing my belief,
> The same prayer make as the repentant thief." [20]

One may be in error with regard to the meaning of
our Blessed Lord's words which he spoke in referring to
the Holy Mysteries and so deny his presence altogether;
such an one can deny and must denounce the worship
of the Sacrament, but if a man affirms a presence of
Christ and refuses to worship Christ thus present, he is
an Arian in heart or mind; he cannot believe in the Incarnation, and to all such we would quote the words of
the Athanasian Creed: "Furthermore, it is necessary to
everlasting salvation that he also believe rightly the
Incarnation of our Lord Jesus Christ."

---

[19] Col. ii. 3.

> [20] " In cruce latebat sola deitas,
> Sid hic latet simul et humanitas,
> Ambo tamen credens atque confitens
> Peto quod petivit latro pœnitens."

The Second Declaration.

OF THE PRIESTHOOD.

THERE does not seem to be any need of considering in this Introduction the general subject of the Apostolical Succession. As is well known there have always been those among us who have held that such succession was only necessary to the well-being of the Church and not to its actual existence, to its *bene-esse* and not to its *esse*. While such an opinion has been and still is held by some, it is not that usually entertained nor is it that intended by the expression "Apostolical Succession," which has always been understood as including the doctrine that ministers not having a share in such a succession have not the powers to perform the work of the priesthood. Although not found in any authoritative document of the Church of England, the expression occurs in a most pronounced and definite shape in our American Prayer Book, where in the office for the "Institution of Ministers" we read, "O holy Jesus who hast purchased to thyself an Universal Church and hast promised to be with the Ministers of Apostolic Succession to the end of the world, etc." This (together with the statement in the Preface to the orders for Ordination, that "no man shall be accounted or taken to be a lawful Bishop, Priest, or Deacon in this Church, or suffered to execute any of the said functions, except he be called, tried, examined and admitted thereunto, according to the form hereafter following, or hath had Episcopal

Consecration or Ordination ") would seem to be sufficient to render any further treatment of this particular of the statement unnecessary. Especially as this lax view has not had any following in this country from the first nor any place in its legislation, having always been considered as contrary to the real doctrine of the Church of England. In evidence of this the following, which was adopted unanimously by the Convention of Maryland in 1783 in its "Declaration of certain fundamental Rights and Liberties," is most interesting and conclusive: "Ever since the Reformation it hath been the received doctrine of the Church whereof we are members that there be these three orders of Ministers in Christ's Church: Bishops, Priests, and Deacons," "and that an Episcopal Ordination and Commission are necessary to the valid administration of the sacraments and the due exercise of the ministerial functions in the said Church."[1] In accordance with this has been all our legislation, and so, too, is the declaration recently made by the House of Bishops, of which more hereafter.

But while this is the case, it may be well to enter somewhat in detail into the reasons which lead us to think this doctrine an important corrective to a class of errors which we find rife around us to-day, and which may be grouped for convenience under the head of Socialism and Communism. No one can doubt that democratical ideas have increased with wonderful rapidity during this century. With the political aspect of this change we have nothing to do, but with the moral results we, as theologians and churchmen, are deeply concerned. Now it will not be denied that just in proportion to the spread of the theory that all power is

---

[1] Reprint of Early Journals, p. 6.

derived from beneath, and resides in the people as its source, being committed by them to certain persons who rule and govern for a period fixed by the people, and in accordance with the popular will, and responsible for their manner of governing to the people, just as these views have gained ground, there has also increased Socialism, Communism, Anarchism, and cognate opinions.

We do not mean to assert that these dangerous views are the proper or necessary result of the democratical principles just referred to, all we mean to assert is the bare fact that with the increase of the one set of ideas has come an increase of the other. Nor can we think this unnatural. Men are made to believe that the people own everything, that the people are all equal, that all power really belongs to them, and from these ideas the step is but small to the declaration that the land is the people's and should be made theirs in fact; that the theoretical equality should be made a reality, by force if not otherwise; that the law should be in the interest of the people, and if it is not, the law should be resisted. The logic may be bad, but, we say, it is not unnatural. We find this same thing has been worked out in the ecclesiastical domain among the different dissenting bodies, in which the ministers are made by the people, derive such powers as they have from the people, exercise their office subject to the control of the people, and give an account of their ministrations to the people. We have asked ourselves what is the remedy for all this? We find it in the unchanging and unchangeable (because divine) constitution of the Catholic Church. Here we have a " kingdom," ruled over by a dynasty which has not changed and which cannot change. In this kingdom all power comes from above, from the Everlasting King, who rules by his vicegerents in a hierarchy of fixed orders, three in number, the powers of which are carefully defined and cannot be exceeded without the offender's being made liable to punishment. In this kingdom the people are to obey and the priesthood are to rule. The priest is reverently to obey his bishop, the deacon is to serve the priest. All spiritual power and jurisdiction resides in this hierarchy, and no one, unless he has a share in this priesthood, has the right to administer the sacraments to the people. The gift of the Confirming Spirit with his sevenfold dower, the food of the soul and the Bread of Immortality, the healing of spiritual sickness and the soothing of the deathbed of the faithful, all these graces can be obtained from the priesthood alone. One Bishop can bestow all these, all the people of the whole world together cannot bestow any one of these graces! It needs no words to shew what an enormous power this hierarchy, so aristocratical, so absolute, so unchanging, so altogether separate from the people, must possess as a bulwark against the Socialism, Communism and Anarchism of the day. It is a power of conservative resistance. It is an organization which cannot change. Amid the changes of the world the Catholic hierarchy stands unchanged, teaching the same principles which it has taught since the beginning and which it received from God the Holy Ghost. "Servants, obey in all things your masters, according to the flesh, not with eye service, as menpleasers; but in singleness of heart, fearing God." [2]

"Wives, submit yourselves unto your own husbands." [3]

"Art thou called being a servant? use it rather, even if thou mayest be made free." [4]

---

[2] Col. iii. 22. [3] Col. iii. 18. [4] I. Cor. vii. 21.

" Masters, give unto your servants that which is just and equal." [5]

" Children obey your parents in all things." [6]

" Do violence to no man, neither accuse any falsely; and be content with your wages." [7]

" Let your women keep silence in the churches; for it is not permitted unto them to speak. If they will learn anything, let them ask their husbands at home." [8]

" Servants, be subject to your masters with all fear; not only to the good and gentle, but also to the froward. For this is thankworthy if a man for conscience towards God, endure grief, suffering wrongfully." [9]

Such are samples of the teaching of the Catholic hierarchy, such are the words of the Divine Scriptures, but they sound strange in our ears to-day, and agree but little with the maxims of "enlightened thought," and of " civil and religious liberty." What, then, our Declaration asserts is, that the Ecclesiastical Hierarchy is, in our belief, a divine institution and a necessary one for the salvation of the world, so much so that without it none of the sacraments could be administered · except only Baptism and Holy Matrimony. Nor can we express this divine origin of the Episcopate better than in the words of the American Bishops in General Convention assembled in the year of grace, 1886: " We do affirm that Christian unity . . . can be restored only by the return of all Christian communions to the principles of union exemplified by the undivided Catholic Church during the first ages of its existence, which principles we believe to be the substantial deposit of Christian faith and order, committed by Christ and his Apostles to

[5] Col. iv. 1. [6] Col. iii. 20. [7] Luke iii. 14. [8] I. Cor. xiv. 34. [9] Col. ii. 18.

the Church unto the end of the world, and therefore incapable of compromise or surrender by those who have been ordained to be its stewards and trustees for the common and equal benefit of all men. As inherent parts of this sacred deposit, and therefore as essential to the restoration of unity . . . we account the following, to wit: . . . the historical episcopate."

It is not intended by anything that has been said to add to this credendum any particulars not contained in it and the writer wishes distinctly to declare that all the person signing this credendum commits himself to is the statement that the priesthood of the Catholic Church is " necessary to the valid administration of all the sacraments except Baptism and Matrimony," and while he is deeply impressed with the cogency of the preceding remarks, they are his alone and for them the Clerical Union is in no sense responsible. We come now to consider the two exceptions mentioned in the declaration, and since there seems much confusion on the subject I think it may be well to treat them more at length.

OF LAY BAPTISM.

IN the discussion of the question of the validity of lay-baptism, there are but two material considerations: 1. Is an ordained minister necessary to the validity of holy baptism? and, 2. If not, and if a layman can validly baptize, is there anything in the peculiar standing of the ministers of the Protestant denominations which deprives them of this power enjoyed by other unordained persons? To this last question we first of all direct our attention. If there exists any such disability it must spring either from their schism, *i. e.*, the fact that they are sectarians, or else from their heresy. But this matter of the effect of heresy or schism upon baptism has been determined once for all by œcumenical authority, and to affirm that such baptism is void is well said by the present archbishop of Canterbury to be "contrary to Scripture principle, Church tradition, and the ruling of the Catholic world." [1]

We pass now to a consideration of the first question, viz: whether lay persons can validly baptize. Of course it is sinful in laymen, whether calling themselves ministers or not, to baptize except in cases of necessity, but it must be remembered that the sacraments work *ex opere operato*, or, as the Articles express it, "be effectual because of Christ's institution and promise, although they be administered by evil men." (Article XXVI.) Kelsall most quaintly sets this forth in his ever-to-be-admired letter as follows: " It is not a new assertion that God so husbands the sinful actions of men as thereby to serve the ends of his providence, the needs of his Church, and the necessities of his servants. Judas and Pilate and the Jews, who conspired against and killed the Lord of Life (such of them as did not afterwards repent and believe in him) are in hell for having done what they did; and yet without it mankind could not have been saved. And this answer I take to be sufficient with respect to all baptisms administered in defiance and opposition to the Christian priesthood by these lay-usurpers, counterfeit ministers of the Gospel, who officiate in fanatical congregations and act without Episcopal ordination."

The Custom of the Greek Church to-day is in conformity with this opinion (*Cf. Duty of Parish Priests*,

---

[1] Sermon at opening of Lambeth Conference of 1888.

Blackmore's trans. c. iii.), and also of the Roman Church
(*vide, e. g.* Konings's *Tractatus de Baptismo,* 1264), and,
we need hardly add, such has always been the custom
of the Episcopal Church. Unless there is reason to
doubt "that the child was baptized with water 'in the
Name of the Father and of the Son and of the Holy
Ghost' (which are essential parts of baptism)," baptisms
by heretics or schismatics, whether clerical or lay, must
not be repeated under pain of violation of the rulings of
the Catholic Church of Christ and of despising her traditions. (*Cf.* rubric at end of Private Baptism Office.)

Perhaps someone will think this custom of allowing
the validity of lay-baptisms is a lax one which has sprung
up in the latter days of the Church, first in the West; and
that the Eastern Church has only by Western influence
been drawn in to acknowledge it. It may be well then
to shew that the same custom prevailed in the East before the time of Photius, and that among all the
points of difference between East and West, which at
that time were exaggerated as much as possible, this
was not so much as mentioned, shewing that there
was then no difference of opinion. The following are
the exact words of the synodical decision, given in the
times of the Patriarch Nicephorus, in the beginning of
the ninth century : "Unbaptized children needs must be
baptized if any be found in a place where there is no
priest. If the father of the child, or anyone else, provided only he be a Christian, baptize him, he commits
no sin."[2] Such was the old law of the Greek Church

[2] Leunclavius, *Jus Græco-Romanum.* Lib. iii. p. 169; cited by
Bingham. The same doctrine is taught in another canon found in
Harmenopulus, *Epitom. Can.* Sect. IV. tit. ii. apud Leunclav.
p. 44.

and despite some few gainsayers such it has continued down to to-day, the Patriarch Jeremy of Constantinople having answered the Tubingen Divines as follows: "When there is a necessity, laymen are permitted to baptize."[3]

In closing this part of the discussion it will be well to recall to the reader's mind the bitter Papal denunciation of those of the French clergy who In mistaken zeal re-baptized the Huguenot converts. It is true that Roman Catholics among English-speaking people are accustomed to re-baptize *sub conditione* all that come to them but this is not on account of any supposed insufficiency of the minister but out of a pretended doubt as to whether the proper form and matter were used. This may be clearly seen by the exception which they are forced to make (in theory at least) in favour of those performed by High Churchmen. Konings's ruling is as follows: "Among Episcopalians the baptism of ritualists is presumed to be rightly performed."

We come now to consider the main question, viz: whether a priest is required for the validity of Holy Baptism. We believe Calvin was the first to embrace such an opinion and it would seem that even he did not very consistently insist upon it. Before proceeding to examine the Divine Scriptures it may be well to state the present use of the whole Catholic Church, which is that it matters not who is the minister of this sacrament, whether man or woman, provided that it be administered with the essential form and matter. This is without controversy the use of East and West and that it is the law of the Church of England has twice been decided in this century (Court of Arches, Kemp *v.* Wickes 1809, and

---

[3] Huttinger *Hist. Eccles.* tom. i. p. 632.

Mastin *v.* Escott, which was also heard by the Judicial Committee in 1841). Anyone wishing to see the Canon Law upon the subject will find it in Lyndewood. The only point upon which a question may arise is as to the validity of baptisms performed in jest ; on this point St. Augustine is doubtful (*De Bapt.* lib. ii. c. 53) and the usual practice is to treat such acts as null.

When we come to the Scriptural consideration there appears no statement requiring the limitation of baptism to the priestly order. From the Old Testament type which was circumcision we are led to infer that as lay-men and even women circumcised under the elder dispensation, so laymen and women can baptize now; the reader will not forget the case of Zipporah, nor of the women of whom we read in I. Macc. i. 60. In evidence of how strongly Calvin felt the force of this argument, it may be interesting to record that he called Zipporah many bad names, among others a "*stulta mulier*" and describes the act so blessed by God as having been done through " weakness of mind " (*ab animi impotentia*) ! It is urged that the commission to baptize was given only to the priesthood, but this would seem to be a wholly gratuitous assumption, "for although (as Card. Bell-armine well remarks) Matthew makes mention only of the eleven Apostles, nevertheless it is probable that there were present many more. For these words seem to have been said upon Ascension Day when there were present with the Apostles the forty brethren, as the Apostle testifies in I. Cor. xv." Moreover it is manifest that the commission to preach had the same restrictions and yet we find Stephen, who was not a priest, preaching; and Philip both preaching and baptizing; and the same thing we find others doing neither priests nor deacons, as

Ananias. Moreover so universal was the practice of lay-baptism in the early Church that no one it would seem can doubt its Apostolic origin. To enter into any proof of this is impossible in our narrow limits but we may refer to Bingham's *Scholastic History of Lay-baptism* for a catena of authorities.

No doubt our readers have been asking themselves, What is the history of the matter in our Church here in America? We cannot give this history better than in the words of good old Bishop White, the first Bishop of Pennsylvania. He writes, in his *Memoirs of the Protestant Episcopal Church*, as follows (p. 211 of 2d edition): "It appears on the Journal [of the Convention of 1811] that two reverend gentlemen made to the Convention an application, the purport of which is not recorded. . . . The object of the two gentlemen alluded to was to procure a declaration of the invalidity of lay-baptism; and they were said to be conscientiously scrupulous of admitting as members of their congregations persons who had received no other. This, of course, precluded accessions, except on condition of compliance with their proposal, from the most numerous denomination in the State, their baptism by the Congregational ministers being considered as performed by laymen. Although the clergymen referred to were singular in carrying the matter so far, yet there has been an increasing tendency in some of the clergy to administer Episcopal baptism to such as desire it, on alleged doubts of the validity of former baptism. Even this is contrary to the rubrics. . . . It is true that this does not settle the question of the sense of Scripture. On the most serious consideration of the subject many years ago, conviction is entertained that the Holy Scriptures and the Church are not at variance in the matter. . . . If the prejudice should prevail, it is very unfortunate that two of our bishops (Dr. Provoost and Dr. Jarvis) never received baptism from an Episcopalian administrator. So that who knows what scruples this may occasion as to the validity of many of our ordinations. . . . Therefore, who can tell to what extent this sentiment may prevail, and what inconveniences it may occasion? There would be no certainty of the existence of a bishop in Christendom. In England the scruple arose in the latter end of the reign of Queen Anne. . . . It was a political measure . . . a reproach was thrown on the electoral family that they were unbaptized Lutherans. . . . Archdeacon Sharp . . . gives an account of a meeting held at Lambeth of the two archbishops and all the bishops who were in town. . . . The assembled prelates determined unanimously in contrariety to the scruple [against lay-baptism administered by dissenters]." The actual decision arrived at is given by Sharp as, "that lay-baptism should be discouraged as much as possible, but if the essentials had been preserved in a baptism by a lay-hand it was not to be repeated." This ruling of the English archbishops and bishops in 1712 was but a setting forth afresh of the old unchanging law of the Catholic world; it is the law of the whole Catholic Church to-day, and has been both the law and practice of the American Church from the first. It is implicitly contained in the overtures to dissenters for union, which have been made not only by our House of Bishops but by the Lambeth Conference. Baptism is, as everyone knows, "the gate of the sacraments," without the passing of which no other sacrament can be received, and yet all recognise the baptism of dissenters as sufficient for the reception of Holy Matrimony; if so, then for any of the sacraments.

To sum up, lay-baptism is, *cæteris paribus*, recognised as valid by the whole Catholic Church, nor does the fact of the lay-person being a sectarian in any way affect the validity of the sacrament, "which is effectual because of Christ's institution and promise." It follows, then, that the vast majority of baptized Protestants are validly baptized, and were made by such baptism "members of Christ, children of God, and inheritors of the kingdom of heaven;" and that while, in particular cases, there may be reasonable doubt as to whether the essential form and matter were used, such doubt can only exist in regard to the few and not to the many; and that, except in such special cases, the repetition of the ceremony is in violation of the law of Christendom and a profanation of the Holy Name.

OF HOLY MATRIMONY.

THE accepted doctrine on the subject of Holy Matrimony is that it is a Sacrament of the New Law, consisting in "the conjugal union of a man and a woman who are capable thereof according to law, and which obliges them to live inseparably the one with the other."[1] Such is the definition of Peter Lombard, and this has been followed by all theologians. When we come to the next point, viz: as to who is the Minister of this Sacrament, there is some difference of opinion. All the School Authors, with the possible exception of William of Paris, teach that the contracting parties are the ministers of the sacrament, and that while the priest joins them together

---

[1] Master of the Sentences, Lib. IV. D. 27.

and gives them his blessing, yet that his presence is not necessary, *necessitate medii*, but only *necessitate præcepti*. It is true that Melchior Canus taught a different doctrine in the sixteenth century and was followed by a few very weighty theologians, but his opinions soon died out and to-day have no followers, the doctrine as stated above being now an article of faith for the Roman obedience, having been so set forth by Pope Pius IX.

When, then, two baptized persons consent together to live as man and wife, according to God's ordinance, until death do them part, and witness this consent by some external sign, they receive the Sacrament of Holy Matrimony; and, if they are not in mortal sin and so precluded from receiving grace, they receive *ex opere operato* the grace proper to this sacrament. Nor, when we come to look at the matter closely, is there any cause for astonishment that such should be the case; for our Lord did not add sacramental marriage to natural marriage, but he elevated natural marriage into a sacrament by making it the type of his own union with his bride, the Church. Now, it is evident that the essence of this union is the mutual consent of the Heavenly Bridegroom and of his earthly bride; and so in the sacramental setting forth of this mystical union, the essence is the mutual consent of the contracting parties. Such has ever been the doctrine of the Church, and the learned reader who wishes to pursue the matter more fully is referred to Denziger's *Ritus Orientalium* in which he will find that the same doctrine is still held by the different heretical bodies in the East, who separated from the Church in the fifth century, thus carrying back the doctrine to within a century of the time that the empire became Christian and the Church's doctrine became practically operative. Such, too, is the custom of the whole Church throughout the entire world to-day. It is an universally accepted doctrine that the current interpretation is the best commentary upon the meaning of the law. This being the case, its application to the matter in hand is obvious, for everywhere marriages contracted between baptized Protestants are treated as valid when one or both of the parties are converted to the Latin, Greek, or Anglican obedience; and no new ceremony is performed, which would certainly be the case had they not already received the sacrament and its grace for a blessed and faithful conjugal life.

Such, then, being the practice of the whole church, it will be well to consider what is the doctrine of that particular part of the church in which the good providence of Almighty God has placed us. And first we remark that the mere fact that our American revisers in 1789 deliberately changed the word " Priest " to " Minister " in all the rubrics of the Marriage Service shews that they intended to allow a deacon (in case of necessity) to perform the office. Nor in doing so did they depart from the usage of the rest of the Church of England, where deacons had solemnized and still do (although as we cannot but think unrubrically) solemnize Holy Matrimony. It is not material to consider here what changes, if any, the deacon should make when he uses the service; nor to question whether a deacon can bless in such forms as are provided in that service; the only point for us to notice is that by the deliberate action of the Church the rubrics restricting the solemnization of marriage to the priest alone have been removed, shewing past all question that by the doctrine of the American

Church a priest is not the exclusive minister of this sacrament.

We now pass to a consideration of the service as used in common by all parts of the Anglican Communion, and here the case is equally clear. The office is nowhere styled "the Ministration of Holy Matrimony," nor is there anything corresponding to the expressions " I baptize thee," or "I absolve thee." While we read of "the Ministration of Public Baptism," of " the Administration of the Lord's Supper " "that Confirmation may be ministered," etc., here we read "the Form of Solemnization of Matrimony." The work of the minister in Holy Baptism is to baptize, in Holy Communion to housel, in Confirmation to confirm, but in Holy Matrimony it is not to marry but to " solemnize the marriage." To make all this still clearer the matter is set forth with legal and theological precision by the office itself in which the officient is made to say: "I pronounce that they are man and wife," not forasmuch as I have joined them together, having administered to them the sacrament of Holy Matrimony, but "forasmuch as M. and N. have consented together . . . and have witnessed the same," etc. There is left here no room for difference of opinion, the words can mean but one thing, the minister only "pronounces" the validity of what the contracting parties have done and afterward bestows his blessing. The priesthood then in Apostolical Succession is not necessary for the valid administration of the Sacrament of Holy Matrimony. Q. E. D.

The Third Declaration.

I T IS manifest that the third of the credenda contains three propositions. First: Sufficient grace is given to every man to escape damnation, *i. e.*, the doctrine of the Sufficiency of Grace. Second: This life is the time in which such grace must be corresponded to, *i. e.*, the denial of any Post-mortem Probation. Third: The results of the acceptance or rejection of this grace are endless, *i. e.*, the doctrine of Everlasting Rewards and Punishments. Of each of these we shall treat in order.

OF THE SUFFICIENCY OF GRACE.

T HE universality of the redemption wrought by our Blessed Lord upon the cross will not be questioned. He died that all might live, and while, indeed, his redemption, as a matter of fact, is effective only to the salvation of the elect who by grace obey the calling, walk in good works, and win the eternal rewards; yet his redemption was sufficient for all, of every age, of every people. But it is evident that universality of redemption carries with it, of necessity, the idea of sufficiency of grace; for since we can do no good thing of ourselves, and in our fallen estate are entirely dependent upon the grace of God to lead us into holiness, unless sufficient grace is given to every human soul to escape damnation, the universality of redemption becomes an unreality. To assert this, however, would be to dishonour God and to throw a slur upon the work of his dear Son. It must be remembered that by grace in theology is meant, not the impulses of kindness, gentleness, etc., etc., which are natural to man, but something which is external to him; something which by nature he cannot have; something which comes to him from without; something which sets him against himself, and which is one combatant in that mighty struggle which is waged in the soul between grace and nature. Nature, then, and grace must be looked upon as utterly separate, the object of grace being to overcome nature. This being the case, grace is defined as a supernatural gift bestowed at the first *gratis* (that is, without anything to deserve it *de condigno*) upon men and angels by Almighty God, to the end that they may attain to their supreme end, which is eternal life.

It does not seem necessary to enter here at length into the many problems and difficulties which have been discussed by the theologians, such as what is to be said of children dying before birth, or of infants dying before baptism. For the answers of the theologians to these questions I will refer the reader to Perrone, in his tractate *De Gratia Christi*,[1] where he will find the matter treated at length. Perhaps I may be allowed to add as my own suggestion (and therefore probably worthless), that we have no way of knowing at how early an age the soul may be capable of resisting grace, which, if corresponded to, would have brought to the waters of baptism; to fix any point after the instant of conception would seem to be quite arbitrary. This and other like questions do present difficulties, and difficulties which will be answered in different ways, and possibly never entirely satisfactorily; but (as the immortal Bishop Butler, quoting

---

[1] Perrone, *Prælectiones. De Gratia Christi*, Pars. I. cap. v.

Origen, says) if we find difficulties which we cannot explain in God's Book of Nature, why should we not expect to find also difficulties in God's Book of Revelation? At all events, whatever may be the difficulties, both the necessity of Holy Baptism and the sufficiency of grace are clearly set forth to us in Holy Scripture, the latter being undoubtedly necessitated by such texts as that Almighty God " desireth not the death of a sinner," and " will have all men to be saved;"[2] by that question which he asks, " what more could I have done unto them that I have not done?" and similar passages, all of which clearly shew that the damnation of any man is because of his evil deeds and of his failure to correspond to the grace given him of God, not because of that grace being not sufficient.

It seems hardly necessary to point out to the reader how this doctrine removes all the difficulties with regard to the salvation of the heathen, and of the practically heathen masses in our midst—difficulties which have so much exercised the minds of men in these last days. We must affirm that Holy Baptism is " generally necessary to salvation;"[3] that " except a man be born again he cannot see the kingdom of God;"[4] that " except a man be born of water and of the Spirit he cannot enter into the kingdom of God;"[5] that " works done before the grace of Christ and the inspiration of his Spirit are not pleasant to God . . . but [that] they have the nature of sin,"[6] that " they are to be had accursed that presume to say that every man shall be saved by the law or sect which he professeth, so that he be diligent to frame his life according to that law and the light of

---

[2] I. Tim. ii. 4. [3] Catechism. [4] Jno. iii. 3. [5] Jno. iii. 5. [6] Art. XIII.

nature."[7] But while all this is true, and while the
heathen will all be damned if they continue heathen to
the end, yet this will not be the fault of Almighty God
for having neglected them, but will be simply and only
because they have rejected the grace which God gave
them, which was quite sufficient to enable them to escape
damnation, and which, if it had been corresponded to,
would have brought them, as it did the Three Holy Kings
and the good Cornelius, to the knowledge of Christ and
to everlasting salvation; "for Holy Scripture doth set
out unto us only the name of Jesus Christ whereby men
must be saved."[8] How God will do this it is not ours
to enquire; enough for us to know that Jesus died for
all, and that he does all things for the salvation of each
soul for which he died. And of all these we may safely
say in the words of Holy Scripture, "But thou sparest
all: for they are thine, O Lord, thou lover of souls."[9]

OF POST-MORTEM PROBATION.

IN any consideration of the subject of the possibility of a further opportunity for probation after
death, the fact that a human soul is not a man must
always be kept conspicuously in the foreground. A man
is made up of a body and a soul, thus as it were uniting
in himself the angelic and the brute nature. Now many
of the greatest temptations that we endure come to us from
the body, and therefore as composite beings; and since
both body and soul are to be saved, the time for our probation, the time in which it will be demonstrated whether
we will subdue the flesh and bring every thought to the
obedience of Christ, must be while soul and body are

---

[7] Art. XVIII. [8] Art. XVIII. [9] Wisdom xi. 26.

united, *i. e.* before the hour of death. If after death those who rejected God in life and followed the lusts of the flesh are to have another chance, and in soul alone (without the burden of the flesh, of which St. Paul so bitterly complained when he cried, " O wretched man that I am, who shall deliver me from the burden of this death !"[1]) are to be subjected to some new kind of a proof, it is clear that they have a decided advantage over those who have tried to heed the word of exhortation, " Now is the accepted time, behold now is the day of salvation."[2] In fact so strongly did this objection weigh with a defender of this post-mortem probation doctrine that his only answer to the question, 'Why then go to the heathen at all?' was, 'I cannot tell, but we are bidden to do so.' He thought it a manifest disadvantage to be born in a Christian country, and yet in our Catechism we are taught to "heartily thank our heavenly Father that he hath called us to this state of salvation [*i. e.*, of being baptized]." Into such absurdities are men drawn who would depart from the revelation of Almighty God as taught by the Church. Any and every doctrine of post-mortem probation we absolutely reject. And we affirm that there is no dogma of the Christian faith more clearly revealed and more necessary to be believed unto eternal salvation than that "according to the works done in the body" every man shall " be eternally rewarded or punished."[3] We reject this so-called "larger hope," firstly, as unnecessary, every soul having been given sufficient grace for salvation; secondly, as illogical and unjust, since a human soul is not a man but only a part of a

---

[1] Rom. vii. 24. [2] II. Cor. vi. 2. [3] Morning Family Prayer, in Prayer Book.

man, and as giving the wicked and the heathen an advantage over the righteous and the Christian; thirdly, as
lacking the support of any one text of Holy Scripture;
fourthly, as contrary to the teaching of the whole Church
of God, and especially as contrary to the express teaching of that part of the Church to which we belong; fifthly,
as leading to immorality and sensualism, and as encourag-
ing men to neglect present opportunities of salvation in
the " larger hope" of those to come; sixthly, as contrary
to the teaching of the Fathers and of all the theologians
of the whole Christian world.

A doctrine open to six objections of such weight
surely can have no following among those who profess
to hold the Catholic Faith, and it does not seem necessary
to pursue this matter any further than to quote a few
passages from the Fathers. St. Cyril of Jerusalem, in his
famous Catechetical Lectures teaches as follows: "And
if it is said, 'The dead praise not thee, O Lord,' this shews
that since in this life only is the appointed time for repentance and pardon, for which they who enjoy it shall
' praise the Lord,' it remains after death for them who
have died in sins, not to give praise as the receivers of a
blessing but to bewail themselves; for praise belongs to
them who give thanks, but to them who are under the
scourge lamentation. Therefore the just shall then offer
praise; but they who have died in sins will have no
further season for acknowledgment."[4]

St. Basil the Great writes: "This life present is the
time for penitence and forgiveness of sins, but the life to
come is that of just judgment and of retribution," and in
another place, "Once departed this life there is no more
time for good works, because God, who is always long-

---

[4] *Catech.* xviii. 14. (Ox. Trans. p. 246).

suffering, has fixed the time of this present life for the accomplishment of that which is necessary to please him."[5]

And to leave the East and come to a Western writer, St. Gregory the Great says: " For those who are departed hence there is in the pit neither confession nor amendment (Ps. vi. 5); for God has limited the time for work to the duration of our sojourn upon the earth, leaving to the life to come the examination of what has been done in this life present."[6]

A longer catena would be quite unnecessary, accordingly I close with a sentence from Chrysostom: " As long as we are in this life present, we can still avoid punishment by amendment; but, once in the other life, it is a pure loss that we weep over our sins."[7]

OF ENDLESS REWARDS AND PUNISHMENTS.

WE are of opinion that no doctrine of the Christian Faith is more necessary to salvation than the endless punishment of the lost. The mystery of the Incarnation, which is so stupendous as to seem folly to the world, and sometimes also to try the powers of faith of the Christian, even when it is remembered that the Divine Son took on him human nature to save the creatures of his hand from God's wrath and everlasting damnation, seems utterly absurd and incredible if there was no such wrath or everlasting damnation to save them from. If, on the other hand, it be said that it is by the virtue of the Incarnation alone that punishment will not be endless, we can only say that a religion which teaches that Judas Iscariot and John the Divine, that Messalina and Mary, that Nero

---

[5] Basil, *Moralia*, Reg. I. capp. ii. and v. [6] *Serm.* xv. [7] *In Psal.* ix. I am indebted to Macarius for these citations.

and St. Louis will reign together in glory to the ages of ages[1] does not appear to us to be the religion of Jesus Christ, nor the religion of the New Testament, nor the religion which has converted the world and filled heaven with converted sinners, nor (if we may say it reverently) a religion which sets forth a moral government of the universe with fitting rewards and punishments. We have endeavoured in our declaration to state this doctrine of the Church in the most explicit and unmistakable manner, and in order to do so we have quoted the words which the Church addresses to the prisoner under sentence of death. Both exhortations in the Office for the Visitation of Prisoners are full of the spirit of true Catholicism on this point and may well be studied. The phrase we have adopted is this, that at the hour of death everyone passes into "an endless and unchangeable state."

At our birth we were in a state of damnation, that is to say, "born in sin and the children of wrath;" but by Holy Baptism we were taken out of the state of damnation, we were made "members of Christ, the children of God, and inheritors of the kingdom of heaven," therefore, we must "heartily thank our heavenly Father that he hath called us to this state of salvation." The baptized, then, are in a state of salvation, but that state may be lost, and then may be gained anew, and so on through the many ups and downs of the spiritual life, and therefore we are taught to "pray unto God to give us his grace that we may continue in the same [state of salvation] unto our life's end."

Our "state," then, before the hour of death is a state that may end at any time, may change at any time. One

---

[1] See this idea beautifully worked out in Dr. Pusey's sermon, *Everlasting Punishment.*

day we may be in a state of grace, the next in a state of loss through the commission of some deadly sin. All this uncertainty ends at death. " Blessed are the dead who die in the Lord . . . their works do follow them." " They rest from their labours," whether those labours be good or evil, they can work no more, they cannot win more merit, but (O joy unspeakable!) they cannot lose what they have won. They have entered upon a condition which is "endless and unchangeable." As they were found at the last hour, so is their state throughout eternity, a state of grace and favour with God, or a state of damnation and alienation from him.

We are far from wishing to deny that many of those who, at the hour of death, pass into an endless and un-changeable state of salvation may have to endure much purification before they are fit to be admitted to the presence of the King; but we believe that their knowl-edge of the fixedness of their eternal estate makes it easy for them to endure the loving pains which are preparing them for their joy and rest in the Beatific Vision of the God whom they have served.

On this whole subject of the endless punishment of the wicked I desire to quote at length from the sermon preached at the opening of the General Convention of Baltimore, in 1892, by the Rt. Rev. the Bishop of Alabama:

" Not only do the ungodly and profane deride the idea of a coming retribution, but, sad to say, some who have been commanded to warn the wicked from their ways, are lulling them into a fatal security. They are sound-ing that note that first tempted man to fall; 'Thou shalt not surely die,' and if thou diest, still there is 'eternal hope.'

"What do we know of the future state save as Christ hath revealed it? Let us draw very near him when he speaks, for life and death are in his words. He was asked the question, 'Lord, are there few that be saved?' His discourse seems to have raised that question, and our preaching, if it be like his, will ever stir the same enquiry. How shall we press men to the enquiry, 'What shall I do to be saved?' unless we convince that, as they now are, they are in peril of being lost? What was our Lord's answer? 'I say unto you strive— agonize—to enter in at the straight gate.' He goes on to give the reason for this urgency—'because straight is the gate and narrow is the way that leadeth unto life, and few there be that find it.' This, then, is a settled question, one that may not be properly brought into discussion among the disciples of Christ. And you may go through the Gospels—I speak advisedly, soberly, and in the fear of God—there is not a sentence, not a word, not a syllable of any saying of Christ's which gives countenance to the modern sentimentalism of 'eternal hope.' And I marvel at the audacity of any ambassador of Christ who ventures to smooth over, neutralize, and falsify the message of his Sovereign.

"If the Fatherhood of God, manifested in his Son, reveals a type of love, as far surpassing that of human love as the divine is above the human, so does his infinite holiness declare an aversion to sin in like proportion. Indeed, the divine compassion for the sufferer from sin is the measure of the divine hatred of that which caused the suffering. In a word the boundlessness of the Father's love is the measure of his hatred of that which estranges his children from himself, renders them unfit for his presence, and leaves them in 'outer darkness' when 'the door is shut.'"

The Fourth Declaration.

OF HOLY SCRIPTURE.

OUR last declaration is on the subject of the Divine
Scriptures. Feeling most deeply that anything
that attacks Holy Writ attacks also the Holy
Spirit who inspired it, we have set forth as clearly as we
could our faith on this point. Our statement contains a
proposition and a necessary corollary. The proposition
is that all the books of the Old and New Testaments are
inspired by God the Holy Ghost in such a way that he is
the author of the books in all their parts. And from
this it follows that they are infallible and undeceivable in
all their statements, so that "whatsoever is contained in
them is true." We therefore reject all such false and
semi-rationalistic statements as that "the authors and not
the books are inspired," or that the Old Testament is
"the history of an inspired race and not the inspired
history of a race." We do not believe that the sacred
writings are a mixture of things human and divine in
which it is left to the wit of man to pick out what is
human and to reject it, and what is divine and to accept it.

While it is, of course, true that in the Holy Scriptures
there is a human element as well as a divine element, by
this we do not mean that certain parts of Holy Scripture
are human and certain parts divine, but we mean that
each and every part is both human and divine, the human
part pertaining to the form, the divine part pertaining to

the substance. As the whole Christ is divine, so the whole of Holy Scripture is divine, every book of it, every chapter of it, every verse of it, every word of it.

We do not say that the Holy Scriptures "contain the Word of God," but (as we have declared at our ordination) we "believe the Holy Scriptures of the Old and New Testaments to be the Word of God." To us, therefore, the name of the person who was used as the penman, and the date at which he lived, are matters of little or no interest, as the Holy Ghost is the author of all the books in all their parts, for we receive the sacred writings "not as the words of men but as they are in very deed the Word of God."

The adversaries to the truth of our corollary are principally of two classes. First: Those who hold that the statements of doctrine and morals in Holy Scripture are inspired but the statements of fact uninspired and subject to correction. Second: Those who teach that our Blessed Lord assumed ignorance and that therefore his statements are not to be looked upon as final or irreformable. (May God forgive me for writing such blasphemy!) This they call the "Kenosis" of God the Son. Both of these opinions we entirely reject, affirming that the Holy Scriptures are true, the Written Word of him who is the Truth as well as the Way and the Life, the direct work of him who is called by our Blessed Lord "the Spirit of Truth."

We do not look in the Holy Scriptures for a scientific digest or statement of dogmatic theology or of moral theology, far less do we look for a scientific statement of astronomical, geological or other facts of natural science. But we do look for, and accept as such, truthful statements of doctrine and morals and so, too, we accept the statements with regard to history and science as truthful, while possibly not scientifically accurate in their expression. The most learned astronomer of our own day, in writing upon another subject, would not hesitate to speak (*e. g.*) of the sun rising and setting, and this without exposing himself to the charge of either ignorance or untruthfulness; why then should it be thought a mark of fallibility that the Divine Scriptures say that God "maketh his sun to rise upon the evil and upon the good?" We deny that science, or history, or comparative philology, or any other human branch of wisdom or learning ever has pointed out or ever will or ever can point out any one false statement made in the Divine Writings of the Sacred Canon. And this being the case, there does not seem to be any reason for further consideration of this point, and we pass on to the last subject for our treatment in this Introduction, viz: the so-called "Kenosis" of our Blessed Lord.

OF THE "KENOSIS" OF GOD THE SON.

BEFORE considering what is the truth in this matter we must first pause to ask what is meant by this word "Kenosis," a word as a technical term unknown to the theology of the Catholic Church. Speaking broadly it is used to denote a supposed assumption of ignorance on the part of our Lord Jesus Christ. One writer, amid a haze of mutually contradictory statements, considers this ignorance not only to have been an ignorance of the human soul of the Lord but an ignorance of the incarnate Godhead, and in defending this extraordinary opinion, he informs us that with him wisdom is only an attribute of God and not a necessary

condition of his being, and that therefore he can be ignorant by a self-imposed limitation of his attribute of
wisdom. Of course this is the most absolute nonsense
that can be conceived of, since it is but saying that God
can make himself not God for a year, or for thirty years,
or for a special purpose, in accordance with his beneficent
will towards mankind. An ignorant God is a contradiction in terms, for the idea of God carries with it
necessarily the idea of All-Wisdom. Nor is it possible to
ascribe ignorance to one person of the Holy Trinity and
not to each of the other two at the same time; for as the
will of the Holy Trinity is one, so too is the wisdom of
the Holy Trinity one. Nor can this be denied without
the denial of that which is the foundation of all Monothe-
ism and which is revealed to us in that sublime formula,
" Hear, O Israel, the Lord thy God is One Lord."

This is more evident if the matter be looked at from
the other side, for if there be one will of the Father and
another will of the Son and another of the Holy Ghost,
then are there Three Gods and not One God. And
again, if there be one wisdom of the Father, and another
wisdom of the Son, and another of the Holy Ghost, then
are there Three Gods and not One God. To affirm,
therefore, a self-imposed ignorance in God the Son is but
affirming Polytheism; and yet by a strange confusion of
thought the very author who thus makes Three Gods
(if an ignorant God can be argued about *per impossibile*)
has seemed to charge the Catholic doctrine of the Holy
Trinity as taught in the chapter of the *Summa Res* of the
Fourth Council of the Lateran with being "the nighest
thing to Tritheism ! "

A less absurd idea was entertained by the same writer
in an earlier book of his[1] to wit: that the human soul

---

[1] *Lux Mundi*, Introduction.

of Christ was not perfectly enlightened by the Divine
Nature to which it was united, so that the Divine Person
could and did by an act of self-limitation deprive his
Sacred Humanity of knowledge which it would otherwise
have possessed; and on the strength of this supposition
he proceeds to consider as inconclusive such statements
made by our Blessed Lord as that " David himself by
Holy Ghost" wrote the first verse of Psalm cx; holding
that the Divine Son concealed from his human soul the
true authorship of that psalm and left it in the prevailing
ignorance of that day. It has been well pointed out that
even so, our Lord would not be free from the guilt of
teaching that which was false, for if a man teaches that
which is false because of an ignorance which is of his
own making, it is exactly the same act, from a moral
point of view, as if he taught that which he knew to be
false.[2]

These and all other views which attribute ignorance to
the Incarnate Son of God, together with every doctrine of a
feigned "Kenosis," other than that of which Holy Church
speaks in Te Deum when, praising her King of Glory, she
sings, "Thou didst not abhor the Virgin's womb," we entirely reject. His "Kenosis" was (as the Apostle says):
"He took upon the form of a servant and was found in the
fashion of man; he humbled himself and became obedi-
ent even unto the death of the Cross."[3] Is not this a
sufficient "emptying of himself" without further impu-
ting to him, without a word of authority from the Holy
Scriptures or from the great Doctors and Fathers of the
Church, of ignorance, and thus introducing into the
Holy Gospels themselves the element of untruth and
fallibility, even into the words of the Lord Jesus!

---

[2] See Archdeacon Denison's admirable treatment of this point.
[3] Philip ii. 8.

With this most dangerous and (as it appears to us) blasphemous opinion is often united an idea which would imply that during the thirty-three years of his flesh here on earth the Eternal Word left the Father's side when proceeding forth to be incarnate for the redemption of the world, contrary to what the Fathers teach, to what the Church sings in the hymn:

> "Verbum supernum prodiens
> Nec-Patris linquens dexteram,"[4]

and to what the Lord himself taught while here on earth, that "the Son of Man is in heaven."[5]

All the doctrines which teach a "Kenosis" other than that recognised by the formularies, conciliar decrees, and teaching of the Doctors of the Church, we look upon as importations from Germany, that hot-bed of rationalism, which, in this matter of the so-called "Kenosis," has but brought to light, in a slightly modified form, one of the old heresies of Origen, for which he was anathematized in the eighth Anathema.

The knowledge of all things, that is to say, infinite knowledge, which we call Omniscience, can pertain to God alone and never to any creature. As God is infinite, so the creature is always finite. Now, the human soul of the Son of God is a creature, and therefore finite, hence it is that no theologian has ever claimed for the human intelligence of God the Son omniscience. On this point there has been and can be no dispute; and while (as Hooker says) the soul of Christ "cannot choose but be privy unto all things which God worketh,

---

[4] "The Eternal Word proceeding forth,
But leaving not the Father's side."

[5] Jno. iii. 13.

and must therefore of necessity be endued with knowledge, so far forth universal, though not with infinite knowledge peculiar to Diety itself";[6] yet Newman's statement cannot be disputed.

"It is the doctrine of the Church that Christ as man was perfect in knowledge from the first, as if ignorance were hardly separable from sin, and were the direct consequence or accompaniment of original sin. 'That ignorance,' says St. Austin, 'I in no wise can suppose existed in that Infant, in whom the Word was made flesh to dwell among us; nor can I suppose that that infirmity of the mind belonged to Christ as a babe which we see in babes. For in consequence of it, when they are troubled with irrational emotions, no reason, no command, but pain sometimes, and the alarm of pain, restrains them,' etc., *de Pecc. Mer.* ii. 48. As to the limits of Christ's perfect knowledge as man, Petavius observes that we must consider that the soul of Christ knew all things that are or ever will be or ever have been, but not what are only *in posse* not in fact. *Incarn.* xi. 3, 6."[7]

It is evident that if we "believe rightly the Incarnation of our Lord Jesus Christ"[8] we will believe that, as the human will was brought into complete conformity with the Divine Will through the Hypostatic Union, and yet that there were two wills, the one the human and the other the divine; so we will believe that the human understanding and wisdom were completely illumined by the Divine understanding and wisdom through the Hypostatic Union, and yet that there were two wisdoms and two understandings, the one the human and the

---

[6] Hooker, *Ecc. Pol.* v. 54 [6]. [7] Note on St. Athan; *C. Ar. Disc.* iii. § 52 Ox. Trans. p. 473. [8] Athanasian Creed.

other the divine; and this doctrine St. Thomas says was defined by the Sixth Synod.

All theologians are agreed that the Hypostatic Union carries with it, as of necessity, the Beatific Vision, but if the soul of Christ enjoyed from the first moment the Beatific Vision it is evident that it had the knowledge of all things which, as finite, it was capable of knowing; any increase in knowledge, therefore, was impossible, whether that increase is supposed to have come after birth during the life of the thirty-three years, or since his ascension into heaven, for some have been blasphemous enough as to suggest that even now the Lord is imperfect, and that his "humanity . . . is, in fact, gradually becoming more and more adequate to the divine nature." Besides this knowledge which our Lord's human soul has as the result of the Beatific Vision, in which he sees all truth and knowledge,[9] and which theologians call his "Beatific Knowledge," he has also infused and experimental knowledge. It does not seem necessary to pause to consider the second kind of knowledge which our Lord enjoys, which is the infused knowledge, a knowledge like that enjoyed by the angels, the direct gift and infusion of God; but we come to the third kind, viz: his experimental knowledge. Now, it is evident that this knowledge "increased" day by day. As the result of this increase, Jesus was no wiser than he was before, for from the first instant of his conception he knew all things; but what before he knew only by Beatific and Infused Wisdom, he now learned by experi-

---

[9] Bp. Wordsworth's Hymn:
> "All truth and knowledge see
> In the Beatific Vision
> Of the Blessed Trinity."

ence. He knew how to speak from the first instant, but he learned to speak by experience; he knew how to walk, but he learned to walk by practice. There was no increase of wisdom, but the wisdom he had acquired already in other ways he was shewing forth as he gained it by experience; and so it was with the favour of God, in which we read he likewise increased. There was, of course, no increase in God's actual favour towards the Son of his bosom, but there was an increase in the clearness with which that favour was manifested. Therefore, our Lord was infallible, and not only so, but also had the knowledge of all things knowable by the finite, and in all matters his word is truth, and his words, as recorded for us in the Sacred Scriptures, are always absolutely reliable upon all subjects upon which he vouchsafed to speak.

When this great distinction between the Beatific and the Infused Wisdom on the one part, and the Experimental Wisdom on the other, is understood, passages in the Fathers, which otherwise would seem to give colour to the error we are refuting, and which are commonly quoted as authorities on that side of the question, are seen to agree entirely with what all other Catholic theologians and teachers have taught. Thus St. Athanasius says, "It was not, then, the Word, considered as the Word, who advanced, who is perfect from the perfect Father, who needs nothing, nay, brings forward others to an advance; but humanly is he here said to advance, since advance belongs to man. Hence, the Evangelist, speaking with cautious exactness, has mentioned stature in the advance; but being Word and God, he is not measured by stature, which belongs to bodies. Of the body, then, is the advance; for, it advancing, in it advanced also the manifestation of the Godhead to those who saw it. And, as the Godhead was more and more revealed, by so much more did his grace as man increase before all men. . . . For thus, the body increasing in stature, there progressed in and with it the manifestation of the Godhead also, and to all was it displayed that the body was God's Temple, and that God was in the body."[10]

So St. Ambrose, still more clearly: " There was increase of age and increase of wisdom, but it was of human wisdom. . . . If he, as man, advanced in age, he must, as man, have advanced in wisdom; the advance in wisdom must have been proportional to that in perception from which it is derived."[11] Here the Saint could refer only to experimental wisdom, since he says it is derived from perception.

Nor are some of the passages of Origen capable only of a bad sense, for no Catholic would reject the following: "We cannot, indeed, say of Wisdom in itself that it was ignorant and acquired knowledge by learning; but it is certainly true of Wisdom as it was in the flesh, for Christ must need learn to stammer and speak like a child with children."[12]

Well says St. Maximus, that whoever he be that says our Lord increased in wisdom by learning more has fallen away to the Nestorian apostasy.[13]

There remains now but one point for consideration, viz: the much-disputed text in St. Mark, xiii. 32, "Of that day and that hour knoweth no man: no, not the angels who are in heaven, neither the Son, but the

---

[10] *C. Arianos.* Disc. iii. 52 (Ox. Trans. p. 473). [11] *De Inc.* vii. 52. [12] Origen, *Hom. in Ter.* i. 8. [13] *Vide* Note (52) to St. Jno. Damasc. *De fide Orth.* Lib. III., Cap. XXII. (ed. Migne).

Father." Of this text there are two explanations possible. First, that of nearly all the Fathers and of all the theologians and doctors of the whole Church, viz: that our Lord as man did know the day and hour of the Day of Judgment, but denied it, speaking "economically," either because he did not know it for the purpose of revealing it, or that he spoke as the head for the members, meaning that the Church does not know that day or hour (so St. Jerome, St. Gregory, and others). The only other possible meaning of the text is that our Lord as man did not know that day and that hour. If such were the case, then it was because that day and that hour can only be known by the infinite, and since our Lord's human soul was finite, he could not as man know that day. In either case, the Catholic doctrine stands unaffected; if it was a piece of information unknowable by the finite, then his finite soul, of course, did not know it; if it was knowable, then he knew it, and spoke economically.[14] This matter cannot be better disposed of than by quoting the words of one who, being dead, yet speaketh, and who sets the whole subject in its true position and shews what is the real heresy of those who attribute ignorance to the Incarnate God, I mean the dear departed Canon Liddon. In a foot-note to his sermon,

---

[14] Perhaps there should have been mentioned also the view that our Lord does not refer to his human knowledge at all, but to his knowledge as the Divine Son, and means to say that as the Son derives his substance from the Father, so also he derives his knowledge from the Father, and that he can reveal only so much as the Father has given him to reveal; therefore, the text means, 'Even the Son of God has not derived from the Father the knowledge of that day and hour so that he is at liberty to reveal it to mankind.' This, however, for practical purposes is identical with the first view.

" The Worth of the Old Testament," he writes as follows:

" On this serious subject there is often a singular confusion between limitation of knowledge and the utter-
ance through ignorance of that which is in fact untrue.
If our Lord *as man* did not know the day and the hour
of the judgment (St. Mark xiii. 32), he did not as man
claim to know it.   Had he told us that the real value of
the books of the Old Testament was hidden from him,
or had he never referred to them, there would have been
no conflict between modern so-called ' critical' specu-
lations and his Divine authority.   But if the Apostles
' beheld his glory,' ' full,' not only ' of grace,' but ' of
truth' (St. John i. 14); if, on the one hand, he knew
what was in man (St. John ii. 25), and, on the other, as
the Only Begotten Son, which is in the bosom of the
Father, ' declared' him whom no man hath seen at any
time (St. John i. 18), is it conceivable that he could say,
' Moses wrote of Me' (St. John v. 46) in utter ignorance
of the (presumed) fact that the book to which he was
principally alluding (Deut. xviii. 13, 14; but *cf.* also
Gen. iii. 15 ; xii. 3 ; xviii. 18 ; xxii. 18 ; xlix. 10) was
really compiled by a ' dramatizing' Jew in the reign of
Josiah; or that he could have referred to Ps. cx. as he
is reported in St. Mark xii. 36, St. Luke xx. 42 (in St.
Matthew he is reported as less directly asserting the
Davidic authorship, xxii. 42–46), if that psalm never
really existed before the date of Simon Maccabæus?

" The hypothesis that, in consequence of imperfect information, our Lord taught erroneously on the subject
of the historical worth of the Old Testament history,
appears to be inconsistent with the Catholic doctrine
of the Incarnation as asserted by the Church against
Nestorius.   According to that doctrine, all the acts and

words of the One Christ are the acts and words of God
the Son, although performed and uttered through the
human nature which he assumed (*cf.* Labbé and Cossart,
Conc. III. 408, Anath. 4). Erroneous teaching is as little
compatible with the Union of his two natures in a single,
and that a Divine, Person, as is sinful action (St. Thomas,
Summa, pt. iii. quæst. xv. a. 3). Language is sometimes
used which appears to imply that, unless our Lord's
human intellect was not only limited in knowledge, but
also liable to error, he did not assume 'a true human
nature.' But this is to forget the very purpose with
which he condescended to become man. As Hooker
observes, 'the very cause of his taking upon him our
nature was to better the quality and to advance the condition thereof, although in no sort to abolish the substance which he took, nor to infuse into it the natural
forces and properties of his Deity. (*Eccl. Pol.*, V. liv. 5).
And thus, 'to be the Way, the Truth and the Life; to
be the Wisdom, Righteousness, Sanctification, Resurrection; to be the Peace of the whole world, the Hope
of the righteous, the Heir of all things; to be that
Supreme Head whereunto all power in heaven and earth
is given—these are not honours common unto Christ
with other men; they are titles above the dignity and
worth of any which were but a mere man, *yet true of
Christ even in that he is man*, but man with whom Deity is
personally joined and unto whom it hath added these
excellencies which make him more than worthy
thereof' (*ibid.*). It is in accordance with this principle
that the Church has hitherto believed him to be an infallible teacher, and especially when he is touching on
matters which, like the Old Testament Scriptures,
directly concern God's revelation of himself to man. To

say that he shews no signs of transcending the historical knowledge of his age is to imply that he shared with the rabbis around him grave errors respecting the real worth of the Old Testament literature, and that he was in this respect inferior to those modern scholars who take the negative side in questions of Old Testament criticism.

"Those persons who unhappily have persuaded themselves that this is the case, and yet happily shrink from rejecting his authority altogether, sometimes attempt to save themselves by projecting a distinction between critical or historical and spiritual truth. If he was in error respecting the historical value of the Pentateuch or Daniel, he could not, they think, err in what he tells us as to the Nature of God or the duty of man. But such persons must know that at this hour his authority in these spiritual matters is as fiercely challenged as in those questions which they somewhat arbitrarily describe as 'critical.' And he himself has taught us that we must receive his teaching as a whole, if we are to receive it at all. 'If I have told you earthly things and ye believe not, how shall ye believe if I tell you of heavenly things?' (St. John iii. 12).

"Perhaps it would be difficult to find a better statement of whatever we know about the knowledge possessed by our Lord's Human Soul than is given in the following words: 'Quia nulla perfectio creaturis exhibita, animæ Christi, quæ est creaturarum excellentissima, deneganda est, convenienter præter cognitionem quâ Dei essentiam vidit, et omnia in ipsâ, triplex alia cognitio est ei attribuenda; una quidem experimentalis sicut aliis hominibus in quantum aliquæ per sensus cognovit, et competit naturæ humanæ; alia vero divinitus infusa ad cognoscenda omnia illa ad quæ naturalis cognitio hominis se extendit vel extendere potest. . . . Sed quia Christus secundum humanam naturam non solum fuit reparator naturæ, sed etiam gratiæ propagator, affuit ei etiam tertia cognitio qua plenissimè cognovit quidquid ad mysteria gratiæ potest pertinere.' He adds: 'Manifestum est quod res sensibiles per temporis successionem magis ac magis sensibus corporis experiendo cognovit, et ideo solum quantum ad cognitionem experimentalem Christus potuit perficere, secundum illud Luc. ii. 52.' (St. Thomas, *Opusc.*, i. 216, Opp. Vol. XVI., ed. Parmæ). On this subject see also Wilberforce, *Doct. of Incarnation*, pp. 97–105 ; and the elaborate discussion in De Lugo *Opp.* iv., *De Myst. Inc.*, dispp. xviii.-xxi., where, however, some exceptions may be taken to the interpretation of St. Mark xiii. 32."

⮲ The Credenda.

¶ *To be signed by every Clergyman before his election to the Union.*

I.

I BELIEVE that our Lord, really and objectively present in the Eucharist under the forms of bread and wine, is to be adored.

II.

I BELIEVE the Priesthood received from Bishops in Apostolical Succession to be necessary to the valid administration of all the sacraments except Baptism and Matrimony.

III.

I BELIEVE that to every human soul God gives during the time of this life sufficient grace to escape damnation; I believe that as Probation consists in the struggle of the soul against sin and Satan, it is limited to this life; and that at the hour of death every soul passes into "an endless and unchangeable state."

IV.

I BELIEVE the Holy Scriptures of the Old and New Testaments to be inspired by God in a manner wholly different from all other writings, and so that they are "the infallible and undeceivable Word of God," and whatever is contained in them is true.

Constitution.

Article i.

OF THE NAME.

THIS Association shall be called the Clerical Union for the Maintenance and Defence of Catholic Principles.

Article ij.

OF THE PRINCIPLES.

1. We hold that to be Catholic in Doctrine, which can be proved to have been implicitly received from the beginning, and that which has been from time to time explicitly declared by the whole Church.

2. We hold that to be Catholic in Practice, which can be proved to have been used by authority in all parts of the Church at any one time.

But we hold that national Churches have a certain power over matters of Practice. (See the XXXIV. Article of Religion.)

3. We hold that to be lawful in Ritual, which can be proved to have been part of the authorized ritual of the Church of England in the second year of the reign of King Edward the Sixth.

Article iij.

OF THE OBJECTS.

1. The defence of the Divine Constitution and supernatural powers of the Church against latitudinarian and rationalizing assaults upon them.

2. The defence of the Catholic claims of the Churches of the Anglican Communion against Roman denials of those claims.

3. The furtherance of the movement in the Church for the elimination of the words "Protestant Episcopal" from her title.

4. The giving of due prominence to the idea of Eucharistic worship in the public services of the Church.

Article iv.

OF THE OFFICERS.

1. There shall be elected annually a President of the whole Union, each member of the Union having one vote in such election.

2. There shall be a Council, composed of two members chosen annually by each local branch, with the President of the Union as Chairman. The Council shall have power to propose the terms of membership and whatever other matters they may judge expedient, provided that all action which they originate shall be approved by two-thirds of the local Clubs, each Club being considered as an entity.

No publications shall be issued nor any action taken in the name of the Union without a vote of the Council; and the President shall have the absolute right of veto upon all publications.

3. There shall be a Secretary and Treasurer elected by the Council.

4. All voting may be done by letter, as well for officers as on any question arising before the Council.

Article v.

OF THE MEANS TO BE EMPLOYED.

1. The publication of papers in aid of the objects of the Union, which may have been read in the meetings of the branches thereof, to be called "Catholic Papers."

2. The calling of public meetings, the preaching of sermons and delivering of lectures, and whatever from time to time may seem best to the Union to promote its objects.

Article vj.

OF ALTERATIONS.

This Constitution shall not be repealed or altered except by two-thirds of the local Clubs voting as in Article iv., Section 2.

Catholic Papers

WRITTEN BY DIFFERENT PERSONS
AND READ AT SEVERAL TIMES
BEFORE THE MEETINGS OF
THE CLERICAL UNION
IN NEW YORK AND
PHILADELPHIA,
U. S. A.

I · DO · BELIEVE · THE · HOLY
SCRIPTURES · OF · THE · OLD
AND · NEW · TESTAMENT · TO
BE · THE · WORD · OF · GOD
AND · TO · CONTAIN · ALL
THINGS · NECESSARY · TO · SAL-
VATION · AND · I · DO · SOL-
EMNLY · ENGAGE · TO · CONFORM
TO · THE · DOCTRINES · AND
WORSHIP · OF · THE · PROTES-
TANT · EPISCOPAL · CHURCH
IN · THE · UNITED · STATES

The Inspiration of Holy Scripture.

I.

IN this present paper I shall endeavour, first, to trace the Church's belief about the Inspiration of the Bible from the earliest times; and, secondly, to point out some considerations which may help to remove some of the difficulties which that belief has occasioned in many minds.

I do not propose to enter into any questions connected with the settlement of the canon of Holy Scripture. That I shall take for granted as it is given to us on the authority of the Church. My concern is solely with the inspiration of those books which we accept as canonical. The two questions, though really quite distinct, are often confounded. It does not follow because there have been disputes about the canonicity of certain books, and the claims of some have been denied, that therefore there has been a denial of the inspiration of Scripture in general. The claims of the Epistle to the Hebrews, and of the Second Epistle of St. Peter, and of the Apocalypse, were disputed in the earliest days of the Church; yet no one ever doubted that what was recognised as Scripture was inspired. I pass by, then, all such questions, and confine myself to the one point of inspiration,

It has been well remarked by Cardinal Manning,[1] that the dogmas of the Church have for the most part passed through three stages. They have had, first, their period of simple affirmation and belief; then of incipient controversy and partial analysis; lastly, of formal contradiction, complete analysis, and final scientific definition. The doctrine of the Inspiration of Holy Scripture is so far no exception to the rule. It, too, has had its period of simple, unquestioned belief, followed by one of controversy and partial analysis; it may hereafter have its final and authoritative settlement. Meanwhile, I wish to enquire what, through the long ages of the Church's history, has been her constant traditional belief on this subject.[2] Let us see.

The Christian Church in inheriting from the Synagogue the Hebrew Canon, inherited along with it the current Jewish belief in its inspiration. That belief was one which extended the Divine operation to the whole substance and form, the sense, and the letter of Holy Scripture. The care of the Rabbis to count every verse and letter in every book of the Old Testament; their belief that a mystery underlay every jot and tittle of the sacred text cannot have resulted from any lower principle. Later Jews, like the Cabbalists or Maimonides, who were infected with rationalism, seem to have invented the theory of various degrees of inspiration, and

---

[1] *Temporal Mission of the Holy Ghost*, p. 135. [2] For many of the quotations from the Ante-Nicene Fathers, I am indebted to a valuable catena printed as an appendix to Dr. Westcott's *Introduction to the Study of the Gospels;* and for much illustrative matter to Lee on *Inspiration*, especially the notes and appendices, and also to a paper of Cardinal Newman's in the *Nineteenth Century*, for February, 1884.

generally to have held looser views; but the more ancient, as all our records shew, esteemed every part of Scripture alike as the express Word of God. A well-known passage of Josephus (*Cont. Apion*, lib. i. c. 8) may be quoted as a fair sample of the belief of all ortho-dox Jews of his own time. "With us," he says, "there is no endless series of works, discordant and contra-dictory: two-and-twenty books contain the annals of all time, and are justly believed to be Divine. . . . From the age of Artaxerxes, it is true, narratives of events, extending to our day, have been written; but they have not been counted of equal credit with books composed at an earlier period, because there has been no accurate succession of Prophets. Facts clearly prove how great trust we repose in our sacred books; for, although so many ages have passed away, no man has dared to add to, or take away from, or alter ought in them. Nay, it is implanted in every Jew from the hour of his birth, to esteem as the ordinances of God, and to stand fast by these writings; and in defence of them, if need be, to die."

This traditional belief as to the inspired character of these books was inherited by the early Christian Fathers, and extended by them to the writings of the New Testa-ment, as they were one by one recognised by the Church. St. Clement quotes many passages from Scripture with the words: "the Holy Spirit saith" (*Ad. Cor.* i. 45), or their equivalent. He exhorts his readers to "look carefully into the Scriptures, which are the true utterances of the Holy Spirit." Again he says (ibid. 53), "Ye know, beloved, ye know well the Sacred Scriptures, and have looked carefully into the oracles of God." In another place (ibid. 8) he speaks of "the ministers of the grace of God" (meaning the Prophets of the Old Testament) who "by the Holy Ghost have spoken of repentance;" and again (ibid. 47) of the blessed Apostle Paul that he "wrote under the inspiration of the Spirit."

St. Justin Martyr (*Cohort.* 12) speaks of the "history which Moses wrote in the Hebrew character by Divine inspiration," while the "Holy Spirit of prophecy taught him" (*Apol.* i. 44). Again, he says (ibid. i. 36), "When you hear the utterances of the Prophets spoken as it were personally, you must not suppose that they are spoken by the inspired themselves, but by the Divine Word who moves them." The Prophets "spoke by the Holy Ghost, and foretold what would happen thereafter, and what is now taking place. And they alone knew and taught the truth" (*Trypho,* 7). Their work is to announce "whatever the Holy Ghost, who descended upon them, chose to teach through them to those who wish to learn the true religion" (*Cohort.* 35). "For neither by nature, nor human conception, is it possible for men to know things so great and Divine, but by the gift which then descended from above upon the holy men, who needed no art of words, nor skill in captious and contentious speaking, but only to offer themselves in purity to the operation of the Divine Spirit, in order that the Divine plectrum itself, descending from heaven, and using righteous men as an instrument like a harp or lyre, might reveal to us the knowledge of things Divine and heavenly" (ibid. 8). This, I believe, is the earliest use of the illustration of the lyre, which is afterwards so common in the writings of the Fathers. Once more Justin held firmly that no Scripture can be contrary to any other; if such appears to be the case, it is in consequence of our not understanding the meaning. Thus in the dialogue with Trypho, in answering an alleged contradiction in the Old Testament, he replies (*Trypho*, 65), " If you spake these words, Trypho, because you thought yourself able to bring our conversation into a difficulty, and to force me to assert that the Scriptures contradict one another, you are in error: for I will never venture either to think or to say such a thing. But if there is any Scripture which can be urged as appearing to be contradictory to some other (for I am persuaded that such is never really the case), I would rather confess that I do not understand its meaning."

Theophilus, Bishop of Antioch, sixth in succession from the Apostles, says (*Ad. Ant.* ii. 9), "The men of God, being borne along by the Holy Spirit, and gifted with prophecy, being inspired and made wise by God, because God-taught, and holy, and righteous, wherefore they were also deemed worthy of receiving this reward, that they should become instruments of God, and contain the wisdom that is from him, by which wisdom they spake of the creation of the world and all other things . . . which happened before their birth, and during their own time, and which are now being accomplished in our days; and so we are convinced that in things to come the event will be as they say." Again, contrasting the value of sacred and profane history, he says (ibid. 33), "We Christians alone have possessed the truth, inasmuch as we are taught by the Holy Spirit, who spake in the holy Prophets, and foretold all things." Moreover, the "contents of the Prophets and of the Gospels are found to be consistent, because all the writers spake by the inspiration of the One Spirit of God" (ibid. iii. 12).

St. Irenæus, speaking of the Apostles, says (*Haer.* iii. i. 1), "After our Lord rose from the dead, and they were clad with the power of the Holy Ghost coming on them from on high, they were filled with all things, and had perfect knowledge;" and again (ibid. iii. v. 1), that "being disciples of the truth, they are beyond all falsehood." Again (ibid. ii. xxviii. 1, 3), speaking of difficulties in Scripture, he tells us that "we ought to leave such things to God, being aware, as the very truth is, that the Scriptures indeed are perfect, as uttered by God's Word and his Spirit, while we, in such measure as we are inferior, and very far removed from God's Word and his Spirit, just so far are we wanting in the knowledge of his mysteries. And no wonder if this befall us in spiritual and heavenly things, and in such as require revelation, since even of those things which lie close in our way (I mean those which make part of this creation, which are both felt and seen by us, and are with us); many have escaped our knowledge." And then, after various illustrations drawn from things we cannot explain in nature, such as the rising of the Nile—the migration of birds—the ebb and flow of the tide—the causes of winds and storms—he says again, "If among the very things of creation some are laid up with God, while some have come also to our knowledge; what hardship is it, if of the points questioned in the Scriptures also (the whole of the Scriptures being spiritual) some by the grace of God we solve, while others must be laid up with God, and that not only in this world, but also in that which is to come, so that God may always be teaching, and man still ever learning from God." Again, Irenæus teaches that the Holy Ghost overrules the very phrases and expressions which the sacred writers employ. Thus, speaking of the Birth of our Lord, he observes (ibid. iii. xvi. 2), "St. Matthew might have said, 'The Birth of *Jesus* was on this wise;' but the Holy Spirit foreseeing corrupters, and providing bulwarks against their deceitfulness, saith by Matthew, 'The Birth of *Christ* was so and so.'" The details of Holy Scripture may seem insignificant; yet (ibid. iv. xxi. 3) "nothing is empty or without meaning with God." There may be difficulties; yet (ibid. ii. xxviii. 2) "all Scripture, inasmuch as it has been given to us by God, will be found to be consistent."

The early Fathers of the Roman Church spake in a similar strain. A fragment preserved in Eusebius (*H. E.* v. 28) and attributed by some to the Presbyter Caius, speaks of the followers of Artemon, "who fearlessly laid their hands on the Divine Scriptures, saying that they corrected them. . . . How great is the daring of their error (he adds) cannot be unknown even to themselves; for either they do not believe that the Divine Scriptures were spoken by the Holy Ghost, and are unbelievers: or they hold themselves wiser than the Holy Spirit, and we must say they rave." Hippolytus, Bishop of Portus (*Cont. Noetum*, ii.), says, "God gave the Law and the Prophets; and in giving them, he made them speak by the Holy Ghost, in order that, being gifted with the inspiration of the Father's power, they might declare the Father's counsel and will." And again (*De Anti-christo* 2), "These Fathers were furnished with the Spirit, and largely honoured by the Word himself; and just as it is with instruments of music, so had they the Word always, like the plectrum, in union with them, and when moved by him the Prophets announced what God willed. For they spake not of their own power (be well assured), neither did they declare what pleased themselves; but first they were endowed with wisdom by the Word, and afterwards well foretaught of the future by

visions, and then, when thus assured, they spake that
which was revealed to them by God alone." The famous
Muratorian fragment on the Canon also, which is almost
certainly a work of the Roman Church of the second
century, has a remarkable passage recognising the inspiration and unity of the four Gospels under divergent
forms. The passage is as follows (*Fragm. de Canone*):
" Although different points (*principia*) are taught us in
the several books of the Gospels, there is no difference
as regards the faith of believers, inasmuch as in all of
them all things which concern the [Lord's] Nativity,
Passion, Resurrection, conversation with his disciples,
and his twofold Advent, are related by one and the self-
same guiding Spirit."

If we enquire of the Fathers of the North African
Church, they will teach us the same doctrine. Tertullian
says (*Apol.* 18), "in order that we might attain an ampler
and more authoritative knowledge of himself, his counsels, and his will, God has added a written Testament.
. . . For from the first he sent messengers into the
world, men whose stainless righteousness made them
worthy to know God and to reveal him—men abundantly
endowed with the Holy Ghost." He calls the books of
Scripture the "writings" (*litteras*) and the "words"
(*voces*) "of God" (*De Anima* 2, Apol. 31). After quoting 1 Cor. iv. 9, he continues (*Adv. Marcion* v. 7):
"The Holy Ghost has providentially explained the meaning of the passage;" and a few lines further on he says
ironically, "of course a man of the noble courage of our
Apostle (to say nothing of the Holy Ghost) was afraid,
when writing to the children whom he had begotten in
the Gospel, to speak freely of the God of the world." In
like manner he quotes 1 Tim. vi. 10, saying (*De Patient.*

7), "the Spirit of the Lord hath declared by the Apostle, that covetousness is the root of all evil." And interpreting 1 Cor. xi. 5, he observes (*De Orat.* 22), "And no wonder that the Apostle, moved surely by the same Spirit by whom, as all Divine Scripture, so also that book of Genesis was composed," etc.

St. Cyprian holds the same language. Quoting Prov. xvi. 6, he says (*De opere et eleemos.* 2), "the Holy Spirit speaks in the Sacred Scriptures and says, 'by almsgiving and faith sins are purged.'" And again (*De Unitate Eccles.* 4), quoting the Song of Solomon, "Which one Church, also, the Holy Spirit in the Song of Songs designated in the person of our Lord, and says, 'My dove, my spotless one, is but one.'" Everywhere throughout his writings we read that the Holy Spirit spake in the Law and in the Gospel, by Prophets, by Apostles and Evangelists.

The Alexandrian Fathers speak in like manner. "God leads us," says St. Clement (*Strom.* vii. 16), "in the inspired Scriptures." He quotes from the Song of Moses (in Deut. xxxii. 10–12) with the introductory words, "Somewhere in song the Holy Spirit says" (*Pæd.* i. 7). "The Law," he says (ibid. i. 7), "was given through Moses; yet not by Moses, but by the Word through Moses as his servant." Again he says (*Cohort. ad Gentes,* 9), "I could adduce ten thousand Scriptures of which not one tittle shall pass away without being fulfilled; for the mouth of the Lord the Holy Spirit hath spoken these things."

Origen, in the opening of his treatise *De Principiis,* lays down the Articles of the Faith, and amongst them this (*De Princip.*, Praefat. 4), "that the Holy Spirit inspired each one of the saints, whether Prophets or

Apostles; and that there was not one Spirit in the men
of the Old Dispensation, and another in those who were
inspired at the Advent of Christ." In the fifth book
against Celsus, chapter 49, he says that "both Jews and
Christians agree that the books [of Scripture] were written by the Spirit of God, though they do not agree about
the meaning of their contents." Again he says (*De
Princip.* iv. 9), "To those who believe that the sacred
books are not the compositions of men, but that they
were composed by inspiration of the Holy Spirit . . .
we must point out the ways [of interpreting them] which
appear [correct] to us." The details of the cosmogony
and the records of the chosen people were, in Origen's
judgment, as truly written by inspiration as the books of
the Prophets. The Gospels are full of meaning in their
minutest details, and are without error, being "accurately
written by the coöperation of the Holy Spirit." In one
of his homilies on the book of Numbers, he says (*Hom.
in Num.* xxvii. 1), "We cannot say of the writings of
the Holy Spirit that anything in them is otiose or superfluous, even if they seem to some obscure." To the
Christian the words of St. Paul are the words of God;
and they only, he tells us, will find contradictions in the
Apostles' writings "who sever the one doctrine of the
Faith into the diverse opinions of sects, and examine only
those testimonies of Scripture which support their peculiar view, regardless of the full and perfect meaning of
such passages as exhibit the opposite side of the truth."

The above quotations give a fair view of the belief of
the earliest Christian writers. That they held a high
doctrine of inspiration cannot be doubted. Scripture
was to them simply and truly the Word of God. The
whole, and every part of it, was directly inspired by the

Holy Ghost, and was therefore absolutely true and full of a Divine life and mystery. Yet they held no bare, mechanical theory of inspiration such as has been advocated by some in later days. They did not conceive of the sacred writers as mere passive instruments of the Holy Spirit; there was a coöperation of their own spirit and intelligence. The Holy Spirit acted not merely upon them, but through them. Even when Justin and others use the metaphor of the lyre or flute, we must remember (as has been well observed) that the character of the tone depends as well upon the nature of the instrument as upon the hand which touches it, or the wind which breathes through it. Athenagoras alone (*Leg. pro Christo* 9), among early writers, appears to speak of the sacred writers as being entranced and deprived of their natural faculties while they spoke or wrote under the influence of the Divine Spirit. But the more usual teaching of the early Fathers (*cf.* Origen *Cont. Celsum* vii. 4) was rather that the reason was cleared, not clouded; exalted, not paralysed by the Divine influence. There was an intermingling of the Divine and human elements, the one completely interpenetrating the other, and the two acting together in one theandric operation. In short, so far as they can be said to have had any express and definite theory, it was what has been called dynamical, rather than mechanical or merely organic.

Origen, however, was the first great Biblical critic, and when we come to him we find traces of a departure in some respects from the views of those who had gone before him. While holding in the main the full inspiration and absolute truth of Holy Scripture in all its parts, he seems to have felt the pressure of difficulties, and to have endeavoured to escape them by his system of interpretation.   He held (*De Princip*. iv. 11) that "as man consists of body, soul, and spirit; so, too, does Scripture which has been given by God for the salvation of man."   Corresponding to this is his threefold system of interpretation, the literal, the moral, and the spiritual.   Pressed by difficulties in the literal understanding of some passage he set it aside, and taught that there were cases in which we must look only for the moral and spiritual meaning.   Some Scriptures, he says (ibid. 12), "do not at all contain the corporeal sense" (τὸ σωματικον), so that in such cases "we must seek only the soul, as it were, and the Spirit of Scripture."   Thus he denies that we ought to understand literally the account given in the early chapters of Genesis of God planting the Garden of Eden, and walking in it in the cool of the evening (ibid. 16).   In like manner he rejects that interpretation of our Lord's Temptation, which supposes that all the kingdoms of the world were placed before his bodily eyes as contiguous to one mountain; and says, "that many other instances similar to this will be found in the Gospels by anyone who will read them with attention, and will observe that in those narratives which appear to be literally recorded, there are inserted and interwoven, things which cannot be admitted historically, but which may be accepted in a spiritual signification."   So again, when dealing with the harmonistic difficulties of the Gospels, he says,[1] "if one were to set them all forth, then would he turn dizzy, and either desist from trying to establish all the Gospels in very truth, and attach himself to one . . .   or admitting the four, grant that their truth does not lie in their corporeal forms."

---

[1] *Comm. in Joan.* Quoted by Westcott.

Upon these last-quoted passages, Archdeacon Lee observes that "the key to the meaning of Origen, when using these and similar expressions—at first sight so opposed to his many unambiguous assertions of the perfect inspiration of Scripture—is to be found in his system of allegorising."[4] And yet he observes it was not so much that system itself as his failure to apply it consistently which was at fault. "It is plain," says the Archdeacon, "if this analogy (of the threefold nature of man to the threefold sense of Scripture) is to be carried out, that in order to form a just conception of what Scripture means, due value must be assigned to each of its three elements, and the relation to each other which they respectively hold must be maintained. The spirit of man confers its vital power upon the material substance into which it has been infused; while the soul, the product, as it were, of this union of the spiritual and corporeal, is that in which consists the real existence of the living man. To consider the material substance alone, or the spirit alone, is at once to abandon the region of actual being. We should then contemplate an inanimate mass, or speculate respecting the nature of an immaterial element which transcends the limit of all human experience. While, if we grasp the full idea of the living man, his material substance becomes the outward, but necessary garb of the spiritual essence; the union of both being expressed by the soul, which derives its vital principle from what is spiritual, and the *condition* of its existence from the bodily organisation— an organisation which (as we learn from the doctrine of the resurrection of the body) is as essential to its future

---

[4] Lee on *Inspiration*. Appendix G., p. 526, note.

as to its present being.   The fixed relation of these
three component parts was what Origen failed to maintain when he proceeded to apply the analogy which he
so accurately pointed out."   Whatever may be the value
of this apology for Origen, it is certain that, in spite of
some inconsistencies, he agrees in the main with the
stream of Catholic tradition.   His usual language is that
of one who believes in the plenary inspiration, and absolute truthfulness of Holy Scripture; and he frequently
answers objections that may be urged against such a
doctrine, by appealing,[5] as Irenæus had done before him,
to analogies drawn from the world of nature.   It was
indeed a remark of Origen's (*Philocal.*) that "he who
believes the Scriptures to have proceeded from him who
is the author of nature, may well expect to find the same
sort of difficulties in it, as are found in the constitution
of nature," which seems to have suggested to Bishop
Butler his great argument in the Analogy.

But we must pass on to the teaching of the later
Fathers.   St. Athanasius says,[6] "The holy and divinely-
inspired Scriptures are sufficient to express the truth."
And again,[7] "Each Psalm has been spoken and composed by the Spirit;" and, "The Lord is in the words of
the Scriptures."   St. Basil says,[8] "All Scripture is inspired by God and profitable, having been composed by
the Spirit for this purpose, that as in a common hospital
of souls, every man may choose out the remedy for his
own disease."   St. Gregory of Nazianzum says,[9] "But
we who extend the accuracy of the Spirit even to every

---

[5] *cf. Cont. Cels.* iv. 7.   [6] *Orat. Cont. Gentes.* t. i. p. 1.   Ed. Paris,
MDCXXVII.   [7] *Ep. ad Marcellin,* t. i. p. 967, ibid. p. 983.   [8] *Hom.
in Psal.* i. t. i. p. 125.   [9] *Orat. Prima,* t. i. p. 41.   Ed. Paris,
MDCXXX.

the least point and line (of the Scriptures), will never
grant, for it is not right we should, that even the least
actions were written without intention." The other St.
Gregory, of Nyssa, writes,[10] "All things whatsoever the
Holy Scripture says, are the utterances of the Holy
Spirit." St. Chrysostom says,[11] "As in gold mines, one
skilful in what relates to them would not endure to over-
look even the smallest vein as producing much wealth,
so in Holy Scriptures it is impossible, without loss, to
pass by one jot or one tittle, we must search into all;
for they are all uttered by the Holy Spirit, and nothing
useless is written in them." In like manner in his homilies on Genesis he says (*Hom.* xv. *in Gen.* ii.), "For they
are not merely words, but the words of the Holy Ghost,
and therefore a great treasure is to be found even in a
single syllable." And again (*Hom.* ii. *in Esai.*), "Certain
illiterate persons taking up the Divine Books, and per-
ceiving statements as to chronology or catalogues of
names, pass such matters by with the remark, 'it is only
names, and there is nothing profitable in it.' What sayest
thou? God speaks, and dost thou dare to say there is
nothing profitable in what he speaks?" St. Chrysostom
also frequently speaks of St. Paul as "the Lyre of the
Spirit;" language which is repeated so late as the Second
Council of Nicæa, A. D. 787.[12] Even the unimpassioned
and critical Eusebius says, "I hold it to be alike rashness
and presumption to venture to prove that the Divine
Scriptures have erred" (*Comment. in Psal.* xxxiv., quoted
by Lee).

These quotations might be extended to any length,
but I must hurry on. I will cite but one passage more,

[10] *Cont. Eunom. Orat.* vi. t. ii. p. 604. Ed. Paris, MDCXXXVIII.
[11] *Hom. in Joan.* xxxvi. 1. [12]*Can.* i. apud Mansi, t. xiii. p. 417.

and that from St. John Damascene, the last of the Greek
Fathers, a theologian to whose opinions the Eastern
Church has ever since paid the highest deference. While
enumerating a catalogue of the Books of Scripture, he
remarks as follows (*De Fide Orthod.* lib. iv. c. 17): "The
Law and the Prophets, the Evangelists and the Apostles,
spoke by the Holy Ghost. All Scripture, therefore, inspired by God is assuredly profitable" (or perhaps "is
inspired throughout and is profitable"), "so that it is a
most excellent thing to search the Divine Scriptures, and
most profitable to the soul."

For the Latin Fathers we may refer especially to St.
Augustine (*Ep. ad. St. Hieron*, 82): "I confess (he says)
that I have learnt to pay such veneration and honour to
those Books which are called canonical, that I most
firmly believe that none of their authors ever fell into
any error in writing them ; that if I meet with anything
in those books which seems to me to be at variance with
the truth, I do not doubt but that either my copy of that
book is faulty, or that the translation which I am using
of it has missed the sense, or that I myself have failed to
understand the true meaning of the writer. And I suppose that you, my brother in Christ (he is writing to St.
Jerome), are of the same mind with me in this matter.
I do not imagine that you desire your own works to be
read with the same regard as those of Prophets and
Apostles, concerning whose writings it is impious to
entertain any doubt that they are altogether free from
error." In another letter (ibid. 40), also written to St.
Jerome, he shews how insecure the whole fabric of the
Christian Faith would eventually become, if the iner-
rancy of Holy Scripture were given up. "If (he says) we
once admit that Scripture (which is designed to be the

standard of our faith) is false, the whole structure will be shaken and totter; and it is not possible to express how great and inextricable would be the evils which would ensue from this admission." And again, in the same letter, he says, " I owe this free allegiance to canonical Scripture, of all books in the world, that I follow it alone, and do not doubt that in nothing were its writers in error."

St. Jerome speaks of the Holy Scripture, "where the very order of the words is a mystery," and he asserts that in Scripture there can be no contradictions.[13]

St. Ambrose, speaking of the sacred writers, says (*Ep. ad Justum*), " They wrote not by art, but by grace, which is beyond all art; for they wrote what the Spirit gave them to speak." And again, in his exposition of the Gospel according to St. Luke, he adopts and almost translates a sentence of Origen's to the effect that the Evangelists wrote without effort, but the Divine Spirit ministering to them a copiousness, both of words and matter, they accomplished their undertaking without trouble."

St. Gregory the Great, speaking of the Book of Job (*Mor. in Job*, praef. i. 2), says, " Who was the author of it, it is very superfluous to enquire, since at any rate the Holy Spirit is confidently believed to have been the author. He then himself wrote them, who dictated the things that should be written. . . . When, then, we understand the matter, and hold that the Holy Spirit was the author, in enquiring about the writer, what else do we than if, in reading a letter, we were to enquire

---

[13] *Ep.* xxxiii. *ad Pammachion. Ep.* xliv. *Paula et Eust. ad Marcel.*

about the pen." And again, "What else is Sacred Scripture than an Epistle of the Omnipotent God to his creature?" (*Ep. ad Theodorum Medicum.*)

This long array of quotations may be taken to represent the belief of the Church down to the close of the sixth century. If there is to be found no exact definition, and little of elaborated theory, it is because none, either among Catholics or heretics, however they might dispute about the Canon of Scripture, questioned its perfect inspiration. The only exception to the truth of this statement appears to have been the case of the Anomœans, the extreme section of the Arian party, who, when pressed by argument from Scripture, were used to reply, as Epiphanius tells us, "The Apostle says this merely as man," or "Why do you quote the Old Testament to me?"

Indeed it is not till we come to the controversies of the sixteenth century that we find the Church framing formal dogmatic propositions to guard a belief which till that time had been held almost without gainsaying or dispute. The Council of Trent is, I believe, the first Council which dealt expressly with the subject of inspiration. The controversies which were the outcome of the New Learning and the Reformation, forced the question upon the notice of the Church. One great principle of the Reformation was "the sufficiency of Scripture for salvation." The authority of Scripture was exalted against the authority of the unwritten tradition of the Church. Naturally this led to a very high estimate of the Bible. An infallible Book was substituted in place of an infallible Church. Accordingly many of the reformers held extreme views on the subject of inspiration. They maintained that not only the entire matter of Holy Scripture, but also its form, even to its very words and their order, and the connexion of the sentences, was directly dictated by Almighty God. The sacred writers were the mere pens, not even the penmen, which God used to write his Word. This is the mechanical theory of inspiration. The younger Buxtorf carried it to such an extent that he asserted the inspired authority of even the Hebrew vowel points and accents.

But at the same time the Reformation had another and an opposite tendency. It was also favourable to the utmost freedom of thought. Criticism soon led to laxer views ; and the Church was forced to draw up dogmatic propositions on the subject both of inspiration and inter-pretation. However, it would take me too far away to write the history of the various opinions of those outside the Church, or of the controversies within the Church her-self. My purpose is but to trace the stream of Catholic tradition. I will only remark that even among Protes-tants outside the Church the belief in the inspiration and infallibility of Holy Scripture has been held to with singular tenacity by all who have not been more or less tainted with rationalism. Luther and Calvin were both orthodox on this point. The former, though dealing very freely with the Canon of Scripture never impugned its perfect inspiration. His rejection of particular books, it has been well remarked,[14] "arose, not from his refusing to acknowledge the Divine origin and character of the Bible, but from his venturing to lay down a certain standard by which to test the claim of *any* composition to have proceeded from God." He set aside external evidence and the authority of the Church, in favour of the purely subjective criterion of his own intuition.

---

[14] Lee on *Inspiration*, Appendix C.

Among Roman theologians, since the Council of Trent, two opinions are held.[15]

1. The first is that of the older writers, who maintain that every word was inspired and dictated by the Holy Spirit, so that not only the whole substance, but the form also, the composition, and style of the language, is to be ascribed to him.

The learned theologian and commentator Estius is among the most noted of those who held this opinion. In his comment on the celebrated text, 2 Tim. iii. 16, he writes as follows: "From this passage it is rightly and truly established that all sacred and canonical Scripture was written at the dictation of the Holy Spirit; and in such a way that not only the sense, but also every word, and the order of the words, and the whole arrangement is from God, as though he were speaking or writing in person. For this is the meaning of the Scripture being Divinely inspired."

2. The other opinion, which is that of Bellarmine and most of the Jesuit theologians and more recent writers, is, that the whole *matter* of Holy Scripture was written by the assistance of the Holy Spirit, but not the whole *form* dictated by him; or, in other words, "*res et sententias*"—the sense and substance; "*non verba et apices*"—not every particular word or letter.

As an example of this opinion, which is the one most widely held in the Roman Communion at the present day, and appears to be most in accordance with the language of the dogmatic decrees of the Tridentine and Vatican Councils, I will quote from one of the most approved of their recent text-books, the *Prælectiones*

---

[15] *Vide* Manning *Temporal Mission of the Holy Ghost*, p. 150.

Theologicæ of F. Perrone (vol. ii., pars, ii., cap. ii.). He first states the following proposition: "With good reason the Council of Trent teaches that One God is the Author of the canonical books of both Testaments, or that those books are sacred, being written by the inspiration of the Holy Spirit, at least so far as belongs to the facts and sense." Upon the concluding words of which he observes: "We have said '*at least so far as belongs to the facts and sense*,' because, inasmuch as the Church has been unwilling to define or settle the question debated in the schools as to whether God dictated also the very words, and their order, and the construction of the sentences; therefore (that we may not rashly mix up a domestic controversy with the doctrine of the Church), we have limited the meaning of the Proposition to the substance of the matter, without which a true inspiration can neither exist, nor be understood." F. Perrone also expressly says that in virtue of their inspiration the Canonical Books are " free from every blot of error however slight;" and that God gave to the sacred writers throughout an "*assistentia positiva*," by which words he means, as he explains, an assistance not merely preserving them from error, but actually suggesting what they were to write and what to omit, so that "God alone in the strict sense ought to be considered the Author of those Books."

If we turn to the Anglican Divines since the Reformation we shall find their testimony is the same. The earlier writers do little more than repeat the traditional utterances of their predecessors respecting the inspiration and veracity of Holy Scripture.

Hooker, speaking of the Prophets,[16] says, "So often as he (that is, God) employed them in this heavenly work

---

[16] *I. Serm. on St. Jude*, 17–21, vol. iii. p. 662, Ed. Keble.

they neither spake nor wrote any word of their own, but uttered syllable by syllable as the Spirit put it into their mouths, no otherwise than the harp or the lute doth give a sound according to the discretion of his hand that holdeth and striketh it with skill." And again, "God which lightened the eyes of their understanding, giving them knowledge by unusual and extraordinary means, did also miraculously himself frame and fashion their words and writings." And again,[17] "Scripture with Christian men being received as the word of God, that for which we have probable, yea, that which we have necessary reason for, yea, that which we see with our eyes, is not thought so sure as that which the Scripture of God teacheth; because we hold that *his* speech revealeth what *himself seeth;* and therefore the strongest proof of all, and the most necessarily assented unto by us, who do thus receive the Scripture—is the Scripture."

Myles Coverdale, Bishop of Exeter, one of the Bishops who assisted at the consecration of Parker, writes in the Prologue to his *Translation of the Bible*[18] much as St. Augustine had done before him, "Now, I will exhort thee, whosoever thou be that readest Scripture, if thou find ought therein that thou understandest not, or that appeareth to be repugnant, give no temerarious nor hasty judgment thereof; but ascribe it to thine own ignorance, not to Scripture : think that thou understandest it not, or that it hath some other meaning, or that it is haply overseen of the interpreter, or wrongly printed." And he quotes with approval the saying of the same Father (ibid. p. 334), " Let us give place and consent

---

[17] E. P. ii., ch. vii. 5, *cf.* also ch. viii. 5.   [18] *Remains*, p. 14.   Ed. Parker Society.

to the Holy Scripture; for it can neither deceive nor be deceived."

James Pilkington, who was associated with Bill, Parker, Cox, Guest, Whitehead and May in the revision of the Book of Common Prayer (1558–9), and was afterwards successively Master of St. John's College, Cambridge, and Regius Professor of Divinity, and the Bishop of Durham, in his *Exposition of the Book of Nehemiah,* writes as follows (*Works*, p. 286. Ed. Parker Society): " I would not have men think that the Scripture taketh his authority and credit of the man that writeth it; but the writer is to be credited for the Holy Ghost's sake, who inspired him with such heavenly knowledge, and whose instrument he is for God to speak by. Scripture cometh not first from man, but from God; and therefore God is to be taken for the Author of it, not man. . . . God, then, is the chiefest Author of this book, as he is of the rest of the Scriptures, and Nehemiah the pen or writer of all these mysteries."

Dr. Whitaker, also Regius Professor of Divinity and Master of St. John's College, Cambridge, a man for whose learning and talents Cardinal Bellarmine had so high an esteem that he kept a portrait of him in his study, in his *Disputation on Holy Scripture,* writes,[19] " We confess that God hath not spoken by himself, but by others. Yet this does not dimish the authority of the Scriptures. For God inspired the Prophets with what they said, and made use of their mouths, tongues, and hands: the Scripture is, therefore, even immediately the voice of God." And again, he says (ibid. p. 289), "Scripture hath for its Author God himself, from whom

---

[19] *Disputation on Scripture,* p. 296. Ed. Parker Society.

it first proceeded and came forth;" and then quoting 2 Tim. iii. 16, he adds, "the whole Scripture is called θεόπνευστος."

Archbishop Bramhall says (*Works*, vol. iv. p. 330. Anglo-Cath. Lib.), "We have not only a national tradition of our own Church for the Divine authority of Holy Scripture, but (what is of much more moment) we have the *perpetual, constant, universal* tradition of the Catholic Church of Christ, ever since Christ himself did tread upon the face of the earth. This is so clear a proof of the universal reception of the Bible for the genuine Word of God, that there cannot justly be any more doubt made of it, than whether there ever was a William the Conqueror or not." And again (ibid. vol. v. p. 115), "Suffer the truth of Sacred Writ to be questioned in a word or syllable, and you weaken the authority, and lessen the venerable estimation of the whole text."

Bishop Pearson says (*Creed*, Art. 1, p. 12. Ed. Burton), "The Prophets were the instruments of Divine Revelation, which they first believed as revealed to them, and then the people as revealed by them: for what they delivered was not the testimony of man, but the testimony of God delivered by man. It was he who 'spake by the mouth of his holy Prophets which have been since the world began;' the mouth, the instrument, the articulation was theirs; but the words were God's. . . . The Prophets, as they did not frame the notions or conceptions themselves of those truths which they delivered from God, so they did not loosen their own tongues of their own instinct, or upon their own motion, but as moved, impelled, and acted upon by God. . . . That, therefore, which they delivered was the Word of God."

And to come to our own day, Bishop Wordsworth, of Lincoln, speaking of the inspiration of the New Testament, says (*N. T. in Greek*, Preface, p. xviii.), "We are firmly persuaded that there are not any, even the least errors or inaccuracies in the New Testament" (ibid. p. xix.). And again, "If, to our fallible sense there *seems* to be any error in Holy Scripture, we are sure that the cause of this seeming error is not in him who wrote what is written, or in that which is written by his agency, but in us, who read what he wrote." And again (*H. Bible*, Introduc. p. xxxi.), "Moses was not free from error as a *man*, but as a *writer of Canonical Scripture* he was preserved from error by the Holy Ghost; and all that he wrote was 'given by inspiration of God,' and was acknowledged to be so by Christ himself, who is God. God used erring men to write Scripture, in order that Scripture, which is unerring, might be known to be not the work of man, but of God." And once more, on the words of Christ that "the Scriptures cannot be broken," he comments (ibid. p. xxvii., note 2), "Scripture is so solidly compacted together as to be *indissoluble*. Surely this assertion of our Lord is irreconcilable with the theory of those who think that by a critical chemistry they can analyse and dissolve the Scriptures into what they call its constituent elements—dogmatic, historic, physical, etc.—and that they may accept the first and reject the others."

And to quote one more example, Bishop Forbes, of Brechin, writes (*Explan. of the xxxix. Articles*. Art. vi.), "Although the Church has never yet ruled in what measure the inspiration of the Word of God is given, or in what way it works, yet from the beginning it has been believed that God the Holy Ghost inspired certain

persons to record certain events; that in accordance with
the promise of our Lord, that the Comforter should
bring to mind all the matters to be recorded, these
authors owed the remembrance of the facts to supernal
illumination, and that therefore there is no room for
allowing of any error, even the slightest . . . either
the Bible must be true in every respect, or not the Word
of God at all."

For the teaching of the orthodox Eastern Church at
the present day, I have not been able to consult many
authorities; but in a Church so conservative of tradition,
it will perhaps be sufficient to refer to a *Treatise on the
Duty of Parish Priests*, composed by George Konnisky,
Bishop of Mogileff, and first printed at St. Petersburg in
1776. This book has been adopted by the whole Russian Church, and all candidates for Holy Orders in the
Diocesan Seminaries are required to have read it, and to
shew their acquaintance with its contents previously to
being ordained. In the twelfth section of the first chapter
we read, " None other books are to be held by us as
Divine Scripture, or called the Word of God, than the
two volumes of the Old and New Testaments. Of this
we are assured by the text itself of the said Testaments,
and by the things therein written: this the Church of
Christ teaches; and the Doctors of the Church attest the
same." And then, by way of comment, it continues,
" The text of the above-mentioned books is not simply
human, but was written by revelation and command of
God, by the Holy Ghost. The Apostle Peter, in his second Epistle, says that 'no prophecy of Scripture is of its
own interpretation; for prophecy came not ever by the
will of man; but holy men of God spake as they were
moved by the Holy Ghost.' . . . And so were revealed things past, as the creation of the world to Moses,

and things future, both to him and to the other Prophets
from God alone. . . . The same Prophets were ordered by the Lord also to write. . . . But the things
committed to writing in the above-named Testaments
surpass all human reason. Let anyone seriously consider the creation of the world, and its order, the miracles
wrought in Egypt, at the Red Sea, and in the wilderness;
or in the New Testament, the Incarnation of Jesus Christ
the Son of God, his miracles, the Resurrection from the
dead, the outpouring of the Holy Ghost on the Apostles,
and the conversion of the Gentiles by their preaching;
all which answers not to the reason or power of man,
nor of any other creature, but to the Almighty power and
unsearchable wisdom of God alone. And thus both the
writing of the text itself, and the things written there,
and the fulfilment of prophecies, give us the strongest
and most incontrovertible assurance that the said two
Testaments are indeed the Word of God."

This, then, has been the " perpetual, constant, universal " (*Bramhall*, quoted above) belief of the Church—of
the Jewish Church first, and then of the Christian Church
in all parts of the world and in all ages from the time of
the Apostles down to the present day—that all Scripture
is the Word of God; that the Holy Ghost, who inspired
it, is its chief author; and that in it there neither is nor
can be falsehood or error. For fifteen centuries this doctrine was questioned by none; Catholics and heretics
alike appealed to the Divine authority of the Bible. There
were, indeed, controversies as to the authority of certain
books, but none doubted the inspiration and infallible
truth of those books which they received. The one
solitary exception is, as I have said above, the case of
the extreme section of the Arian party; and their denial

of it St. Epiphanius stigmatises as an outrage unheard of in controversy before.[20]

From the fifteenth century downwards we have a consensus of approved writers in every branch of the Church maintaining the same Catholic tradition. Greek, Roman and Anglican theologians are on this point at one. Protestant leaders, like Luther and Calvin, held firmly to the same doctrine; and if their followers have departed from it, and have more or less completely given up belief in inspiration, they have had for the real parents of their error the rationalising Jew, Moses Maimonides,[21] and the infidel philosopher,[22] Benedict Spinoza. In short,

---

[20] It has been maintained by some that Theodore of Mopsuestia is also an exception. But Archdeacon Lee argues that there is good reason for believing that such a charge against him is entirely without foundation. At any rate, when his doctrinal views were condemned by the Fifth General Council, and when in after times his memory was assailed by every calumny that could be brought against him, no charge was ever made of his having denied the authority or inspiration of the Sacred writings; the whole controversy turned upon his errors as an expositor. These errors had their root in a reaction from the extreme allegorizing of another school, which led him to assert the exclusive validity of the literal meaning, in consequence of which he regarded the primary meaning of the Old Testament prophecies as their complete and sole meaning. Hence he was often charged with Judaising.—*Vide* Lee on *Inspiration*, p. 71, 72, and Appendix G, p. 527. [21] Maimonides, A. D. 1135–1204. Spinoza, A. D. 1602–1677. *cf.* Lee on *Inspiration*, Appendix G, p. 453, sq. [22] Quinet has truly said: "L'homme qui de nos jours a fait faire le plus grand pas à l'Allemagne, ce n'est ni Kant, ni Lessing, ni le grand Frédéric; c'est Benedict Spinoza." He has been followed in the same line by Le Clerc, Semler, Töllner, and in more recent times by Schleiermacher and the host of his disciples both in Germany and England. It is remarkable that Schleiermacher sacrificed a lock of his hair as a token of veneration on the grave of Spinoza.—Quoted by Lee, p. 453.

it may be affirmed that there has never been any approved writer in any part of the Catholic Church, or in any age —nay, that there is hardly an instance of any respectable Protestant—who has not firmly held that all Holy Scripture is the Word of God, that the Holy Ghost is its Author, and that in it there is no error of any kind.

This, then, is the belief to which we, as Catholic Christians, are bound to pay the utmost deference and respect.[23]

II.

I come now to the second part of my task. I wish to point out some considerations and cautions which may help to remove difficulties felt by many in this doctrine of the Plenary Inspiration of Holy Scripture and its consequent freedom from error.

---

[23] It is sometimes asserted that the Church of England leaves the doctrine of Inspiration an open question. This is refuted by the use of the word "canonical" in Art. VI. The framers of that Article knew but one sense of the word—a sense consecrated by the usage of centuries—as equivalent to "Scripture given by inspiration of God." This, which is the basis of the distinction between the "canonical" books, and those which were merely "ecclesiastical," was the meaning of "canonical" among the Jews, and is its constant sense with the Fathers. *Vide* the quotations in Lee on *Inspiration*, Appendix G, pp. 498–500, and note 2. He also quotes the following from Erasmus: "Hebræi trifariam distinguunt omnem Scripturam. Canonicam appellant citra controversiam afflatu S. Spiritus proditam;" and also refers to the "Wirtemburgh Confession," which the framers of our Article had before them, and the words of which they use: "Sacram Scripturam vocamus eos canonicos libros Vet. et Nov. Testamenti, de quorum autoritate in ecclesia nunquam dubitatum est. Hanc Scripturam credimus et confitemur esse oraculum Spiritus Sancti."

And, first, let it be clearly understood that we are not bound by Catholic tradition to hold any specific theory as to the *modus operandi* of inspiration. We are not bound, for instance, to the mechanical or purely organic theory; the theory which affirms that the authors of the various books had no share in their composition beyond the mere mechanical act of writing; that every word, every syllable, every letter was directly dictated to them; that they were in fact the mere passive instruments—the pens, not even the penmen of the Holy Ghost. If there are a few isolated expressions and metaphors in some early Christian writers which may seem to countenance such a theory, yet the general language and teaching of the Fathers admits, what is plainly the case, the coëxistence of a human with the Divine agency in the composition of Scripture. It is mainly since the Reformation and among Protestants outside the Church that this extreme mechanical or dictation theory has been insisted upon as of vital importance. When men had broken away from the Church, which God had given to be the infallible Teacher of his Truth, and the Keeper and Interpreter of his Written Word, it was natural that they should look for infallible guidance in the Bible, and seek to exalt its authority by maintaining this theory of inspiration as an article of faith. And however the devout scholar, patiently and laboriously examining into the sacred text, and discovering its marvellous inner harmonies and correspondences, its delicate and consistent usages of words and phrases, may be led to believe for himself in its most minute verbal inspiration, it cannot be denied that to insist upon such a belief among the unlearned, especially when, as has so often been the case, it has been explained on the extreme mechanical theory of inspiration, is attended with great danger, and has actually led to much unbelief. An able English writer (Row, *Bampton Lectures*) bears weighty testimony to the extent of this result among the working classes. He says that in a period of six years he was present at discussions at which he heard not less than 100 addresses, made by unbelievers who belong to this class of society, on points which they considered to involve the truth of Christianity; and of their objections he records his conviction that at least two-thirds of them owe their entire plausibility to their identification of the mechanical theory of inspiration with the truth of a Divine Revelation. To this theory they believe Christianity to be pledged, and consequently that every objection which can be urged against the Old Testament on the ground that its language is not scientifically correct; or that its moral teaching is imperfect; or that it attributes to God the passions of humanity; or against the New Testament on the ground that discrepancies exist in the Gospels which are hard to reconcile— in a word, that everything in the Bible which is at variance with mechanical verbal accuracy is fatal to its claim to be considered inspired by God.

Another theory of inspiration, sometimes called the Dynamical, has been proposed. This theory is certainly much more in accordance with the general teaching of the Fathers, and with the phenomena which Scripture itself presents. It leaves room for that human element which is so obviously present in the language of the Bible. No one can read its different books carefully and intelligently without seeing how the individuality of the various writers is preserved in their style and diction, and manner of treatment of their subject. Isaiah and Jeremiah, St. Luke and St. John, St. Peter and St. Paul, each

have their marked peculiarities which are quite inconsistent with their being the mere penmen of the Holy
Ghost. The Dynamic theory of inspiration leaves room
for this fact. While recognising the Divine energy, it
does not annihilate the human coöperation. Rather the
two are combined in one theandric operation. To borrow
the words of Archdeacon Lee (p. 144): "The Holy
Ghost employs man's faculties in conformity with their
natural laws; at the same time animating, guiding,
moulding them so as to accomplish the Divine purpose;
just as in nature, the principle of life, when annexed to
certain portions of matter, exhibits its vital energy in
accordance with conditions which that matter imposes;
while it governs and directs at the same time the organism with which it is combined." Thus, "the human
element becomes an integral part of the agency employed. Nay, more, the peculiar type of each writer's
nature was even essential to the due reception of that
particular phase of truth presented by his statements;
and his characteristic form of expression was absolutely
requisite for the adequate conveyance of his Divine message." There may be imperfections in the form—the imperfections inherent in all human language; there can be
none in the substance of the facts and truths set down.

And if this be so—if there has been in the process of
inspiration a blending and interpenetration of two ener-
gies, the Spirit of God acting through the subordinate
agency of man, using but not annihilating or paralysing
it—various consequences will naturally result, which I
proceed to notice.

First, we shall not be surprised if a double meaning is
often to be found in the text of Holy Scripture. For

instance,[24] Sarah had her literal meaning when she said, "Cast out the bondwoman and her son;" but St. Paul tells us that the Holy Ghost had another and deeper spiritual meaning which he, inspired by the same Holy Ghost, expounds in his Epistle to the Galatians. Abraham, too, had his meaning when in answer to his son's question as to where was the victim for the sacrifice, he replied, "My son, God will provide himself a lamb for a burnt offering;" and yet those words were a prophecy of a far distant and infinitely solemn event. Indeed, this double sense is a principle which underlies a great deal of Scripture prophecy, which is so framed that a present or near historical event is frequently brought forward as the pledge and type, so to speak, of something more remote. And this principle, if it be borne in mind, will go far to explain the method in which the writers of the New Testament quote the prophecies of the Old. "The Holy Spirit," it has been well said (Lee on *Inspiration*, p. 339), "when inspiring God's servants in former times, had infused a deeper significance into their words than the men who uttered them, or who committed them to writing, perceived." That deeper meaning was afterwards brought out by the New Testament writers, under the guidance of the same Holy Spirit by whom it had been originally infused. And it has been remarked that the very freedom with which the New Testament writers quote the Old Testament is itself a very striking proof of the inspiration both of the one and of the other. Believing firmly as they did in the inspiration of the Old Testament, they would never have dared to alter its

---

[24] These instances are given by Card. Newman in a paper on *Inspiration* in the *Nineteenth Century*, Feb., 1884.

words, unless they had been acting under the guidance of the Holy Spirit in doing so. While at the same time the manner in which they quote and apply it, brings out in the strongest light, the depth and fullness of meaning which is often contained beneath the mere sense of the letter and its primary application.[25] The whole system of typology, which runs throughout the Bible, is another instance of the same sort of thing, where the hidden meanings contained in ordinances and events of the Old Testament, are only brought to light by the Holy Spirit guiding the writers of the New Testament to unfold and explain them.

Again, another consequence which would seem to follow from the admission of the coöperation of a twofold agency in the production of Holy Scripture is this: that an inspired book need not be in all parts the original composition of its reputed writer. Not only may the sacred writers have used, as indeed they sometimes plainly tell us they have done, already existing records and authorities; but there is nothing to prevent them

---

[25] Rudelbach (quoted by Lee, *Inspiration*, p. 340, note 3) has truly observed that "a *hyponoia*—a deeper sense, intended by the Holy Ghost—must be allowed, in the interpretation of Scripture, by all who have a clear apprehension of the *objectivity* of the Holy Spirit's influence upon the Prophets." *Cf.* also the good remarks of Beck (also quoted by Lee, p. 350, note 3), "The question is not whether Divine sayings already promulgated have been quoted with rigid adherence to their mere *letter*, but whether they have been given anew, true to their spirit . . . a repetition, in which the original sense is not falsified, but, in which the sense of its Author, the Spirit, is now developed farther and more profoundly." *Cf.* also the teaching of St. Thomas, discussing the question, "Utrum Sacra Scriptura sub una litera plures habeat sensus," *Pars Prima*, Q. i., Art. X.

from having incorporated portions of such existing materials into their work. Hence, as Cardinal Newman reminds us (*Nineteenth Century*, Feb., 1884), "we have no reason to be surprised, nor is it against the faith to hold, that a canonical book may be composed not only from, but even of, preëxisting documents, it being always borne in mind, as a necessary condition, that an inspired mind has exercised a supreme and an ultimate judgment on the work, determining what was to be selected and embodied in it, in order to its truth in all ' matters of faith and morals pertaining to the edification of Christian doctrine,'[26] and its unadulterated truth."

We need not, then, be perplexed at the conclusions of the critical school affirming that Moses incorporated into the Pentateuch portions of earlier documents. The existing Pentateuch, with all its miracles, is inspired, because those earlier documents, whatever they were, have passed through the mind of one who was inspired. In like manner St. Luke's Gospel is inspired, though the sources whence he drew his narrative were not necessarily so at all. And the same is the case with many other instances where the critics fancy they have discovered proof of different authorship in parts of the same book. It is not necessary for inspiration that a book should be

---

[26] Cardinal Newman is saying what is the *least* a Catholic is bound to hold on the subject of the Inspiration of Scripture, and is therefore laying stress upon the words of the Vatican Council on the interpretation of Scripture. But he is also careful to state in the same Paper, that "we are not to conclude that the record of facts in Scripture does not come under the guarantee of Inspiration; for the Sacred narrative carried on through so many ages is the very matter for our faith and rule of our obedience." " The Bible history," therefore, " is in its substantial fullness to be accepted *de fide* as true."

homogeneous throughout. What is necessary is that the whole material shall have passed through the mind of an inspired editor.

And so, again, to mention another point which belongs to criticism—It is not necessary to maintain that the titles of the various books and their reputed authorship are in all cases correct or to be taken literally. These, as not being integral portions of the books, do not necessarily come within the scope of inspiration. The Book of Job, for instance, need not be maintained to be the work of him whose name it bears; nor if it should ever be proved that the Second Epistle of St. Peter was wrongly attributed to that Apostle would its inspiration and authority be any the less. On this point Melchior Canus says (*Loci. Theol.*, p. 44, quoted by Newman): "It does not much matter to the Catholic Faith, that a book was written by this or that writer, so long as the Spirit of God is believed to be the Author of it; which Gregory delivers and explains in his *Preface to Job*, 'It matters not with what pen the king has written his letter, if it be true that he has written it.'"

Once more, we must bear in mind, what is often forgotten, that we are not bound to any particular system of chronology; for none is laid down in the Sacred Books. With regard to the Old Testament the date of the building of Solomon's Temple is tolerably certain, but beyond this we soon get lost in obscurity. Not only are the numbers in our existing MSS. subject to suspicion, but as has been well pointed out (Row, *Bampton Lectures*), "for a long interval the sole authority is a list of persons, who are said at a certain age to have begotten their sons, some of whose names bear every appearance of not being the designations of individuals but of nations." Moreover, we know very little of the Jewish system, or want of system, in recording genealogies. We know that three names are, for some reason or other, omitted in the genealogy of our Lord given by St. Matthew; why may not the same thing have been done in the Old Testament genealogies? And with regard to the New Testament, many of the objections brought against the Gospels on the score of chronological inaccuracies, lose all their force when we remember that three at least of the evangelical narratives make no claim to be considered histories, in the strict sense of the term, but are rather memoirs compiled with a view of preserving the oral teaching of the Apostles. We need not then expect them to follow the sequence of time and place as a professed historian must do. Other arrangements of their materials might be more to their purpose. St. Matthew evidently uses mainly a topical arrangement, grouping together parables and discourses of our Lord, so as to exhibit their teaching in connexion one with the other. Even St. Luke's Gospel, which might seem to make a claim to chronological system (Lk. i. 3, καθεξῆς, *vide* Alford, *in loc.*), does not necessarily imply this. He *traced* the events in order as they happened; but he may have arranged them as other considerations led him.

Again, the principle laid down by St. Augustine in his letter to St. Jerome, quoted above, is as available as an answer to many objections in our own day as it was in his. The difficulty may be due to an error in the MS. For we must, of course, remember that all that any-one says about there being no errors in Holy Scripture, applies in its strictness only to the original autographs of the sacred writers. We have no right to assume that God would work a perpetual miracle to preserve all scribes and copyists from mistakes, and as a matter of fact we know, from the numerous variations in the MSS., that he has not done so.   Many of the difficulties connected with the numbers in Holy Scripture are no doubt due to this source.   They are at once accounted for as errors of transcribers in copying early Hebrew MSS., in which numbers are expressed by letters, often so nearly alike as to be easily confounded.

Or, in other cases, it may be not the text itself that is in error, but our translation of it; or if not that, then possibly our interpretation.   On this point Dr. Whewell makes some good remarks in his *Philosophy of the Inductive Sciences* (vol. i., p. 403).   He says: " The meaning which any generation puts upon the phrases of Scripture depends, more than is at first sight supposed, upon the received philosophy of the time.   Hence, while men imagine that they are contending for Revelation, they are, in fact, contending for their own interpretation of Revelation, unconsciously adapted to what they believe to be rationally probable.   And the new interpretation, which the new philosophy requires, and which appears to the older school to be a fatal violence done to the Authority of Religion, is accepted by their successors without the dangerous results which were apprehended."   The instance of Galileo is a striking case in point.   The theologians of his day were firmly persuaded that to assert that the sun was fixed and the earth moved round it was to contradict the Bible.   We now know that what it contradicted was not the Bible, but only the current interpretation of the Bible.   Or to take an instance nearer to our own day; the results of geological science when first published to the world were thought to overthrow the truth of Scripture; but we have now learnt to accommodate our interpretation to the facts of science, and are surprised that it could ever have been thought necessary to maintain that the six days of creation were literal days of twenty-four hours each. And in like manner if ever the hypothesis of evolution comes to be a proved scientific fact, we shall find perhaps that some of our interpretations of Scripture were mistaken, but not that Scripture itself contradicts it." A remark of Bishop Butler's on the light which history as it comes to pass may yet throw upon dark and obscure portions of Holy Scripture, is just as true if for "the events of history" we substitute "the progress of science." The passage will then read as follows (*Analogy*, pt. ii., ch. iii.), "Nor is it at all incredible, that a book, which has been so long in the possession of mankind, should contain many truths as yet undiscovered. For, all the same phenomena, and the same faculties of investigation, from which such great discoveries in natural knowledge have been made in the present and last age, were equally in the possession of mankind several thousand years before. And possibly it might be intended that *the progress of science* should open and ascertain the meaning of several parts of Scripture." Thus the advance of science may have a very material part to play in the interpretation of the Bible.[77] Meanwhile what we have to remember is that "no Scripture is of any *private interpretation*," and till the Church, the only authorised and infallible interpreter of the Word of God, has definitely and authoritatively declared a given interpretation to be the true one, it is useless to talk of science contradicting the Bible, because it may

[77] *Cf.* Bacon, *Advancement of Learning,* p. 53.

seem opposed to our own, or even to the hitherto generally accepted interpretation.[28]

Another most important point to bear in mind is the distinction between Revelation and Inspiration. "All Scripture is given by inspiration of God;" but all Scripture is not a Revelation. The Bible contains many things which, from their supernatural character, or the circumstances of the writer, could only be known to him by a special communication from God. These are matters of Revelation. But the Bible also contains many other things the knowledge of which might be and was derived by the writers from the ordinary sources of information. In this case there was no need of a Revelation, but only of Inspiration, that they might record them correctly and according to the will of God. The observance of this distinction will furnish an answer to a large number of the objections brought against the Divine character of Holy Scripture. These objections will often be found to proceed upon the assumption that everything recorded in the Bible is a revelation from God; while the truth is that a great deal is nothing more than simple matters of fact and history set down under the guidance and direction of the Holy Spirit. For example, it has been objected[29] that the speeches of

---

[28] Of course as Catholics we should be very cautious how we dissent from any interpretation which has the weight of a consensus of the Fathers, especially when that interpretation is closely related to doctrine and matters of faith. In such cases a consensus of authorities is practically as dogmatic as if it were expressed in a formal conciliar decree; but in questions of interpretation bearing upon physical science it would seem that Butler's remark, as quoted and applied above, is plainly entitled to consideration.

[29] Coleridge, *Confessions of an Enquiring Spirit*, Letter iii. p., 38.

Job's friends, with all their "hollow truisms, their un-sufficing half-truths, their false assumptions and malignant insinuations," could not have been "dictated by an infallible Intelligence;" and it is supposed by the objector that this forms a crucial instance of the absurdity of maintaining that all Scripture is inspired. This objection rests entirely upon a confusion of Revelation and Inspiration, as if the two were identical and coextensive; and it at once loses all its force when we bear in mind their distinction. The words objected to are not a revelation of truth "dictated by" God himself; they are merely the words, whether actually spoken or imagined, of fallible and imperfect men committed to writing under the inspiration of the Holy Spirit. Again, to take another instance from the same book (ch. xxix. 18), it has been supposed by several modern interpreters that Job, in a certain passage, refers to the legend of the Phœnix, and that this is conclusive evidence against the plenary inspiration of the book in which Job's speech is recorded. It could only be so on the assumption that everything contained in the book was a revelation from God, who must then be held to authenticate the legend as a fact. On the other hand, if we remember that what is recorded under the influence of inspiration is not therefore of necessity a revealed truth, we shall at once see that the supposed reference to an Egyptian fable, granting it to be such, no more affects the authority of the book in which it is recorded, than does the report of the speeches of the tempter; or than the inspiration of St. Paul's Epistles is affected by his quotation from the heathen poets, Menander and Epimenides.

A similar confusion of thought has been the source of many of the objections made to the inspiration of the

Bible on the ground that some of its statements be-
tray a complete ignorance of the proved facts of science.
I shall have more to say upon this point further on; but
meanwhile I will just remark that such objections often
tacitly assume that the statements in question are direct
revelations from God, and were intended to teach us the
truths of physical science, whereas in reality they are
often only the inspired narrative of facts and phenomena
faithfully recorded *as they appeared to the writer*.

Another large class of objections against the inspiration of the Bible on the score of the imperfect morality
contained in portions of it, may be met by the simple and
obvious consideration that if the Bible records the history
of God's education of the human race in moral and
spiritual truth, it must from the very nature of the case,
like all educational processes, have been gradual and
progressive.   Such objections proceed upon the assumption that if ever, God speaks he must speak his whole
mind, and if ever he grants a revelation it must be at
once perfect and complete.   Yet nothing is more certain
than that the Bible itself professes to be a *gradual* revelation, "line upon line, and precept upon precept, here a little
and there a little;" each fresh revelation making clearer
and more complete that which went before, while mankind were meanwhile trained and taught to apprehend
and to appreciate it.   For example, Holy Scripture
expressly declares that the Mosaic Code was not given
as a perfect and final law.   It was in many points pro-
visional only; a law fit for a people "of a stiff neck, and
hard heart," who could not yet bear a higher and more
perfect code.   Thus our Lord speaks of the law of divorce
which was permitted under the Mosaic dispensation, "for
the hardness of your hearts Moses wrote you this

precept," and then he himself enacts the higher Christian
law forbidding divorce altogether. And this had really
been God's whole mind about the matter all along. It
was the original law "from the beginning of the creation," though in condescension to the weakness of man
a relaxation was conceded for a time. This common-
sense principle of God's progressive teaching and train-
ing of mankind will furnish a complete answer to num-
berless objections made against the morality of the Old
Testament, whether it be against the laws which God
gave, on the ground of their imperfection, or against the
actions of men which God passed over without condemnation, or even at times approved. The laws were
the best men could then bear; and the actions, however
faulty when tried by an absolute standard, were nevertheless so far good that they may have been an advance
upon man's previous conduct, or may have had in them,
however imperfectly, something of a true and religious
motive. And with regard to such express commands of
God as that which bade Abraham to slay his son, or the
Israelites to spoil the Egyptians, which are often objected
to as immoral, the answer of Bishop Butler leaves nothing to be desired. He admits that "there are some particular precepts in Scripture, given to particular persons,
requiring actions, which would be immoral and vicious,
were it not for such precepts. But (he answers) it is easy
to see that all these are of such a kind as that the precept changes the whole nature of the case and of the
action; and both constitutes, and shews that not to be
unjust or immoral, which, prior to the precept, must have
appeared and really have been so; which may well be,
since none of these precepts are contrary to immutable

morality.[30]   If it were commanded to cultivate the principles and act from the spirit of treachery, and ingrati-
tude, or cruelty; the command would not alter the nature
of the case, or of the action, in any of these instances.
But it is quite otherwise in precepts, which require only
the doing an external action: for instance, taking away
the property or life of any.   For men have no right to
either life or property, but what arises solely from the
grant of God: when this grant is revoked, they cease to
have any right at all in either: and when this revocation
is made known, as surely it is possible it may be, it
ceases to be unjust to deprive them of either.   And
though a course of external acts, which without command would be immoral, must make an immoral habit,
yet a few detached commands have no such tendency."

And perhaps it may be alleged, that in spite of all that
has been said, there are manifest contradictions in the
Bible which are fatal to its claim to be so inspired that it
contains no error—contradictions between the statements
of the sacred writers themselves; contradictions again
between these and the facts of secular history; contradictions lastly between the language of Scripture and the

---

[30] "Under such circumstances as these there arises what theologians call a '*mutatio materiæ*;' a change of the object-matter whereon
a moral judgment has to be formed.   By means of that '*mutatio
materiæ*,' a certain external act, which *was* intrinsically wrong,
ceases to be so and becomes lawful.   Then the command of God
supervening is a kind of *positive* command; and I owe to it obedience, on the same principle which obliges me to obey any *other*
Positive Precept, imposed by my Creator."—*On nature and grace;
Bk. I., Philosophical Introduction*, p. 168, sq., by W. G. Ward.
And *cf.* Suarez, *De Legibus*, Lib. ii., cap. 15, "Utrum Deus dis-
pensare possit in Lege Naturali etiam de absolutâ potestate,"
where he discusses the very instances given above.

ascertained truths of physical science. With a brief answer to these charges I must conclude this paper.

And first as to the charge that the sacred writers contradict themselves or one another. It is said that there are numerous cases, in the Gospels, for instance, where there can be no reasonable doubt as to the correctness of the text, and yet its various statements cannot be harmonised. The objections brought against the narratives of the Resurrection of our Lord on this score will occur to our minds at once.

In reply, let it first be remarked that these objections are not new. They were urged by Celsus and other opponents of Christianity in ancient times, as well as by Strauss or Renan in our own day. The Fathers, therefore, were not ignorant of them, and yet they were assured of the perfect veracity of the Evangelists. For instance, Julius Africanus, a very early Christian writer (A.D. 220), while proposing a very ingenious mode of harmonising the genealogies of Christ in St. Matthew and St. Luke, concludes his remarks by saying, whether this explanation be correct or not, "it cannot be doubted that the Evangelical narrative is true" (Eusebius, *H. E.* i. 7). Nor must we imagine that the Fathers were so uncritical in their method of dealing with difficulties in Holy Scripture as is sometimes insinuated. St. Augustine's Treatise *De Consensu Evangelistarum*, and the critical labours of Origen and St. Jerome are all instances to the very contrary. Some of the difficulties they met with they were enabled to solve by closer study; others they left as difficulties. Yet they never doubted that if we were in possession of all the facts the various accounts would be found to be perfectly true and capable of reconciliation. And this is the right principle on which to take our stand in all such cases of alleged contradiction. Historical narratives may be difficult and even impossible for us, with our limited knowledge of the facts, to reconcile, and yet they may be true. The additional knowledge of some one particular may often supply the missing link and make all plain. Illustrations of the validity of this principle are constantly occurring. Every lawyer who is accustomed to examining witnesses in court would, I suppose, furnish numbers of instances where the testimony of two or more seemed to be quite irreconcilable till some other fact, sometimes a very small and seemingly unimportant one, was brought to light.

So, again, with respect to the variations in the reports of our Lord's discourses, or the difficulties raised by the different versions of the words in which he instituted the Blessed Sacrament, or of the Title on the Cross, we may reply in the wise words of St. Augustine (*De Consensu Evangelist.*, ii. 6, 7): "There are varieties, but not contrarieties, in the Gospels; and by means of these variations we may learn some very useful and necessary truths. We are thus reminded that the main thing for us is to ascertain the *meaning*, to which the *words* are ministerial; and we are not to imagine, that the sacred writers deceive us, because they do not give us the precise words of him, whose meaning they desire to express. Otherwise we shall be like mere miserable catchers at syllables, who imagine that the truth is to be tied to the points of letters; whereas, not in words only, but also in all other symbols of the mind, it is the mind itself which is to be sought for." Nor can I refrain from quoting the excellent remarks of Bishop Wordsworth on the same subject. He says (*Greek Test. Introduction* p. xlvi. sq.): "Holy

Scripture was not written to tell us merely that which Christ taught by means of words, which are only human coinage, but to unlock the inner treasury of Wisdom of him who is Divine. If the Holy Spirit had given us only one verbal account of Christ's sayings, he would have given a far less clear view of Christ's mind than we now possess. This arises, not from any imperfection in the working of the Spirit, but from our imperfection, and from that of the instrument to be used by the Spirit for the conveyance of a knowledge of Christ's mind to us— namely human language. He has given to us a fuller knowledge of that mind, by presenting its sense to us in different points of view; just as a painter gives us a clearer idea of a countenance or a landscape, by representing it to us from different sides." Thus by the varieties of expression the limitations and inadequacy of human language are to some extent compensated.

I pass now to the charge of discrepancies between the statements of the Bible and the facts of secular history.

And, first, I would remark upon the readiness with which it is too often assumed by hostile critics that in all such cases the secular historian must be right, and the sacred writer wrong. Everything in favour of the accuracy of the uninspired writer is made the most of; his statements are accepted without requiring corroboration, whereas the statements of Scripture in similar circumstances are ruthlessly thrust aside as utterly unworthy of credit. For instance, St. Luke has been charged with historical inaccuracy, because in his report of the speech of Gamaliel he mentions Theudas as the leader of a revolt, whereas Josephus says that an insurrection was headed by Theudas, in the reign of Claudius, and

Procuratorship of Fadus, more than ten years after the time of this speech of Gamaliel. But what forbids us to believe that St. Luke and Josephus are speaking of two different persons bearing the same name? The name was quite a common Jewish one; and moreover the circumstances along with which the two historians mention it are very different. The Theudas mentioned by St. Luke (Acts v. 36) had only about 400 followers, whereas Josephus says that his Theudas gained over a very large multitude. The one was quite a small affair; the other a serious insurrection (Jo. *Ant.* 5, 1).

But indeed the accuracy of Scripture in matters of history is constantly receiving wonderful confirmation from the researches of the learned. "Time," it has been said, "is an excellent interpreter;" and the truth of this remark has been abundantly illustrated of late years. I must content myself, however, with referring to one or two notable instances.

In the beginning of the second chapter of his Gospel St. Luke speaks of a census made at the time of our Lord's birth while Cyrenius was Governor of Syria. It has often been asserted that St. Luke has here fallen into a glaring mistake, because Tacitus says that Cyrenius, or Quirinius, was for the first time sent as Proconsul to Syria eleven or twelve years after the birth of Christ. And on the ground of this alleged blunder the whole credibility of St. Luke's Gospel as an authentic narrative has been called in question. Yet in 1854 Augustus Zumpt published a Dissertation on the subject,[31] in which he brings evidence to shew that though Cyrenius

---

[31] *Commentationes Epigraphicæ*, vol. ii. Quoted by Merivale, *History of the Romans under the Empire*, vol. iv., p. 457.

was Governor of Syria at the date given by Tacitus, and made a census then, he had also been Governor of that same Province once before at the very date of our Lord's birth. This evidence has been accepted as conclusive by Mr. Merivale and most modern historians and scholars. Perhaps a still more striking instance is afforded by a passage in the Acts (xiii. 7). In the thirteenth chapter St. Luke speaks of Sergius Paulus, the Governor of the Island of Cyprus, and gives him the title of Proconsul. Here, again, it was asserted by many that St. Luke had fallen into an inaccuracy, and that he ought to have used the title Proprætor, which was the one invariably given to the Governors of Imperial Provinces. But in course of time a passage of Dio Cassius came to light which shewed that St. Luke was right and his critics wrong. For Dio Cassius tells us that Augustus converted the island into a Senatorian Province, under a Proconsul.[32] And this statement has been recently confirmed by the discovery in the island of inscriptions and coins of the age of Caligula and Claudius, which give the title of Proconsul to a governor, who must have been the immediate predecessor of the Sergius Paulus mentioned by St. Luke. I may refer also, before leaving this point, to the wonderful confirmations of the truth and accuracy of Scripture which are almost daily being received from the researches of travellers and archæologists, and especially from the deciphering of such ancient monuments as the cuneiform inscriptions.

I pass on now to the last point on which I will touch ; the alleged contradictions between the language of the

---

[32] Καὶ οὕτως ἀνθύπατοι (the precise word used by St. Luke) καὶ ἐς ἐκεῖνα τὰ ἔθνη πέμπεσθαι ἤρξαντο. *Hist. Rom.* liv. 5.

Bible, and the ascertained truths of physical science. I
have already alluded to this subject, and pointed out that
in many cases it is not the Bible, but our interpretation
of the Bible, which has been at variance with the truths
of science. When the scientific fact was proved, then
we found that the statements of Scripture were capable
of being interpreted in conformity with it. Moreover,
we must remember that nature may be misinterpreted
as well as Scripture. For many hundred years, as every
one now admits, nature was misinterpreted. Therefore,
when it is alleged that the statements of Scripture are at
variance with the facts of science, we are fairly entitled
to ask whether these alleged facts are really facts, and
not mere hypotheses. There is often a tendency in scientific men to overstep the strict logic of induction, and
to treat what is after all only a working hypothesis, as if
it were an ascertained and verified truth. Believing, as
we do, that Scripture is Divine, we may be sure that its
statements will ultimately be proved to be in perfect harmony with every real fact of physical science. If there
seems for a time to be any inconsistency, it is because
we are misinterpreting either Scripture, or nature, or
possibly both.

Something, too, has already been said on this subject
while treating of the distinction to be observed between
Revelation and Inspiration. It was there pointed out
that many of the objections against the Inspiration of
Scripture which we are now considering proceed upon
the tacit assumption that every statement contained in
the Bible is a revelation from God, so that the very
language in which it is conveyed must be held to be the
direct language of God, and therefore the expression of
absolute truth as it is in itself. One of the most signal

instances of this confusion of thought is to be found in
the case of those who have objected to the inspiration
of the Bible on the ground that in recounting the
miracle wrought at the prayer of Joshua it describes
the sun as standing still. If the Bible were inspired, it
is said, God must have known that the sun does not
really move, and must therefore have used language
which was strictly in accordance with the scientific fact.
The answer, of course, is that the statement objected to
is not a revelation from God, designed to teach us a fact
of science, but merely an inspired narrative of an event
faithfully recorded as it appeared to an eye-witness. If
we bear in mind this distinction, we shall see that there
is no need to maintain that the Bible ought to use the
strict language of science. If the Bible had been intended to be a revelation of scientific knowledge, there
would have been point in the objection, not otherwise.
The truth is, that on these matters the Bible uses the
ordinary language of sense, just as we to this day habi-
tually speak of the sun as rising and setting because it
appears to our senses so to do, though we well know
that in reality it is the earth that moves and not the sun.
If the strict language of science had been used by the
Holy Spirit, the Bible must have been actually unin-
telligible to generations of persons who have gone before
us, and probably also in a great measure to ourselves.

And surely it will not be out of place here to call attention to the marvellous superiority of the Mosaic Cosmogony to all those of the most learned philosophers
for thousands of years afterwards, and to ask how this
can be accounted for except on the supposition of a
miraculous inspiration? It has been confessed by one
of the writers in *"Essays and Reviews"* (p. 253), that

" Moses *anticipated* the highest revelation of modern enquiry—the unity of the design of the world, and its subordination to one sole Maker and Lawgiver." And another writer, of high repute for eminent scientific attainments, has well said (Prof. Dana, quoted by Wordsworth), " There is so much in Genesis that the most recent readings of science have for the first time explained that the idea of man being its author is truly incomprehensible." And if there are still some unexplained, and seemingly unexplainable, difficulties in the Biblical account of the origin of the world, let me quote once more the words of Dr. Whewell, who reminds us (*Philosophy of the Inductive Sciences*, vol. i., p. 687), " That in the sciences which trace the progress of natural occurrences, we can in no case go back to an origin, but in every instance appear to find ourselves separated from it by a state of things, and an order of events, of a kind altogether different from those which come under our experience. The thread of induction respecting the natural course of the world snaps in our fingers when we try to ascertain where its beginning is. Since, then, science can teach us nothing positive respecting the beginning of things, she can neither contradict nor confirm what is taught by Scripture on that subject; and thus, as it is unworthy timidity in the lover of Scripture to fear contradiction, so is it ungrounded presumption to look for confirmation in such cases."

And now I must draw these remarks to a close. I have but touched upon some of the principal forms of objection which are made to the doctrine of the Plenary Inspiration of Holy Scriptures, and hope that I may have said something which may at least tend to dilute them, if not in every case to remove them. The subject

is so vast and complicated that within the limits of a
single paper we must be content to pass over many
points and arguments which might be brought forward.
I will only add that in the course of writing this essay
I have been led to take a higher view of inspiration than
that with which I began. What study and thought I
have been able to give to the subject has constantly
deepened the conviction that the Holy Scriptures are in
very truth the word of God inspired throughout by the
Holy Ghost; that they are, *in their originals*, entirely
without errors of any kind; and that whatever inaccuracies or errors there may seem to be, exist only in
the medium of transcription, translation, interpretation
or comment, through which alone we are able to view
those originals. And this I take to have been the belief
and teaching of the most approved Catholic writers from
the earliest times down to our own day.

Whether the Holy Spirit has also watched over and
directed every word and letter, seems to me to be a question for the patient investigation of the devout scholar;
and a belief to be held, if he should be led to hold it, for
his own edification and increased interest and delight in
the study of the sacred text, rather than to be proclaimed
to the world, or, still less, to be imposed as an article of
faith upon others. I can but record my own growing
conviction that, at least in some portions, its language is,
to use the words of one who studied it very deeply for
many years, " minutely, scrupulously, marvellously accurate in every word, and syllable, and letter " (Sewell,
Microscope of the N. T., p. 7).

The Deutero=Canonical Books
of the Old Testament and the
Ante-Nicene Fathers.

WE hear on all sides the Fathers of the first three centuries cited in defence of matters of faith or practice; we hear a great deal about the undivided church, and of that primitive and pure age, while the church was being persecuted, and before (as we are told) she had joined forces with and been corrupted by the world. We are very apt to hear the Fathers of this age quoted where it is convenient, and forgotten where it is inconvenient. In no case is this more conspicuous than as regards their opinion of the deutero-canonical books of the Old Testament; here undoubtedly they are not quoted with any degree of fairness.

We are told they use very general and careless language, or even if they meant to be exact, that they had not critical minds; that they did not understand the principles of modern criticism; that they knew little about Hebrew, and were only familiar with the Septuagint; that they were not competent to give an opinion in the case.

Putting all this aside, let us try and find out what the opinion of the Ante-Nicene Fathers is as regards the deutero-canonical books, how they quote them, with what authority and intention; whether they thought they were in any sense Scripture or not; whether inspired by the

Holy Ghost in at all the same sense in which they under-stood the other books of the Bible to be inspired.

I have been able to find in all about 316 references to these books in the extant writings of those who wrote before A. D. 325, nearly all of these references are direct quotations, and the probability is that there are quite a number that have escaped me, a large number I have rejected as being doubtful; two-thirds of these are from three books: Ecclesiasticus (which is quoted or referred to 138 times), Wisdom (ninety-eight times) and Tobit (twenty-four times).[1] When we examine these quota-tions, the great majority of them are made without any reference to the book or author, but occur mixed up with quotations from the canonical books of Holy Script-ure made in the same way, frequently they occur in controversial works where the simplest reply would have been, "you are quoting from a book, which has no authority."

For instance, Clement in *The Instructor* says, " Misap-prehending, as appears, the *Scripture* which says, 'and he that feareth the Lord will turn to his heart.' "[2] (Ecclus. xxi. 6.)

---

[1] The number of references to the other books are Baruch 12, Susanna and II. Maccabees 11 each, I Mac. 9, Judith 6, Bel and the Dragon and The Song of the Three Children each 4, and also The Prayer of Manasses 1, and I. Esdras 1, II. Esdras 2.
[2] Clement *Instructor*, i. viii. c. ed. i. 155. In each case the refer-ence will be given to the page in the Ante-Nicene Library, pub-lished by Clark of Edinburgh, as well as to the treatise, chapter and section. The Edinburgh edition is used instead of the Amer-ican reprint, as in that edition the quotations from the Deutero-Canonical books are omitted from the index of texts, except in the first volume. If the editor of that edition had so tender a con-science that he could not put the references where they are in

So Origen, to prove the immortality of the soul, "For we must not imagine because he was drowned that therefore he had completely (*substantialiter*) perished, 'for in the hand of God are both we and our words: all wisdom also and knowledge of workmanship' (Wisd. vii. 16), as Scripture declares."[3] And again in the Apostolical Constitutions, "'For precious in the sight of the Lord is the death of his saints' (Ps. cxvi. 15), and again: 'O my soul, return unto thy rest, for the Lord hath done thee good' (Ps. cxv. 7), and elsewhere: 'The memory of the just is with encomiums' (Prov. x. 7), and, 'The souls of the righteous are in the hand of God.' (Wisd. iii. 1)."[4] I have quoted this passage rather at length, as it is a good illustration of how quotations from the proto-canonical and deutero-canonical books are mixed up and quoted with like force. Even more striking a case occurs where this same passage from Wisdom is quoted with Matt. xxii. 32, as an argument for prayers for the dead: "The God of Abraham, the God of Isaac, and the God of Jacob, who art the God of them, not as of dead, but as of living persons: for the souls of all men live with thee, and the spirits of the righteous are in thy hand, which no torment can touch,"[5] or even more strongly Cyprian says, "The *Lord* speaks,

---

Clark's edition after the reference from the minor Prophets, he might at least have had the honesty to reprint them by themselves, it being "the understanding with the public: they were to be presented with the Edinburgh series, free from appreciable colour or alloy," as it is now, the American edition is just so far worthless for work on the Deutero-Canonical books. [3] Origen *de Prin*. iii. i. 14. c. ed. i. 191. "As Scripture declares," is in the Latin text. *Apost. Const.* vi. xxx. C. ed. 175. *Apost. Const.* viii. xii. C. ed. 251.

saying, 'and I will give . . .' (Jer. iii. 15), and again it is written, 'whoso despiseth discipline is miserable.'"[6] (Wisd. iii. 11).

Such use of the deutero-canonical books occurs not only in the later writers of the period, but also in the earlier ones. Thus Clement of Rome quotes Wisdom: "Who shall say unto him, What hast thou done? or, Who shall resist the power of his strength"[7] (Wisd. xii. 12), and the same book is quoted by Irenæus: "But immortality renders one nigh unto God"[8] (Wisd. vi. 19). Tertullian quotes Baruch as the words of Jeremiah: "For they remembered also the words of Jeremias writing to those over whom that captivity was impending, 'And now ye shall see borne upon [men's] shoulders the gods of the Babylonians,'"[9] etc. (Baruch, vi. 3); and Irenæus quotes more than a chapter of the same book in the same way: "And Jeremiah the Prophet has pointed out . . . saying, 'Look around Jerusalem,'"[10] etc. (Baruch, ii. 36 and v.). There is a mass of such quota-

---

[6] Cyprian, Ep. lxi., c. ed. i. 205. [7] Clement, *1 Cor.* xxvii. c. ed. 26. [8] Iren., *ag. Heresies* iv. 33, 3, c. ed. ii. 44. [9] Irenæus, *ag. Christian Heresies* v. 35, i. c. ed. ii. 152. [10] Clement, *The Instructor.* Quotations from Ecclus. i. viii. c. 156: i. viii. c. 160: i. viii. c. 161: i. ix. c. 168: i. ix. c. 169: i. ix. c. 172: i. xiii. c. 184: ii. i. c. 191: ii. ii. c. 203-210: ii. vi. 224, 225: ii. vii. 225-229: ii. viii. 235, 239: ii. x. 250, 253: ii. xi. 259: iii. iv. 293. The same writer quotes Wisdom in *The Miscellanies:* ii. ii. c. ii. 4: iii. xii. c. ii. 360: iv. xi. 175: iv. xvi. 187: v. xiv. 274: vi. xi. 357, 358: vi. xiv. 368, 370. Wisdom quoted by Origen against Celsus, all in controversy and usually on doctrinal points: iii. lx. c. ii. 140: iii. lxxii. 150: iv. xxviii. 188: iv. xxxvii. 201: v. xxix. 298: vi. xiii. 350: vii. viii. 432: vii. l. 473: viii. xiv. 502: viii. xxxii. 518. Wisdom quoted by Cyprian, *Treatise against the Jews:* 14 c. ii. 112: 16, 152, 153: 53, 175: 58, 178: 59, 179: 66, 185: 112, 196. *Glory of Martyrdom:* 11, 233: 16, 242. Maccabees quoted by Cyprian

tions and I simply give a few references to shew their frequency. Many of the references contain two or even more quotations, and notice they are often in controversial treatises like that of Cyprian against the Jews, and Origen against Celsus, and frequently on doctrinal points.

We find repeatedly a simple reference or allusion to some character or event in the books, but it is often as strong testimony as a quotation, or even stronger. Thus Tertullian evidently refers to the Song of the Three Holy Children in his treatise against Hermogenes, and never questions its authenticity; he says: " Even he whom we believe to be existent everywhere, and everywhere apparent, whose praises all things chant, even inanimate things and things incorporeal according to Daniel." [11] Again, Clement of Rome refers to the Book of Judith: " Many women also, being strengthened by the grace of God, have performed numerous manly exploits. The blessed Judith, when her city was besieged, asked of the elders permission," etc. (Judith, viii. 30).[12] Immediately before Esther is mentioned, and both are referred to in the same way; Irenæus evidently accepts the story of Bel and the Dragon, when he says: " Whom also Daniel, the Prophet, when Cyrus, King of the Persians, said to him, ' Why dost thou not worship Bel ? ' did proclaim, saying, ' Because I do not worship idols made with hands,' " [13] etc.

---

against the Jews : III. 4, c. 143 : 15, 152 : 17, 156 : 53, 175. To-bit quoted by Cyprian *against the Jews :* 1, 136, 137 : 6, 144 : 62, 183. *Works and Alms :* 5, c. ii. 5 : 20, 15, 16. *Exh. to Martyr-dom :* ii. c. ii. 69. [11] *Ag. Hermogenes,* xli. c. ii. 116. [12] Clement, Ep. lv. c. 46. [13] Irenæus, *ag. the Heresies,* iv. v. 2 : c. i. 387.

It will be sufficient simply to give in a foot-note a few references to this sort of use of the deutero-canonical books.[14]

We come now to the more important passages where these books are distinctly and with emphasis quoted as "Scripture," "Holy Scripture," "Sacred Scripture," the "Word of God," the "Divine Oracles," the "Divine Word." I will take up some of the books in turn and give the more striking passages, taking first the book of Ecclesiasticus. Cyprian says, "Holy Scripture teaches and forewarns, saying, 'My son, when thou comest to the service of God,'" etc.[15] (Ecclus. ii. 1–4). "The Holy Spirit speaks in the Sacred Scriptures and says, 'By alms-giving,' etc. (Prov. xvi. 6). . . . Moreover, he says again, 'As water,'" etc.[16] (Ecclus. iii. 30); and Origen, "Now the North wind is described in Holy Scripture as cold, according to the statement in the Book of Wisdom, 'That cold North wind'"[17] (Ecclus. xliii. 20), and again notice how he puts Ecclesiasticus on a par with St. Peter's Epistles, "But he ought to know that those who wish to live according to the Holy Scriptures understand the saying, 'The knowledge of the unwise is as talk without sense' (Ecclus. xxi. 18), and have learnt 'to be ready always to give an answer to every one that asketh us a reason for a hope that is in us'"[18] (1 Pet. iii. 15),

---

[14] Maccabees by Cyprian, *Exh. to Martyr.* ii. c. 70–73; by Tertullian, *Ans. to the Jews*, iv. c. iii. 213; *Apost. Const.* vii. xxxvii. c. 198; Judith, *Apost. Const.* iii. vii. c. 98: vi. xx. 143: by Methodius, *Banq. of Virgins*, ix. 2, 113; Susanna by Hippolytus, *Com.* c. i. 483; by Methodius, *Banq. of Virgins*, ix. 2, 113; *Apost. Const.* ii. xxxvii. 67: ii. xlix. 77. Bel and the Dragon, by Tertullian, *on Fasting*, vii. 135. Cyprian, Ep. lv. i. 184: and others. [15] *On Mortality*, vii. 9, 475. [16] *On Works and Alms*, 2, ii. 2. [17] *De Prin.* ii. viii. 3, 123. [18] *Ag. Celsus*, vii. xii. 11, 435.

and again, " Finally see if you can easily find a place in
Holy Scripture where the soul is properly mentioned in
terms of praise; it frequently occurs, on the contrary,
accompanied with expressions of censure, as in the passage, 'An evil soul ruins him who possesses it'"[19]
(Ecclus. vi. 4), and again he quotes it as the Divine
word, " For the Divine Word says, ' What is an honourable seed?'"[20] etc. (Ecclus. x. 19), and at least in one
other place as "Scripture."[21] Clement of Alexandria
frequently quotes it as "Scripture" in *The Instructor*.
"'The crown of old men is great experience' (Ecclus.
xxv. 6) says the Scripture."[22] "' For the fear of the Lord
drives away sin, and he that is without fear cannot be justified' (Ecclus. i. 27, 28), says the Scripture."[23] " Other
finger-rings are to be cast off, since, according to the
Scripture, 'instruction is a golden ornament for a wise
man'"[24] (Ecclus. xx. 24), and so in several more places.[25]

But it is to be noticed that this book is not only spoken
of as " Holy Scripture," " Sacred Scripture " or " Scripture," but as the "Divine Oracles" and directly attributed
to God who speaks by the author. " But listen to the
Divine Oracles: 'The works of the Lord,'" etc.[26] (Ecclus.
xvi. 26, 27). "As the word spake by the prophet saying
'O son, do not delight, etc.'"[27] (Ecclus. xvi. 1–2). " For
thus he (*God*) says, 'Look my son upon the nations,
etc.'"[28] (Ecclus. ii. 10–11).

---

[19] *De Prin.* ii. viii. 3, 123. [20] *Ag. Celsus*, viii. l. 11, 534. [21] *Ag.
Celsus*, vi. vii. 11, 344. [22] *The Instructor*, iii. iii. 1, 285. [23] Ibid.
1, 1, vii. 159. [24] Ibid. iii. 21, 1, 316. [25] Ibid, iii. iv. 1, 294: iii. xi.
1, 331: iii. iii. 288: ii. viii. 235; Methodius *on Things Created*, ix.
182; Ep. of Callistus. Hipp. 11, 205. [26] Dionysius, Bp. of Alex.
Ag. the Epicur. 3, c. 179. [27] Cyprian. Ep. liv. 15, 175. [28] *Ag.
Novatian* by an Anon. Writer, 18, cii. 445, 11.

"Solomon also shews that it is the Word of God, and no other, by whose hands these works of the world were made. 'I,' he says, 'came forth out of the mouth of the Most High'" etc.[29] (Ecclus. xxiv. 5–7). In the same way Wisdom is quoted as Scripture in the most unmistakable way, thus, "And again, where the Sacred Scripture speaks of the virtues which consecrate God's martyrs, and sanctify them in the very trial,'" etc.[30] (Wisd. iii. 4–8).

Could any expression be stronger than this by Methodius, "And that you may not take refuge behind a safe wall, bringing forward the scripture which says 'As for the children of the adulterers,'"etc.[31] (Wisd. iii. 16), or this of Cyprian's, "Since Holy Scripture says, 'What hath pride profited us,'" etc.[32] (Wisd. v. 8); and so in other places.[33] This book is also quoted both as inspired by the "Word" and by the "Holy Ghost," by these same writers, e. g., "Are blamed by the Word, which says, in the Book of Wisdom, a book full of all virtue, 'His heart is ashes, his hope,'" etc.[34] (Wisd. xv. 10), and "The Holy Spirit shews and predicts by Solomon, saying 'and although in the sight of men,'" etc.[35] (Wisd. iii. 4: 8). Twice they are cited by Cyprian as though inspired.[36]

Twice at least the books of the Maccabees are quoted as Scripture, once the first, and once the second book, and that by two early writers, one a Father whose

---

[29] Lactant. *The Divine Inst.* iv. viii. 1, 226. [30] Cyprian's Ep. lxxx. 326. [31] Methodius. *Banq. of Virgins*, ii. iii. 14. [32] Cyprian, *Dress of Virgins*, 10, 1, 340. [33] Origen *de Prin.* ii. ix. 1, 127. Methodius. *Banq. of Virgins*, 1. iii. C. S; Clement, *The Instructor*, ii. x. 244. *The Miscellanies*, v. xiv. 285. [34] Methodius, *Banq. Ten Virgins*, ii. vii. 19. [35] Cyprian. *Exhor. to Martyr.* 12, ii. 74. [36] Cyprian. Ep. xli. 1, 46. *On Dress of Virgins*, 1, 334.

authority and learning are undoubted, the other that writer whom the modern school of criticism holds in such high opinion, viz: Cyprien and Origen, as follows:

"Since Holy Scripture meets and warns us saying, 'But he who,' etc. (Hab. ii. 5), and again, 'and fear not the word,' " etc.[37] (I Mac. ii. 62, 63). "But that we may believe on the authority of Holy Scripture that such is the case hear how in the book of the Maccabees, where the mother of seven martyrs exhorts her son to endure torture, this truth is confirmed, for she says, 'I ask of thee, my son, to look,' " etc.[38] (II Mac. vii. 28).

In the same way the Song of the Three Children is quoted as Scripture, both times by Cyprian. "Ananias, Azarias and Misael, the illustrious and noble youths, even amid the flames. . . . Even amid the glorious martyrdoms of their virtues. The Sacred Scripture speaks saying 'Azarias stood up and prayed,' " etc.,[39] and again, "This law of prayer the three children observed when they were shut up in the furnace, speaking together in prayer, and being of one heart in the agreement of the Spirit, and this the faith of the Sacred Scripture assures us, in telling how such as they prayed, gives an example which we ought to follow in our prayers, in order that we may be such as they were. 'Then these three,' it says, 'as if from one mouth,' " etc.[40] (v. 28).

So Tobit also is quoted as Scripture, "And thus Holy Scripture instructs us saying, 'Prayer is good with fasting and almsgiving' "[41] (Tobit, xii. 8), and the same passage by Clement, "Having heard the Scripture which says, 'Fasting with prayer is a good thing,' "[42] and again,

---

[37] Cyprian, Ep. liv. 3. 1, 162. [38] Origen *de Prin.* ii. ii. 5, 1, 77. [39] Cyprian *on the Lapsed*, 31, 1, 373. [40] Cyprian *on Lord's Prayer*, 8, 1, 403. [41] Ibid. 32, 419, [42] Clement, *the Miscellanies*, vi. 12, 362.

" Whence the Sacred Scripture says well, ' Do not that to another which thou wouldest not have done to thyself.' "[43] Moreover this book is quoted twice at least as revelation.[44]

One passage where Baruch is quoted as Scripture is worth noticing, " Excellently, therefore, the Divine Scripture addressing boasters and lovers of their own selves says ' Where are the rulers of the nations ' "[45] etc. (Bar. ii. 15–19), and twice more it is quoted with the force of Scripture,[46] as is also the History of Susanna.[47]

There is yet another method of quotation which strengthens, if possible, the testimony which these early Fathers give to the authority of the deutero-canonical books, they quote them as the words of Daniel, Jeremiah or Solomon as the case may be. This has already been shewn to a certain extent by the historical quotations, where we have seen these books quoted as authentic history under the evident supposition that Daniel or Solomon wrote them.

But still more strongly they are directly ascribed to these inspired writers. Thus the Song of the Three Children to Daniel, " Moreover in Daniel, 'And we are lowly this day,' "[48] etc. (Song 14–19). To the same writer Susanna is ascribed by both Irenæus and Cyprian, "And they shall hear those words as found in Daniel the Prophet, 'O thou seed of Canaan, and not of Judah, beauty hath deceived thee,' "[49] etc. (Hist. Sus. 56), and,

---

[43] Callistus, Ep. v. c. Hippol. ii. 213. [44] Cyprian *on Mortality*, vii. 10; 1. 458 (two quotations). Epistle, li. 22, 145. [45] Clement, *the Instructor*, ii. iii. 1. 212. [46] *Apost. Const.* vi. xxiii, 169: Hippolytus *ag. Noetus.* 2, ii, 52. [47] *Apost. Const.* ii. li. 79. [48] Cyprian, *Test. ag. Jews*, ii. 20; 160. [49] Irenæus, *ag. Heresies*, iv. xxvi. iii. 463.

"Also in Daniel 'There was a man dwelling in Baby-lon,'"[50] etc. (Hist. Sus. 1–3).

Two passages have already been quoted where Bel and the Dragon is ascribed to "Daniel the Prophet,"[51] and there is another passage in Tertullian too long and involved to quote.[52]

Baruch is quoted as by Jeremiah, "Moreover in Jere-miah 'This is our God,'"[53] etc. (Bar. iii. 35–37). "By Jeremiah, he sets forth prudence, when he says, 'Blessed are we of Israel,'"[54] etc. (Bar. iv. 4; also iii. 9 and iii. 13). "He (Jeremiah) says, 'Learn where is wisdom,'"[55] (Bar. iii. 14, 15). And twice more by Tertullian[56] and Ire-næus.[57]

Wisdom is often quoted as Solomon's. "The Holy Spirit who of God is in all things"[58] (Wisd. xii. i.) "And again Solomon says concerning Christ and the Jews, that, 'When the righteous shall stand,'"[59] etc. (Wisd. v. 19). It is to be noticed here that Hippolytus is quoting thus, in a treatise against the Jews, the words of Solomon in the Book of Wisdom as an inspired pro-phecy about Christ, and in the same treatise[60] is a pas-sage which, although rather long, is so important that I quote it in full: "I produce now the prophecy of Sol-omon, which speaketh of Christ, and announces clearly and perspicuously things concerning the Jews, and those which not only are befalling them at the present time, but

---

[50] Cyprian, Test. ag. Jews, ii. 20, 160. [51] Irenæus, ag. Heresies, iv. v. 2; i. 387. Cyprian, Eph. lv. i. 184. [52] Tertullian, on Fast-ing, vii. iii. 135. [53] Cyprian, Test. ag. Jews, ii. 6, 104. [54] Clement, the Instructor, i. x. 176. [55] Methodius, Banq. Virgins, viii. 3, 69. [56] Tertullian, Scorpiace, 8; i. 396. [57] Irenæus, ag. Heresies, v. 35, i. ii. 152. [58] Methodius, 229. [59] Hippolytus against the Jews, 10, c. ii. 45. [60] Ibid. 9, c. ii. 44.

those, too, which shall befall them in the future age, on account of the contumacy and audacity which they exhibited toward the Prince of Life; for the Prophet says, 'The ungodly said, reasoning with themselves, but not aright,' that is, about Christ, 'Let us lie in wait,'" etc. (Wisd. ii. 12, 13); also, in a number of other places.[61]

The Prayer of Manasseh is ascribed to him in the Apostolical Constitutions and is given in full,[62] in the same work Judith is said to prophesy, "Now women prophesied also of old, Miriam, the sister of Moses, and Aaron, and after her Deborah, and after these Huldah and Judith,"[63] and Tobit is certainly classed as a Prophet by Irenæus.[64] It is also to be noticed that Lactantius, Cyprian, and Clement quote Ecclesiasticus as the words of Solomon, thus: "And the Holy Ghost speaks by Solomon, saying, 'a perverse,' etc. (Prov. xvi. 27); also, again, he warneth us and says, 'Hedge in thy ears'"[65] (Ecclus. xxviii. 24). "Moreover Solomon, established in the Holy Spirit, testifies and teaches what is the priestly authority and power, saying, 'Fear the Lord with all thy soul,'"[66] etc. (Ecclus. vii. 29). "Solomon also shews that it is the Word of God, and no other, by whose hands these works of the world were made. 'I,' he says, 'came forth out of the mouth of the most high,'"[67] etc. (Ecclus. xxiv. 5–7), and so Clement of Alex. in two places.[68]

---

[61] Clement, *Miscellanies*, vi. xiv. ii. 370, 368; vi. xv. ii. 374, 375: vi. xi. ii. 358. Origen *ag. Celsus*, v. xxix. 298. [62] *Apost. Const*. ii. x. xii; 57. [63] Ibid. viii. ii. 211. [64] Irenæus *ag. Heresies*, i. xxx. ii. c. i. 110. [65] Cyprian Ep. liv. i. 179. [66] Cyprian, Ep. lxiv. i. 227. [67] Lactantius, *The Divine Inst*. iv. viii. i. 226. [68] Clement, *Miscellanies*, ii. v. 15.

I have contented myself largely with giving the quotations and letting them speak for themselves, only the most striking have been quoted, and yet there are many others which are fully as strong when considered in connection with the context, and many of those which I have quoted are more forcible when not torn away from the text.

That the Ante-Nicene Fathers considered the deutero-canonical books to be inspired, that they believed them to be the words of inspired men, that they treat them as they do other books of the Bible, that they quote them in defence of doctrine, discipline, and worship, and that in controversial treatises, frequently in controversy with the Jews, cannot it seems to me be denied.

In the three lists of the books of the Bible, which are all that we have of those who wrote before 325 A. D., Melito does not mention the deutero-canonical books at all,[69] neither does he the book of Lamentations or Esther; Origen does mention them and says " besides these there are also the Maccabees."[70]   The Apostolical Constitutions[71] leave out the Lamentations, put in Esther, give three books of Maccabees, put in or leave out Judith according to different manuscripts, put in Ecclesiasticus in a class by itself, and ignore the other books ; it is possible that the omitted books may be included under some other book, as Lamentations under Jeremiah.

That these lists are comparatively if not absolutely worthless as testimony against the books, is true first on account of their negative character and from the fact that they omit books recognised as canonical, secondly because the author of the list in the case of Origen, and

---

[69] Eusebius, *Eccl. Hist.* v. 26.   [70] Ibid. vi. 25.   [71] *Apost. Const.* viii. 85, 268.

other parts of the same book in the case of the Apostolical canons, quote the deutero-canonical books frequently
as Scripture; the Apostolical Constitutions quoting the
books at least twenty-six times, while Origen quotes
them more than forty-eight times: at least eight
of these quotations being introduced with the expression
"Holy Scripture,"[72] or "Divine Word"[73] besides which
he wrote a lengthy letter to Africanus defending both
the authenticity and inspiration of those deutero-canonical portions of the Prophet Daniel.[74]

In addition to these three lists is a curious fragment,
known as the Canon Muratorianus, ascribed to Caius, a
Presbyter of Rome, and believed to belong to the latter
half of the second century, I will quote from this all that
affects the testimony concerning these books, "And the
[book of] Wisdom, written by the friends of Solomon in
his honour [is admitted]. We receive also the Apocalypse of John and [that of] Peter, though some amongst
us will not have this latter read in the Church. The
Pastor, moreover, did Hermas write very recently in our
times in the city of Rome, while his brother Pius sat in
the chair of the Church of Rome, and therefore it also
ought to be read; but it cannot be made public in the
Church to the people, nor [placed] among the Prophets,
as their number is complete, nor among the Apostles to
the end of time."[75]

As is seen the testimony of this fragment is very uncertain; it apparently admits the Book of Wisdom, but
beside that it mentions two other books, the Apocalypse
of Peter and The Pastor, of Hermas.

---

[72] Origen *ag. Celsus*, vi. vii. 344: vii. xii. 435. *De Princip.* ii.
ii. 5, 77 : ii. viii. 3, 123 : ii. ix. 127 : iii. i. 191. [73] Origen *ag. Celsus*,
viii. l. 534. [74] C. ed. Origen, i. 371. [75] C. ed. Irenæus, ii. 162.

This brings before us the almost universal reply to this argument for the deutero-canonical books based on their use by the Ante-Nicene Fathers, namely that other books also such as Enoch, and The Pastor, of Hermas, are by the same writers quoted as Scripture in the same way. Thus Bishop Cosin in a few words tries to sweep all this testimony to one side; he says: " Sometimes he [Origen] citeth under the general name of Scriptures, the book of Tobit, and the Maccabees; but this is no greater argument that he held them to be canonical Scriptures, than it is to say that he held the book of Enoch, and Hermas his Pastor, to be canonical, because we find them also often alleged by him under the same general name of the Scriptures." [76]

There is no doubt that the early writers of this age looked upon these two books, together with the Epistle of Barnabas and those of Clement, as of sufficient value to be read in the Church and quoted with inspired writings; at the same time there is an evident discrimination, as we have just seen in the passage quoted from Caius, or whoever it may have been.

The two strongest passages that can be quoted in favour of Enoch are from Tertullian, " These things, therefore, the Holy Spirit, foreseeing from the beginning, fore-chanted through the most ancient Prophet Enoch," [77] and in his Treatise on Female Dress,[78] he defends the book quite at length as prophecying of Christ and as quoted by St. Jude; in another place he quotes it in connexion with Isaiah.[79] Anatolius[80] and Irenæus[81] quote

---

[76] *A Schol. Hist. of the Canon*, Ox. Ed. 40. [77] Tertullian *on Idolatry*, xv. i. 164. [78] i. iii. 307. [79] *On Idolatry*, iv. i. 145. [80] Anatolius, v. 415. [81] *Ag. the Heresies*, iv. 16, 2, 423.

it in a general sort of way, and Origen quotes it and Hermas in the same passage, and rather contrasts them with Scripture,[82] and in another place he says, "Which we see pointed out moreover in the little book of the Shepherd, which seems to be despised by some."[83] Several times he makes simple quotations from Hermas, and so does Clement of Alexandria,[84] while Tertullian quotes him evidently not as Scripture.[85]

But these quotations are very few, are confined to at the most five writers; and Enoch alone is quoted with any force as Scripture. There were many reasons why they should have been deceived as to that work, the apparent reference to it by St. Jude, and the fact that some such book did exist, which was, or was strongly supposed to be authentic; these cases are, however, not at all parallel as Cosin would make out.

Summing up the evidence, we find an enormous number of quotations from the deutero-canonical books, and (mark!) the argument is a cumulative one, if ten, twenty or even more of the quotations prove to be false, or the writings in which they appear of doubtful authenticity, it does not invalidate the argument, although it may weaken it. Not only are there a large number of quotations, but they are from many writers, extending over a period of more than two centuries, on all sorts of subjects. These writers quote the books as history, they quote them as the works of inspired writers, they quote them as of authority in controversies touching the faith, they quote them as the words of God and of the Holy Ghost, and prophecies of Christ and the Church, they

---

[82] *De Prin*. i. iii. 3, 134. [83] Ibid. ii. i. 5 : i. 77 : iv. i. 35: i. 352. *Miscellanies* I. xvii. I : i. 408 : ii. ix. ii. 28 : ii. xii : ii. 34. [85] *On Prayer*, xvi. i. 190.

quote them with the most solemn assertions of their being the Sacred and Holy Scriptures, the Word of God, they quote them against the Jews as well as against heretics and heathen, they do not question far less deny their inspiration nor their authenticity.

Is it conceivable that they could have quoted them with more authority, or in terms which should more fully express their inspiration as the Word of God? Well then has the Anglican Communion followed in their footsteps, when in her VI. Article of Religion on Holy Scripture she places the deutero-canonical books. (In a list by themselves as not contained in the present Hebrew canon, it is true, but this she does on St. Jerome's authority.) She binds them in her Bible with the other canonical books of Holy Scripture, she reads them to her children not only on ferias but on feast days.

In her Homilies she quotes them as "The infallible and undeceivable Word of God," [86] "As the Word of God testifieth," [87] (Wisd. xiv.), "As the Scripture teacheth," [88] (Wisd. xiii. xiv.), "The same lesson doth the Holy Ghost teach in sundry places of the Scripture, saying, ' Mercifulness,' " [89] etc. (Tob. iv.).

She quotes them in her liturgy, and in the *Necessary Doctrine and Erudition for any Christian Man* (one of her authoritative documents, accepted and put forth by Convocation) she refers to the Book of Maccabees in defence of prayers for the dead.[90]

One cannot but feel it is a pity her children do not read and study these books more thoroughly, of which, if one might judge, as some men judge of the inspiration

---

[86] I B. x. I. [87] 2 B. ii. 3. [88] Ibid. [89] 2 B. xi. 2. [90] *Formularies of the Faith*, Ox. 1856, 375.

of the Bible, by the way in which it appeals to their inner consciousness, the inspiration would not be doubted.

Few books of the Old Testament are as helpful or suggestive as Wisdom and Ecclesiasticus, few if any approach so near to the spirit of the New Testament.

[It should be remarked, in reference to the foot-note on p. 55, that this Essay was published soon after it was written, and that the publishers of the American edition of the "Ante-Nicene Christian Library" wrote to the author to say that they would see to it that all the omitted references should be found in the Index of Texts, which would be in the last volume, a promise which they kept.—ED.]

Science and Miracles.

IT is a trite remark with which to begin my essay, that the relations between Science and Religion (or rather between those who call themselves scientists and Christians) are not what they should be, and that the cause of the strained relations may be traced to faults on both sides.

Scientists on the one hand are not generally remarkable either for humility, modesty, or consistency ; perhaps they might defend themselves in regard to the first two virtues, by saying that humility and modesty are Christian graces, and therefore have nothing to do with scientists, which would probably be true, but in addition to these they are greatly wanting in consistency in the charges which they bring against religion, and surely consistency is a jewel which scientists would claim as belonging to their treasury.

For instance their favourite point of attack is the unfortunate mistake which the Roman Church made in persecuting Galileo for holding the Copernican instead of the Ptolemaic theory of astronomy.

It is not uncommon to read an article against religion clearly divided into two parts. The first being filled with denunciations of the wickedness and folly of the Church in its action in the case of Galileo; the second being a similar denunciation of the still greater folly of the Church in the present day in not at once accepting the dogmas which science promulgates.

This kind of treatment we have experienced from science so long, that perhaps some of us have failed to see how delightfully inconsistent it is; for if we reduce these two charges to a careful statement of facts, does it not come to this, that in Galileo's time the Church made the mistake of being over-credulous in accepting the dogmas of science, and propagating the theories of the scientists of those days, and of all previous days. When Galileo was punished for not accepting the Ptolemaic theory of the planetary system, was not that the scientific theory which was accepted by a great majority of teachers, and instead of the Church having put herself in opposition to science on that occasion was not her fault that she too readily listened to science, over-credulity in trusting science not obstinate refusal to accept its teachings, and is it not, to say the least, inconsistent in the scientist of to-day to abuse us for being credulous in the time of Galileo, and for being incredulous in our own day? May we not say that having trusted to science once, and having found ourselves deceived, we may fairly claim the right to be very slow in accepting its conclusions to-day, especially as they are still being changed or modified every decade?

If scientists desire to be consistent and accurate let them cease from charging the Church with always opposing science, and let them remember that in the matter of the Ptolemaic theory of astronomy, where she accepted a scientific theory, she had cause to repent of it.

But I said there were faults on both sides and if the attitude of science to religion is inconsistent, I must admit that the position of many religious persons towards science is not free from blame. It seems to me that such persons commonly fall into one of two errors : (1) either an abject surrender to every demand of so-called science or (2) an obstinate and prejudiced hostility to every discovery which science proclaims.

The many mistakes which have been made in the name of science forbid the first, while the debt of gratitude which we owe for the discovery of much scientific truth and the dispersion of still more error demands better treatment than the second. We should recognise surely that many scientists at least are seekers after truth, though often blinded and led astray by pride. We should accept their statements with great caution, but surely we should shew ourselves willing to investigate their arguments, and, at least so far, to meet them on their own ground.

One of the greatest objections of scientists to Christianity is that it is a religion demanding a belief in miracles, and there are two mistakes which are commonly made in meeting the objection.

(1) Minimising the number and character of the miracles of Christianity, shewing for instance that some of them at least may be accounted for by causes with which we have become familiar. Surely this is most illogical or rather is not a meeting of the difficulty at all, when we still believe that upon one miracle Christianity absolutely depends, I mean of course the miracle of our Lord's Resurrection, and there can be no kind of advantage gained to us, nor can we overcome the scientists' objections by practically giving up a number of miracles, if we still hold, as we do, the most stupendous, the Resurrection of our Lord from the dead, as a positive fact, and a necessary dogma of the Christian faith.

Matthew Arnold somewhere has rather wittily described this class of apologists, as saying that while it is quite incredible, in the story of Cinderella, that the pumpkin was changed into a coach and six, there is not the same difficulty in believing that it may have been changed into a one-horse chaise.

These apologists fail to see that no amount of minimising the number and character of the Christian miracles could ever affect the *a priori* difficulty of scientists in accepting a religion which is founded on the doctrine of the resurrection.

(2) The second class err almost as greatly, to my mind, by refusing to discuss the question, practically saying, " Well you do not believe in miracles and I do, and it is hopeless and useless for us to discuss the question." Would it not be more charitable, more courageous, and a sign perhaps of greater faith in our own position for us to say to the scientist, " Well, now, tell me your objections to miracles, and I will see how I can meet them, not by evading the question or by explaining away miracles, but by fairly and squarely taking the one central miracle of the Resurrection of Christ, and considering how far I can meet and answer the scientific objection to it."

While the scientist in theory would say the truth of a miracle must be decided by the evidence for it, yet as a matter of practical fact he would say, " A miracle is an impossibility, because it is an interference with that law of continuity in nature, which has never been broken, and which is the most universal and best recognised of all nature's laws; and no amount of evidence in an age believing in the miraculous can be sufficient to prove what is an *a priori* impossibility."

. I have tried to state the scientific objection to miracles as fairly and as strongly as I can, now let us investigate it carefully and see how we can answer it.

In the first place it is evident that what is regarded as miraculous by one person is not a miracle to another, and that the miraculous really only implies an ignorance of the cause of any strange phenomenon; when we can account for it, however wonderful it may be, it ceases to be a miracle.

Next I would ask the scientist to tell me what he means by " nature," when he speaks of an interference with the laws of nature. Probably he would reply, as many people do, by sharply dividing all things into two spheres which he would call the natural and supernatural; the former of which he would claim as his domain, the latter he would be willing to leave to theology on the condition that it confined itself strictly to its limits. By " natural" he would probably mean things which could be observed, and to some extent accounted for and registered, and therefore known ; and by " supernatural or moral " he would mean all outside of this class. Now at the outset I entirely deny this antithesis, and claim that the definition does not really define, because evidently as our knowledge became greater we should be continually subtracting from the supernatural, and adding to the natural. For instance we can imagine how our forefathers would have classed according to this definition among supernatural things, many which now we know to be entirely natural, such as some of the manifold effects of electricity, or hypnotism, or steam, so that the line of demarcation which the scientist thinks so clear, on closer examination wavers more and more, and to my mind finally disappears altogether.

Bishop Butler has a far truer view of what " natural " means : " It is," he says, " that which is stated, fixed and settled, in other words something which is familiar," and he adds, "From hence it must follow that a person's notions of what is natural vary in proportion to their greater knowledge of the works of God." The distinction then is not absolute but relative to our growing knowledge; to perfect knowledge, God's working in the physical and moral world must be all natural. It cannot be partly one and partly the other; for the moment we accept such a definition as the scientist has given, we practically recognise the existence of a power other than God, and then while nature becomes the expression of order, law, and rational procedure, God is represented as the antithesis of this, as motiveless volition, as a principle of indeterminateness, which is hard to distinguish from caprice.

Here I must protest again most earnestly against the word "interference." There are not and cannot be any divine interferences in nature, for God cannot interfere with himself. His creative activity is present everywhere, there is no division of labour between God and nature, or God and Law, nor, do I think, can the scientist even from his own point of view justify the term "interference," for to talk of interference with the laws of nature is to assume a knowledge of *all* the laws of nature, whereas science at best has only succeeded in discovering and registering a few of them, and even her own investigations must have taught her that almost every phenomenon of nature is produced by a combination of laws, which the scientist would hardly say were interfering with one another, although the effect is often the resultant of opposing forces so delicately balanced, that we can easily see that any alteration in their relation, or the introduction of a new force, would perfectly naturally produce a most marvellous result. And so a miracle would be better defined, even by the scientist, as the intervention of some principle or law with which he is not familiar.

And again, not only does science not know all the laws of nature, it does not know what is behind nature; for the so-called laws are themselves results, not causes, and there is something behind, which the scientist may, if he pleases, call the Unknowable or the First Cause, but which is absolutely necessary to account for the smallest law.

There was a time not long ago when scientists wished to deify "matter," and then nature would have been with them another term for the laws of matter, but this position has been given up, and matter admitted to be but the phenomena of force; and further, there is rapidly growing a recognition of what is called the unification of force, and this one force, which is behind all nature, and which science calls by various names, our Creed tells us is God, Almightiness, and it is well to bear in mind how scientifically accurate the Creed is when in the original it uses the word " Pantokrator " to describe this attribute of God, not as the Latin translation " *Omnipotens*" which may imply, "able to do all things," but rather the source and fountain of all force, so that nothing can be done without him.

Let us take man as an illustration, since in him the two spheres at least to some extent meet, and he may be regarded as a microcosm.

The scientist explains to his own satisfaction the origin of man's body, its gradual development by evolution from protoplasm till it appears the last production of nature, but its greatest, the flower and crown of all that has gone before. But in man the scientist has to recognise a new force, an intelligent will—a soul, we should say—whose origin the scientist cannot explain, but whose existence he cannot ignore. He observes further how this will directs and governs man's physical actions—in a word, is *the force* behind human life. The scientist goes on next to observe the working of this will, that, as in lower nature, he may reduce it to a system, may register its laws so as to be able to foretell its future acts. The fascinating study of psychology promises a science of human history, and a science of human character, but its promises fail.

Take a family inheriting the same tendencies, brought up under the same circumstances. One child turns out very good, another very bad; a third child has been thrown upon the street to bring himself up, and he grows up a noble, honest man; a fourth has a tender mother's care and turns out a disgrace to society. How can the scientist account for this breach, so to speak, in law? He can only say that he does not know all the laws of the moral world; and yet it is those laws which are behind human life, even in its physical aspects.

I said that, since the theory of the materialists had given place to the newer opinion that matter is but the phenomena of force, there had arisen among many scientific men a growing conviction that all force may ultimately be reduced to one force; and this force, on which all nature depends, Christianity tells us is God's Will, the motive power of the universe, working more uniformly than man's will, and yet able, on occasion, to vary, and indeed, as a matter of fact, manifesting this variation in certain very marked ways, to which I am shortly about to refer.

This law, too, of continuity from which some scientists derive the impossibility of miracles, to others in the first rank of science, to the authors of "the unseen universe," is the very law which postulates just such an unseen kingdom, stretching out into eternity, as the Christian revelation teaches.

With these exceptions to the scientist's use of the terms "interference" and "nature" in his definition, I shall now go on to shew further that miracles are not even a breach of the law of continuity, but are in the strictest analogy with the phenomena which science has already examined and classified, in the region of what it is pleased to call "natural law."

The great scientific doctrine of evolution may, I suppose, be described as the gradual progress through many a struggle of the protoplasmic germ till culminating in man: but does not another evolution begin here—that of the moral world? And do we not find in each miracles?—not interferences, but revelations and prophecies of something higher, anticipatory forces belonging to another and higher order, but all in strictest analogy to what science has already discovered in the lower kingdoms of nature.

Let me illustrate by example what I mean. Take the two great divisions of matter, organic and inorganic. Fancy yourself with a scientist living in the Azoic period, and, together with him, watching and registering the phenomena of the inorganic world. In the way in which the dead world proceeds day by day you recognise the great law of continuity. You say it has no breaks; it is inexorable in its monotony. But one day, in the rocks which border the St. Lawrence river, you observe a strange phenomenon, and on closer examination in the limestone there you find the Eozoon Canadense, the first manifestation of organic life. But here is a distinct breach in your law of continuity, a most marked interference with the hitherto unalterable law of nature. Here, in a word, is a miracle as great—nay, greater—than the resurrection of the body, for the body has lived once, while here out of what was lifeless, life has come—from whence, in what manner, by whose agency? Science is dumb and cannot answer. Religion says from God.

Pass on some ages, and take for the next sphere of your investigation the vegetable world. What is it doing? Why, it is stooping down and taking out of dead, inorganic matter certain properties with which to build up its various organisms, and, as in the carboniferous period, you see all around you the magnificent flora of that age, you see on a gigantic scale one kingdom interfering with another—the vegetable kingdom interfering with the inorganic and taking up into itself miraculously the dead world, with which we started our investigations.

Pass to another kingdom. How is it that certain kinds of orchids depend for their fertilization on the operations of insect life? Is this an interference of the entomological kingdom with the vegetable? Another breach in the law of continuity, as we first read it; another instance of miracles. Miracles, of course I mean at the time when the phenomenon first appeared in the process of evolution.

So you find the world developed one step at a time, but each step being at that time what you might call an interference with the laws of the previous period. Then comes man, and man revolutionises everything, combining all sorts of laws, and so introducing mechanism and appliances which have transformed the whole world.

But with man you will admit the moral kingdom begins;
and do you think that its beginning is also its ending?
Do you think that because man has discovered so much
that therefore there is no more to be discovered? Do
you think because everything so far has worked up to
you, as a human being, that therefore you are the absolute end of all things? No. Revelation and science
alike say that you are only the beginning of the moral
kingdom, and revelation goes on alone to say that
there is another life beyond, of which as yet we know
but little, but of which the resurrection from the dead is
a prophecy and revelation, just as the eozoon was a
prophecy of the introduction of the lower organic life.
But, mark well, to stop here is unscientific; for to stop
here is the real breach in the law of continuity. For
science has seen the higher kingdoms of nature continually stooping down and taking out of the lower that
which is necessary to the development and manifestation
of their own life, and that man is the flower and crown
of this long series of progress, as far as his body is concerned, but that his moral nature is the germ or seed of
a new kingdom; and why should science call on us to
halt here? Is there any instance in the past of a halt in
the law of progress? No! Now religion steps in and
teaches us that in the Incarnation a new kingdom begins, that God stoops to take unto himself man, and
through him all the lower kingdoms of creation, and
lifts man up to a higher sphere. And the necessary consequence of the Incarnation is the Resurrection. Observe
with what scientific accuracy it is explained by St. Peter
in Acts ii. 24: "Whom God hath raised up, having
loosed the pains of death, because it was not possible
that he should be holden of it." For there is no

instance of the lower kingdom holding down in its embrace the higher, but, on the contrary, the higher lifts up with it the lower; and revelation, still in strictest accord with the analogy of the lower world, tells us that into this sphere we shall one day be lifted.

In all this there is nothing contrary to science, though it may be beyond the province of science. Trᴜe science can only be negative in regard to miracles; it can say of any one miracle that it does not consider the evidence sufficient to justify belief in it, but it cannot claim that a miracle is impossible; it cannot disprove the miraculous.

In evolution science is positive, and many of its positive statements we can gratefully accept; but its negatives, like all negatives, cannot disprove.

To take the scientific statement with which we began, That a miracle is impossible because it is an interference with the laws of nature, a break in that continuity which has known no exception," we see how entirely it fails on examination.

First, the laws of nature cannot be separated from the other laws of God, or, if you prefer it, of the supernatural.

Second, the very fact of nature having laws is a recognition of a force behind nature, and points to the probability of an intelligent will, which cannot interfere with itself.

Then, thirdly, it is not true to say that there have been no breaches in the law of continuity, for the introduction of life was such a breach, and thus breaches or miracles have always occurred as the prophecy, or revelation, or introduction of an approaching higher kingdom. And so we have a right to claim, in the light of the scientific discoveries of the past, that the so-called miracles of

Christianity, and especially the miracle of the resurrection, is exactly what the law of continuity, in its larger generalisation, would lead us to expect, as the prophecy of that higher moral kingdom, the Kingdom of our Lord and of his Christ, in which all the laws of so-called nature, as well as the supernatural, all the kingdoms of this world, will find their consummation and perfection.

The Doctrinal System

Underlying the Prayer Book and Articles.

IT is a well-recognised principle that the *lex suppli-candi* is the *lex credendi.*[1] What more sure witness to the Church's teaching can be found than the words with which she addresses God, and with which she administers the rites of religion? The writings of individuals may be valuable as indicating with more or less certainty the received teaching of the Church, but the language of the Church herself in her liturgical formularies will signify more than a thousand quotations from individual writers. Moreover the Prayer Book has ever been regarded, as not only setting forth a liturgical system, but as also being a formal expression, by the Church herself, of her dogmatic teaching. The history of the successive revisions which the Prayer Book has undergone; the dislike with which it has been regarded by all thoughtful and consistent Protestants; the persistent attacks which have been made upon it by unbelievers; the obstinate refusal of the Church to make any radical changes—she preferring the secession of large numbers of the discontented rather than make the desired concessions; and it might also be added, the overruling Providence which has thus far preserved it intact

---

[1] Pope Coelestine I. *Epistola xxi. ad. Episcopos Galliæ.*

from the eviscerating influence of latitudinarianism, are so many proofs of its dogmatic character.

Next to the Book of Common Prayer, we have the Articles of Religion. Although subscription to them is no longer required by canon as a condition for the susception of Holy Orders, they are undoubtedly part of the Church's teaching, and as such they cannot be ignored or lightly set aside; and therefore any attempt to set forth the Church's doctrinal system which passed them over, could not be regarded but as partial and unsatisfactory. "Coloured as they are in language and form by the peculiar circumstances under which they were originally drawn up,"[2] we may be permitted to think that the "omission of a few clauses in a few of the Articles would render the whole body free from any imputation of injustice or harshness towards those who differ from us,"[3] but because they are recognised standards of doctrine, no teacher of the Church may formally deny any of the theological propositions contained in them without incurring the charge of at least grave temerity.

Any doubt, however, which there might be as to the formally dogmatic character of both the Prayer Book and the Articles is answered by the encyclical letter of our bishops assembled at Lambeth. After declaring their unfeigned adhesion to "the one Faith revealed in Holy Writ, defined in the creeds maintained by the primitive Church, and affirmed by the undisputed Œcumenical Councils," they add, that they "recognise the Prayer Book with its Catechism, the Ordinal, and the

---

[2] *Encyclical Letter of the Lambeth Conference of 1888.* [3] *Report of the Committee on Authoritative Standards appointed by the Lambeth Conference.*

Thirty-nine Articles " " as standards of doctrine and worship alike," and they express the desire "that these standards should be set before the foreign churches in their purity and simplicity." Moreover, while granting that it would be unreasonable to require the *ipsissima verba* of the Articles as conditions of communion in the cases of native and growing churches, they nevertheless most emphatically declare that in order to such communion these churches must hold substantially the same doctrine as that set forth in the Prayer Book and Articles. The words of the conference on this point are: " It would be impossible for us to share with them in the matter of Holy Orders, as in complete intercommunion, without satisfactory evidence that they hold *substantially the same form of doctrine as ourselves.* It ought not to be difficult, much less impossible, to formulate articles, *in accordance* with our own standards of doctrine and worship, the acceptance of which should be required of all ordained in such churches."

Now, while the Prayer Book and Articles are manifestly not a systematic body of divinity, indeed, from their very nature they could not be, yet their doctrinal statements, scattered and often incidental, are undoubtedly the more or less complete expression of some underlying system. What is this system? Is it Catholicism or is it Protestantism? To answer this question is the object of this essay. We shall begin by stating as briefly as possible the characteristics of these two systems, and afterward we shall be able to judge which is the system of our formularies.

In the first place, then, the system of Catholic doctrine may be briefly stated thus: As man came forth from the hand of God he possessed not only every possible physical and intellectual perfection, but his soul was also endued with the gifts of immortality, free will, and the capacity to know and love God. All these gifts were natural to man, and essential to the integrity of his human nature, and constituted him *the image* of God. The tendency of the body, however, from the very constitution of its nature, was to seek a material good. In order that this inclination of man's lower nature might never dominate over his higher nature, God freely bestowed upon him the supernatural gift of grace. By this gift the reason was illuminated to know God perfectly, and the will, while left perfectly free, was so supported that, conforming perfectly to the will of God, it was enabled to hold all the lower inclinations in perfect subjection. Man was now not only the image of God, but also the very *likeness* of God. Let it be carefully noted—for upon this point hinge all the controversies between Catholics and Protestants on the subject of Original Sin and Justification—that this gift of grace was a *supernatural* gift; it added nothing to the essential integrity of human nature. The Fall was the exercise of man's free will by which he rebelled against the commandment of God. His punishment was the deprivation of this supernatural gift of grace, and consequently of the vision of God, both in time and in eternity. Let it be noted here, that man was *wholly* deprived of supernatural grace. The words of St. Thomas on this point are very clear: By the sin of Adam "the whole gift of original righteousness has been taken away"; and again, "the good of nature [*i. e.*, the *donum originalis justitiæ*] has been wholly taken away by the sin of our first parent." *

---

* *Summa*, P. I⁰. 2ᵐ, Q. lxxxii. A. 4, and Q. lxxxv. A. 1.

But, let it be also noted, that man by the Fall lost no natural gift; the essential integrity of his human nature remained unimpaired. That nature was indeed displaced from the proper end for which it was created, and hence resulted the wounds of ignorance, inordinate concupiscence, proneness to evil, and physical decay and death, but it was not so completely displaced that it was wholly inclined to evil, or wholly averse to good. *The likeness* of God was lost, but *the image* of God remained still. If man is to be again made acceptable to God, he must again receive the supernatural gift which he had before his fall; but man being unable to do anything to properly merit this favour, it is freely bestowed upon him out of God's loving munificence. The sacrament of baptism is the instrument by which he receives the *infusion* of supernatural life which removes from his person both the guilt of sin and the liability to its penalty, and makes him really and truly just and holy.† Concupiscence does indeed remain after baptism, but it can only stain the soul when the will consents to its suggestions; and this the will, by the power of grace, may refrain from ever doing. In the regenerate after baptism, therefore, there is nothing which is properly sin. And he is accounted righteous before God, because the righteousness of Christ has become inherent in him. By virtue of the life which he now has, he has not only obtained remission of all his sins, but has also been brought into a union with Jesus Christ so close and intimate that he is said to be 'of his body, of his flesh, and of his bones,'[4] or as St. Peter boldly expresses it, he has become 'partaker of the divine nature.'[5] So that he can truly say to

---

† When this supernatural life is again lost after baptism, it is restored by penitence.   [4] Ephesians, v. 30.   [5] II. Peter, i. 4.

God with the psalmist, " Preserve thou my soul, for *I am holy*." [6]   His Christian life afterwards consists in the development of the supernatural principle received in baptism, and the reducing to order of all those passions which were thrown into disorder by the Fall. So that gradually he that is just becomes more just, and he that is holy becomes more holy, until at length he attains unto the fulness of the stature of Christ. Now, this is what is known as justification by an infused righteousness, and it is the system of Catholicism. Once grant that it is true; once admit that the justified are in a true and real sense members of Christ and the children of God, and the whole devotional and practical system of the Catholic religion must logically and irresistibly follow.

Note some of the logical and necessary results of this doctrine of justification by an infused righteousness.   In the first place see how it necessitates the still further doctrine that there is a visible organism, out of which there is no salvation. If the justified are one by a corporate union with Christ, it follows that there must be a real and vital union between all faithful souls, therefore the apostle says : " We being many are *one body in Christ*."[7] To be united to this body of the faithful is to be united to Christ, to be separated from it is to be separated from Christ.

This common life of believers implies, too, a common sympathy, and interest the one for the other.   Each will have a share in all the prayers and good works of every other member. And as the union between Christ and the justified soul is not broken by death, neither can the

---

[6] Psalms, lxxxvi. 2.   [7] Romans xii. 5.

union which exists between the members be broken. As our good works and prayers assisted our brethren while on earth, so will they continue to assist them when they have passed into the Church Expectant; and as they had an interest in our salvation while they were still in the body, so will they continue to interest themselves in us when they are in the presence of God, and all by virtue of the union with Christ, "from whom the whole body fitly joined together and compacted *by that which every joint supplieth according to the effectual working in the measure of every part*, maketh increase of the body unto the edifying of itself in love."[8] We can understand, therefore, how natural the practice of prayers for the dead, and the belief in the virtue of the intercessions of the Saints is to a Catholic.

Note another practical deduction from this doctrine. If the justified possess the very life of God, it follows that he can keep the commandments, and that none of them can be impossible to him. Nay more, not only will all the commandments of God be possible to him, but, if he have the divine calling, he may without any presumption undertake to follow even the counsels of God, and by vows bind himself to a life of poverty, chastity, and obedience in the religious state. And as he is the son of God, all his good works must have a necessarily meritorious character, so that they become the condition of his receiving further supplies of grace in this life, and of his final reward in the life to come.[9]

---

[8] Ephesians iv. 16. [9] Concerning the doctrine of the possibility of the regenerate fulfilling the law—a doctrine most clearly taught by the Prayer Book, as we shall shew further on—it may be well to say, that while all Catholic theologians insist upon it—as a necessary principle underlying the very idea of Chris-

In distinct contradiction to Catholicism stands out the system of Protestantism. According to the teaching of the Reformers and Protestant Confessions, none of the gifts bestowed upon the first man were supernatural, but all were natural and created (*concreata*) with him. The Fall, therefore, was not the deprivation of something distinct from human nature, but it was the destruction of the integrity of man's essential being in every part. It was not only that human nature being left without the help of grace was diverted from its supernatural end, and made corrupt and prone to evil, but it was the extinction of everything to which the adjective "good" could be applied. Hence the habit of concupiscence, which Catholic theologians regard as a natural power in disorder, is by Protestants regarded as being in itself positively sinful, quite apart from the consideration of the will consenting or not consenting to its motions. Man, therefore, being but one mass of sin, and unable to even think anything good, all his actions are truly sinful. Of course in the work of his justification there can be no real coöperation

---

tian obligation, they do not mean to imply that anyone has so perfectly fulfilled the law that he could be said to be without sin. Of all of us the words of Article XV. are true, "that we offend in many things; and if we say we have no sin we deceive ourselves, and the truth is not in us," and in the mouth of no one is the acknowledgment untrue that "we have offended against thy holy laws. We have left undone those things which we ought to have done; and we have done those things which we ought not to have done." But while there is no one who has fulfilled the law so as to be free from venial failings, the *possibility* of so fulfilling the law that one may be free from all grave violations of it exists, and must exist, if it be true, as Article VII. says, that no Christian man whatsoever is free from the obedience of the commandments which are called moral;" for it is of faith that God does not command impossibilities, and that his grace is sufficient for the fulfilment of

on his part; he remains perfectly passive. Justification becomes simply the forensic act of God by which he grants to the sinner remission of sins, as far as their penalty is concerned, for the sake of the righteousness of Christ. This righteousness is *not* infused into him, in order to become the ground of his justification, but it remains external to him, and is simply *imputed* to him to veil his unrighteousness. The Protestant theory of justification, therefore, " has its foundation in this—that God now outwardly declares that man righteous, *without any new thing being implanted within the man himself.*"[10] In other words, justification does not, as it does by Catholic

---

every obligation he lays upon us. Hence St. Augustine, while denying that there is a sinless man, nevertheless says : " If the question were asked of me, whether it is possible for a man in this life to be without sin, I should acknowledge it to be possible, by the grace of God, and the man's own free will ; having no doubt that even free will itself is to be referred to the grace of God, and is to be classed with God's gifts—not only as to its existence, but also as to its being good, that is to its conversion to doing the commandments of the Lord. It is in this way that God's grace not only sets forth what is to be done, but also assists to the possibility of accomplishing what is set forth." Then after quoting a number of texts of Scripture bearing upon the point, he adds : " From these, and very many other testimonies of like character, I cannot doubt, that God has commanded man to do nothing that is impossible ; and that by God's help and assistance, by which is wrought that which he commands, nothing is impossible of fulfilment." (*De Peccatorum Meritis et Remissione*, Lib. II. 7.) It must be remembered that all statements of St. Augustine's with regard to the actual sinfulness of all men must be understood as being subject to one limitation which he himself lays down, viz : " We must except the holy Virgin Mary, concerning whom I wish to raise no question when we are treating of sin, out of honour to the Lord." (*De Natura et Gratia*, c. 36.) [10] Martensen, *Christian Dogmatics*, p. 392.

teaching, imply sanctification ; sin still remains in the person and hence the man is as really a sinner after the act of justification as he was before.. By sanctification Protestants understand the gradual stripping off of the sinfulness of the justified; a work which the Formula of Concord tells us will only "fully come to pass in the resurrection unto blessedness."[11]

Of course on this theory, the assertion that it is impossible for the regenerate to observe the commandments becomes a logical necessity; and therefore the moral law can only be regarded as an ideal standard, impossible of attainment in this life.   And if the regenerate man is unable to keep the commandments, it would be a manifest absurdity—nay, an impious presumption to bind himself by vows to keep the evangelical counsels. We can understand, therefore, the acrimony and appreciate the consistency with which all the reformers attacked the religious life and the doctrine of condign merit, for in attacking these doctrines they were striking at the whole practical system of Catholicism.

Now of these two systems, which is the system of the Prayer Book and Articles ?   In the first place let us ascertain what the Church's doctrine is with regard to Original Sin, for her teaching upon this point will determine to a very great extent her teaching with regard to man's justification.   As to the existence of original sin the Church distinctly declares that "all men are conceived and born in sin,"[12] and "being by nature born in sin," they are "the children of wrath,"[13] and this "original sin standeth *not* in the following (*imitatione*)

---

[11] Francke, *Libri Symbolici Eccl. Luth*. P. III. p. 22.   [12] First Exhortation of Baptismal Office.   [13] Catechism.

of Adam, as the Pelagians do vainly talk; but it is the fault and corruption of every man, *that naturally is engendered of the offspring of Adam.*[14] Thus far she states but what is held by all Catholics, and by the old Protestants. We say, old Protestants, because the doctrine of the existence of original sin, of its transmission by propagation, of its deserving God's wrath, is either formally or tacitly rejected in much of the latitudinarian literature of the day. It has come to pass that by many sin is no longer regarded as a great spiritual disease bringing eternal death, but as nothing more than a physical or social disorder which may be corrected by purely philanthropic and humanitarian agencies. This, of course, is the most advanced Pelagianism, and must lead—aye, does lead, to the denial of the necessity of the death of Christ. In the face of such a theory the doctrine of the Church is clear and decisive. She teaches that "all men are conceived and born in sin, and they who are in the flesh *cannot* please God;"[15] that "works done before the grace of Christ, and the inspiration of his spirit are not pleasant to God;"[16] that man "cannot turn and prepare himself, by his own natural strength and good works, to faith and calling upon God,"[17] and, therefore, she declares that they "are to be had *accursed* that presume to say, that every man shall be saved by the law or sect which he professeth, so that he be diligent to frame his life according to that law, and the light of

---

[14] Art. IX.   [15] Office of Baptism of those of Riper Years.   [16] Art. XIII.   [17] Art. X. This Article, however, does not deny man's free will, for so far is it from implying that grace acts upon a merely passive subject that it distinctly says that it "works *with* us," (*co-operante*).

nature. For Holy Scripture doth set out unto us *only* the name of Jesus Christ, whereby men must be saved."[18]

So far, we have said, Catholics and the Protestant Confessions are agreed. It is only when we come to consider the effects of original sin more particularly that the divergence begins. We have seen that the characteristic of the Protestant doctrine of original sin is the total depravity of human nature, and the consequent assertion that concupiscence is truly and properly sin. Does the Prayer Book or do the Articles anywhere teach or even imply that the unregenerate man is wholly depraved? Article IX. declares that "man is very far gone from original righteousness, and is of his own nature inclined to evil." Here is a form of statement which is utterly unlike the phraseology used by the Lutheran and Reformed Confessions. The important word in this statement which clearly distinguishes it from the Protestant doctrine, is not *quam longissime*, but *distet*. This word implies a clean distinction between man and grace, and that man did not cease to be naturally what he was before his fall; he is still "man" although "very far gone (*distet*) from original righteousness." Observe the terms which the article uses to describe man's condition after his separation from original righteousness. He is said to be "of his own nature *inclined* to evil," and "his flesh *lusteth* always contrary to the spirit." But it is not said, that man is so depraved that he is ever accomplishing the evil to which his nature inclines him, and after which his flesh lusteth. These are the strongest expressions of the Church with regard to the state of the unregen-

---

[18] Art. XVIII.

erate, and how inadequate they are to express the
Protestant doctrine will be manifest when they are
compared with the parallel statements in the Protestant
Confessions.

According to the Augsburg Confession, man after
his fall would seem to have ceased to be naturally what
he was when created, and to have become something
akin to a devil; for it says that he is not only " born
without trust in God and with concupiscence," but he
is even " without the fear of God."[19]   The Formula of
Concord is more explicit; its words are: " We reject
and condemn that dogma by which it is asserted—that
man's nature and essence are not utterly corrupt, but
that there is something of good still remaining in
man."[20]   The Reformed Confessions are no less positive in declaring that man is wholly depraved.   The
Second Helvetic Confession says: " We understand
sin to be the native corruption of man, engendered in
us all from our first parents, by which, being immersed
in wicked concupiscence, made averse to good, inclined
to *all* evil, filled with *all* iniquity, disobedience, contempt,
and hatred of God, we are unable ourselves to do or
even so much as to think anything good."[21]   The Gallic
Confession of 1559 declares man's " nature is totally
corrupt.   And being blinded in his spirit, and depraved
in heart he has lost, without any exception, *all* integrity,
and there is no good in him."[22]   The larger Westminster
Catechism is in the same strain; it declares that by
original sin "we are *utterly* indisposed, disabled, and

---

[19] Francke, *Lib. Sym. Eccl. Luth.* i. p. 13.   [20] *Ibid.* iii. p. 23.
[21] Niemeyer, *Collectio Confessionum*, p. 477.   [22] Niemeyer, *Collectio
Confessionum*, p. 331.

made opposite to *all* good, and *wholly* inclined to all evil."[23]   And the Westminster Confession tells us that the corruption of nature or concupiscence is "truly and properly sin."[24]   Now no possible stretching of the words of our article will make it teach the doctrine set forth in these Confessions.   It declares, indeed, that man "is of his own nature inclined to evil," but it does not say that he is "without the fear of God;" or that man is "utterly corrupt;" or that he has "lost all integrity, and there is no good in him;"   or that he is "utterly indisposed, disabled, and made opposite to all good, and wholly inclined to all evil."   The article does indeed teach that concupiscence "is not subject to the law of God," and hence the inference is easy that it hath "the nature of sin," but it does not say that it is "truly and properly sin," which would import guilt and penalty. And therefore the Assembly of Divines proposed to revise this article by inserting, instead of the words "hath of itself the nature of sin," the words "is truly and properly sin."[25]   Clearly, therefore, the doctrine of original sin set forth in the IX. Article of Religion is not the Protestant doctrine, "even our enemies themselves being judges."

Our next step will be to ascertain the teaching of our formularies with regard to the Justification of man.   At the very threshold of our enquiry we are met by Article XI., which says that "We are accounted righteous before God, only for the merit of our Lord and Saviour Jesus Christ, by faith, and not for own works or deservings."

That the righteousness of Christ is the only meritorious cause of our being accounted righteous before God—

---

[23] *Ibid.* App. p. 51.   [24] *Ibid.* p. 11.   [25] Hardwick, *History of the Articles*, Notes p. 376.

which justification, theologians call the first justification
—no teacher in the Church of God ever disputed. But
how is it the meritorious cause? Are we accounted
righteous because the righteousness of Christ has been
infused into us, and so has made us really just and holy,
and *worthy* of being accounted righteous before God, as
Catholics teach; or are we accounted righteous because
the righteousness of Christ has simply been *imputed* to
us to veil our unrighteousness, as Protestants teach?
And when the article says, "that we are justified by
faith only," does it mean what Protestants mean by faith,
that is a trust or assurance of God's mercy in our behalf;
or does it mean by faith an infused virtue by which the
soul is enabled to assent to all that God has revealed?
Taking faith in this latter sense Catholic theologians
have not hesitated to teach that we are justified by faith;
for instance: St. Thomas says, "*By faith* the passion of
Christ is applied to us so that we become partakers of its
fruit, as says Romans iii. 25: 'Whom God, hath set
forth to be a propitiation through faith in his blood.'"
But the faith by which we are cleansed from sin, is not
the unliving faith (*fides informis*), which is able to exist
along with sin, but the faith living (*fides formata*) by
charity, so that the passion of Christ is applied to us not
only through the intellect, but also through the affections."[26] And the Council of Trent declares that "we
are said to be justified *by faith*, because faith is the beginning of man's salvation, the foundation and root of
all justification, without which it is impossible to please
God, and to come to the fellowship of his children; but
we are said to be justified freely, because none of those

---

[26] *Summa*, P. III. Q. xlix. A. i.

things which precede justification, whether faith or works, merit the grace itself of justification. For 'if by grace, then is it no more of works; otherwise,' as the apostle adds, 'grace is no more grace.' " [27]

Now when our article says we are justified "by faith," is it using the term in the sense in which St. Thomas and Catholic theologians use it, or is it using it in the Protestant sense for personal assurance or trust? It has been answered that the article is derived from a corresponding one in the Augsburg Confession, and therefore the term "faith" must be understood in the same sense as it is used in that Confession. It is true that our Article is evidently drawn from the Augsburg Confession, but it is also true, that it did not adopt its peculiar definition of faith. The Lutheran Article on Justification stands thus: " Men cannot be justified before God by their own strength, deservings, or works, but they are justified freely for Christ's sake by faith *when they believe themselves to have been received into grace, and their sins forgiven for Christ's sake*, who by his own death made satisfaction for our sins   *This faith* God *imputes* for righteousness before him." [28]   Here the faith which justifies is very clearly defined to be a personal assurance. The first part of this Article was plainly the source of our own article, but the latter part with its clear definition of what Protestants understand by " faith " and the catch word " to impute," the key-note to the whole Protestant system, were carefully excluded and find no place in our Article. It cannot therefore be argued that by "faith," our Article means what is meant by Lutherans, when their definition was refused a place therein.

Session vi. *De Justificatione*, cap. viii.   [28] Francke, *Lib. Sym. Eccl. Luth.* P. I. p. 14.

There is another consideration which leaves no doubt that the Article uses the term "faith" in the old scholastic sense of an infused virtue by which the mind is enabled to assent to all that God has revealed. We are referred to the homily where the doctrine of justification is more largely expressed. In this Homily on Salvation we find that justification and the grace of holy baptism are evidently regarded as one and the same thing; for example, it says: "Infants *being baptized* and dying in their infancy, are by this sacrifice washed from their sins, brought to God's favour, and made his children, and inheritors of his kingdom of heaven;" and, "we must trust only in God's mercy, and that sacrifice which our High Priest and Saviour Christ Jesus, the Son of God, once offered for us upon the Cross, to obtain thereby God's grace and remission, as well of our original sin *in baptism*, as of all actual sin committed by us after baptism, if we truly repent, and turn unfeignedly to him again;" and again, "Our office is not to pass the time of this present life unfruitfully and idly, after that we are *baptized or justified*." If then to say we are baptized is all one with saying we are justified, baptism must be the instrument of our justification. And indeed this is precisely what it is declared to be. Article XXVII. says that it is "an instrument," by which we are grafted into the Church, or as the Catechism puts it, by which "we are made members of Christ, the children of God, and inheritors of the kingdom of heaven." And its inward grace is said to be "[a] A death unto sin, and [b] a new birth unto righteousness." These two effects are what Catholics understand, as we have shewn before, by Justification. The meaning of the Article is therefore made clear: by Justification it means the reception of the grace of holy baptism; and when it says we are justified by faith, it means by faith a gift which comes through baptism. Here again we will adduce the Assembly of Divines as witnesses. They seem to have fully appreciated the obviousness of this interpretation of the Article when read by the light of the Homily for in their proposed revision of it, they omitted all reference to the Homily, and so altered it that it read: "We are justified, that is we are accounted righteous before God, and have remission of sins, not for, nor by our own works or deservings, but freely by his grace, only for our Lord and Saviour Jesus Christ's sake, his whole obedience and satisfaction being by God *imputed unto us*, and Christ with his righteousness being apprehended and rested on by faith only." The Article is also unsatisfactory to the "Reformed Episcopalians" and inadequate to express their doctrine, for they too have carefully omitted all reference to the Homily, and added five entirely new articles in order to set forth their teaching on Justification and its kindred subjects.

We next turn to the baptismal offices to illustrate these two points, viz.: that baptism is the ordinary instrument of justification, and that this justification consists in "a death unto sin, and a new birth unto righteousness," or in other words, is both the complete remission of all sin, and also sanctification. An adult comes to receive holy baptism; he has repentance whereby he has forsaken sin; he believes all that God has revealed, particularly "the promises of God made to him in that sacrament;" he may have everything which on Protestant principles would be sufficient for his justification, and yet when he approaches the font, he will be told that he was "conceived and born in sin;" and that because he is in the flesh he "cannot please God;" and that he cannot "enter into the kingdom of heaven except he be regenerate and born anew of water and of the Holy Ghost." And the minister will call upon those present to pray "that he may be baptized with water and the Holy Ghost," and "being delivered from God's wrath, may be received into the ark of Christ's Church." But once the sacrament has been administered, it will be declared in the most unequivocal terms that the baptized person is "*regenerate*, and grafted into the body of Christ's Church," that he is "*now* born again, and made an heir of everlasting salvation," and "has *now by baptism* put on Christ," which is nothing more nor less than saying that he is in a "state of salvation," and hence is justified.

Examining the baptismal offices still further as to the nature of Justification, we find that the Catholic doctrine is clearly set forth, and that it is regarded not merely as [a] the remission of sin, but as also [b] the renewal or regeneration of the baptized by the sanctification of the Holy Ghost. In the first prayer of the Office for the Public Baptism of an Infant, God is asked [a] to "wash him and [b] sanctify him with the Holy Ghost;" and in the prayer following: "that he coming to thy holy baptism may receive [a] remission of sin, by [b] spiritual regeneration." In the second exhortation to the God-parents it is said: "ye have prayed that our Lord Jesus Christ would vouchsafe to receive him, [a] to release him from sin, [b] to sanctify him with the Holy Ghost, etc." At the blessing of the font, the priest prays: "Sanctify this water [a] to the mystical washing away of sin; and grant that this child now to be baptized therein, may receive [b] the fulness of thy grace." In the prayer of thanksgiving: "he [a] being dead unto sin, and [b] living unto righteousness." In the Office for the Baptism of Adults, we are bidden to "earnestly believe" that God will give to those rightly coming to holy baptism [a] "remission of their sins, and [b] bestow upon them the Holy Ghost." Finally in the Form of Consecration of a Church or Chapel, the bishop prays, "that whosoever shall be dedicated to thee in this house by baptism, may be [b] sanctified by the Holy Ghost, [a] delivered from thy wrath and eternal death."

Since baptism is then clearly the means by which we are justified, and this justification is nothing less than the complete cleansing of sin, and the inpouring of the Holy Ghost, "*the great necessity* of this sacrament where it may be had,"[29] is very evident. Accordingly the Church manifests the greatest solicitude that no one under her care departs out of this world unbaptized. She directs that, "The minister of every parish shall *often* admonish the people, that they defer not the baptism of their children longer than the first or second Sunday next after their birth, or other holy day falling between, unless upon a great and reasonable cause."[30] And in case of imminent danger of death he is to omit all the preparatory parts of the baptismal office, only using so many of the collects "*as the time and present exigence will suffer.*"[31] Still further evidence and illustration of the Church's faith is seen in the way she regards those who have died unbaptized. She has no word of hope for them, but classes them with the ex-

[29] Second Exhortation in Office for Baptism of Adults. [30] First rubric in Office of Private Baptism. [31] Third rubric in Office of Private Baptism.

communicate, and suicides, and peremptorily forbids her priests to give them Christian burial.

Since justification by an *infused* righteousness is clearly a doctrine of our Church, let us next enquire whether any of those doctrines, which, as we have shewn in the earlier part of this essay, are a logical deduction from the Catholic doctrine of justification; are set forth in our formularies. In the first place, we find that the doctrine of the possibility of the regenerate keeping the commandments is taken for granted throughout the Book of Common Prayer. For example, the Church prays to God that we " may *cheerfully accomplish* those things which thou commandest;"[32] that we may give up ourselves *obediently to fulfil* thy holy commandments;"[33] "that *all* our doings, being ordered by thy governance, *may be righteous in thy sight;*"[34] "that we may shew forth thy praise . . . by walking before thee in *holiness and righteousness all our days;*"[35] that we may "serve thee *in holiness and pureness of living,* to thy honour and glory;"[36] that "we may *in all things* obey thy blessed will;"[37] that thy people "may both perceive and know what things they ought to do, and also may have grace and power *faithfully to fulfil the same;*"[38] that "we may ever obey thy godly motions *in righteousness and true holiness* to thy honour and glory;"[39] "that we may *perfectly love* thee;"[40] that we may have "the spirit to think and *to do always* such things as are

---

[32] Twentieth Sun. aft. Trin. [33] St. Andrew. Thanksgiving for restoring public peace at home. [34] A Collect for Grace. [35] A Genl. Thanksgiving. Prayer in behalf of those present at the Visitation of the Sick. [36] The Litany. First Sun. aft. Easter. [37] The Circumcision. [38] First Sun. aft. Epip. [39] First Sun. in Lent. [40] Collect for Purity.

right;"[41] and that "we, forsaking all worldly and carnal affections, may be evermore *ready to follow* thy holy commandments;"[42] and that we may have "the help of thy grace, that in keeping thy commandments we may please thee, both in will and deed."[43]   All these petitions would be manifestly absurd if the keeping of the commandments was an impossibility.[44]   And whatever may be thought of the liturgical fitness of the Decalogue as part of our Eucharistic Office, its periodical recitation, with the repeated miserere because of its violation, and the prayer that God would incline our hearts to keep each one of its commands, is a distinct recognition of the obligation of the law, and certainly implies that none of its commands are impossible to the regenerate.   Pursuing our enquiry still further, we find that at baptism each sponsor, in answer to the demand, "Wilt thou then *obediently keep God's holy will and commandments*, and walk in the same *all* the days of thy life?" is directed to say, "*I will*, by God's help."   And when the Church asks the baptized child, "Dost thou not think that thou art bound *to believe* and *to do* as they have promised for thee?" that is, to believe the Creed and to keep all the Commandments, she puts into the child's mouth the answer, "Yes, verily; and by God's help *so I will.*"

Now, the doctrine set forth in these quotations is most explicitly denied in the Protestant confessions; and this

---

[41] Ninth Sun. aft. Trinity.   [42] St. James.   [43] First Sun. aft. Trin.
[44] In the Collect for the Fifth Sun. aft.Epiphany it is said "that by reason of the fraility of our nature we cannot always stand upright," but it is speaking of human nature unaided by grace, for it immediately adds, "Grant to us such strength and protection as may support us in *all* dangers, and carry us through *all* temptations."   So also in the Collect for Fifteenth Sun. aft. Trinity.

denial is made necessary, as we have seen, by their theory of justification. Their language is, "*No one* is able to do as much as the law requires;"[45] "The doctrine of the papists and monks is rejected which teaches that a man, after he is regenerated, is able to fulfil the law of God perfectly in this life;"[46] "We are able to do no work which is not polluted by the sin of the flesh, and therefore worthy of punishment;"[47] "Our best works in the present life are all imperfect and stained with sin."[48] If it be true that the fulfilment of the law is an impossibility, the law is practically abrogated. And, indeed, Luther boldly asserted this consequence, which he could not but see was the logical inference from his own premises. In the fourth chapter of his *Commentary on Galatians*, he says: "If we have the knowledge that the law is abrogated, it is a great help towards establishing our doctrine on faith, and of bringing sure and certain consolation to consciences, especially in times of great anguish. I have often said before, and now repeat it (for this is a subject which cannot be sufficiently insisted upon), that the Christian who by faith lays hold of the benefit of Christ is subject to no manner of law, but so far as he is concerned the whole law is abrogated, together with its terrors and annoyances. . . . The Thomists and other schoolmen when they speak concerning the abrogation of the law, say that the law touching civil affairs and ceremonies (*judicalia et ceremonialia*) being pernicious after [the death of] Christ, was on that account abrogated, but not so with the law which has reference to morals (*moralia*). But they are ignorant of

---

[45] *Apol. A. C.* Ed. Francke, P. I. p. 191. [46] *Formula of Concord*, Ed. Francke, P. III. p. 118. [47] *Belgic Confession*, Ed. Niemeyer, p. 376. [48] *Heid. Catech.* Ed. Niemeyer, p. 443.

that whereof they speak.   Now, when thou speakest of
the abrogation of the law, be particular to treat of the
law in its strict significance, that is, of the spiritual law,
and understand thereby the whole law, making no distinction between the civil, ceremonial, and moral law.
For when Paul saith that we are set free from the curse
of the law, he speaketh certainly of the whole law, and
especially of the moral law, since it alone accuses, curses,
and condemns consciences, and the other two kinds of
law do not do so.   Therefore, we say that the law of the
Ten Commandments hath no right to accuse and terrify
the conscience in which Christ reigns by grace, because
Christ hath made this right old." [49]   How different from
this is the whole tenor of the teaching of our Prayer
Book, and the clear and positive declaration of the VII.
Article of Religion, which, adopting the very distinction
of the schoolmen between the law which has reference to
ceremonies and civil affairs and the law which has
reference to morals, says of the former that it does "not
bind Christian men," but of the latter that "*no Christian
man whatsoever* is free from the obedience of the commandments which are called moral (*moralia*)."   This
declaration of the obligation of the moral law implies
that every Christian man has the power to keep the law,
and the doctrine of the possibility of the justified keeping the law is one wholly incompatible with the Protestant theory of Justification.

In the next place we find that consistently with her
belief in justification by an infused righteousness, the
Church teaches the meritoriousness of good works.   Article XII. declares that good works which "follow after

---

[49] D. Mart. Lutheri *Commentarium in Epis. ad Galatas.*   Cura-
vit, Dr. Joan. C. Irmischer, T. II.

justification" are "pleasing and acceptable to God in Christ." And the Prayer Book teaches us to pray to God, "that we running the way of thy commandments, *may obtain thy gracious promises, and be made partakers of thy heavenly treasure ;*"[50] "that we may so faithfully serve thee in this life, *that we fail not finally to attain thy heavenly promises ;*"[51] and again: "Stir up, we beseech thee, O Lord, the wills of thy faithful people ; that they, plenteously bringing forth the fruit of good works, *may by thee be plenteously rewarded.*"[52] Moreover, the very sorrows and afflictions of life are regarded as having a meritorious or even expiatory character. ·For example, the Church prays for her sick member that God would vouchsafe to "*consider* his contrition, *accept* his tears ;" and in the Office for the Visitation of Prisoners, "that the pains and punishments which these thy servants endure through their bodily confinement, *may tend to setting free their souls from the chains of sin.*" And again in the exhortation which the priest is directed to address to the sick person who is visited occur these words: " For what cause soever this sickness be sent unto you ; whether it be to try your patience for the example of others, and that your faith may be found, in the day of the Lord, laudable, glorious, and honourable, *to the increase of glory and endless felicity ;* or else it be sent unto you to correct and amend in you whatsoever doth offend the eyes of your heavenly Father." The teaching of this exhortation is very evident. The sick man is told that his sickness is sent either as a chastisement, or it is sent to try his patience ; and if he will bear it patiently

---

[50] Eleventh Sunday after Trinity. [51] Thirteenth Sunday after Trinity. [52] Twenty-fifth Sunday after Trinity.

in the spirit of penitence, it will turn to his profit, and he will be rewarded by the increase of glory and endless felicity. The phrase "the increase of glory" is most noteworthy and its meaning is unmistakable. It is the technical term to express one of the rewards of merit, and as such occurs in the XXXII. Canon of the VI. Session of the Council of Trent: "If anyone shall say that the good works of one that is justified are in such manner the gift of God, as that they are not also the good merits of him that is justified; or that the justified by the good works which he does by the grace of God and the merit of Jesus Christ, whose living member he is, does not truly merit the increase of grace, everlasting life, and the attainment of that eternal life (provided however that he depart this life in grace), and also *the increase of glory;* let him be anathema."

We might go on, and take up one by one all the other statements of the Prayer Book and Articles which bear upon the relation existing between God and man, and we would find that every one of them is but the logical outcome of the doctrine of justification by an infused righteousness, or is, at least, consistent with it. Nowhere does the Protestant theory of justification by imputation find any expression. The system underlying the Prayer Book and Articles is the system of Catholicism and no other. These formularies do not indeed set forth that system in its full development, for in the sixteenth century many of the branches of the tree of Catholic doctrine and practice were lopped off, and therefore we miss, and miss with regret, many things which other parts of the Church of God enjoy. Let us remember, however, that the roots of the system which has produced every Catholic doctrine and practice in the past are still embedded in our

"Standards of doctrine and worship." These roots run
thróugh every collect and prayer; manifest themselves
in the rubrics; and underlie the Articles, although here
hidden by the accumulated glosses which three hundred
years of Protestantism have put upon them. They
are now putting forth branches. The tribunal of penance,
with its concomitant doctrines of the spiritual nature of
sin, of the distinction between mortal and venial sins, of
absolution supplying the defect of attrition, and of penitential satisfaction, has become a necessary and integral
part of the work of very many parishes. The religious
life, which Article XXXII. calls "the estate of single
life,"[65] with its necessarily implied doctrines of the distinction between precepts and counsels, of the merits of
virginity, of the obligation of vows, is an established institution amongst us. Indeed the whole cycle of Catholic doctrine is boldly taught and widely practiced. When
we consider all the theological principles involved in the
advances which have been made, and all the practical
consequences flowing from them; and when we consider
that all these advances have been brought to pass in this
country in the short space of little more than twenty-five
years, and that, too, in the face of the most determined
opposition of every kind, we may truly say, conscious of
our own helplessness to have accomplished such results,
"The Lord hath done great things for us already,
whereof we rejoice." Compared with our successes
how puny and insignificant are the efforts of those who
oppose us. And if so much has been accomplished in
the few years which have gone by, what may we not
hope for in the future? Only one thing can prevent the

[65] Just as the married life is called "the *estate* of matrimony."

still further growth and development of the Catholic system, and that is the destruction of its roots. If, when the Catholic revival began it had been found to be inconsistent with our formularies, it would have withered away of itself. But here has been the secret of our strength from the very first. The practices of the Catholic religion are found to be perfectly consistent with the doctrinal statements of the Prayer Book and Articles, indeed but the logical carrying out of their underlying principles. Hence the efforts which have been made in the past to dilute the Prayer Book and hence the desire on the part of the Broad School now to do away with the Articles. Thus far, through God's infinite mercy, the Prayer Book and Articles remain intact. But we must be on our guard, and zealously scrutinise every proposed emendation to our formularies, and firmly resist every effort to lower in the slightest degree the Church's statements of doctrine. Surely it behooves us to pay heed to the warning given to the Church in Thyatira : " That which ye have *already*, hold fast till I come." As long as our fomularies remain intact the Catholic system will continue to develop, until at length "his branches shall spread, and his beauty shall be as the olive tree, and his smell as Lebanon. They that dwell under his shadow shall return ; they shall revive as the corn, and grow as the vine ; the scent thereof shall be as the wine of Lebanon." [54]

---

[54] Hosea, xiv. 7.

✣ Fasting Reception of the Holy Communion.

IN beginning this paper upon the Fasting Reception of the Sacrament of our Saviour's Body and Blood, it may not be amiss briefly to recall two striking incidents from the elder Scriptures, the first, the finding of the Book of the Law in the days of King Josiah;[1] and the second, the reading of the book to the assembled multitude at the time of Ezra.[2] The effect produced upon both of these occasions was most marked. Josiah rent his clothes, and forthwith set out to purge Jerusalem and Bethel from idolatry; completing his work with the greatest and most exact Passover that had been kept since the days of Moses; and when Ezra, one hundred and eighty years after, read in the ears of the Jews the words of their neglected and well-nigh forgotten Law, all the people wept at what they heard—grieving, it would seem, not only at the departure of their former glory, but chiefly through a penitent consciousness of their own guilt.

If these men of old time and of a former dispensation were thus stricken with remorse as they beheld how far they had departed from the Law of their fathers, what should be the feeling of the devout and loyal Churchman of to-day when he compares the teaching of the church —*in all ages and in every land*—upon this matter of

---

[1] II. Chron. xxxiv. [2] Neh. viii.

fasting before Communion with the practice of the great majority of our congregations? and when he sees that a custom has crept in among us which " tends to the dese- cration of the highest rite of our holy religion?"[3] As the decay of missionary power in the church has been attributed[4] to the neglect of fasting in general, so may not the lack of spiritual force among our communicants be due to an improper preparation? For this cause, also, many may be spiritually weak and sickly among us. "If the Church of England is to recover spiritual vigour in a wide sense," says Canon Liddon, " early communions," [and therefore fasting communions] "must be the main cause and chief symbol of such recovery. They are the real remedy for many of our evils."[5]

But against fasting reception it is at once urged that our Blessed Lord instituted the Holy Sacrament at night, and administered it to his disciples almost immediately after they had eaten.

When we examine this objection, however, we see that it not only proves too much for those who offer it, but it brings into greater and more remarkable prominence the early and universal adoption by the church of *precisely the opposite* rule.

Without pressing the matter of the exact hour of the institution, two things should be distinctly borne in mind: first, that the Jewish day began, not when ours does, but at six o'clock in the evening; and, second, that it is hardly probable that our Blessed Lord instituted the Holy Sacrament until *after* midnight. This latter point is treated at length by Gresswell,[6] and Grueber in his *Catechism of Worship* has the following note: "The paschal

---

[3] Bp. Wilberforce. [4] Blunt. [5] *Evening Communions*, p. 24. [6] *Dissertations*, Vol. iii. Diss. 41, pp. 170-172.

lamb was killed 'between the two evenings' that is, between three and six P. M. (Ex. xii. 6). For some time it was hung up; the tasting of the blood being strictly forbidden (Gen. ix. 4; Lev. vii. 27). Then there was the preparation before being 'roasted with fire,' and the time the roasting took (Ex. xii. 8, 9; Deut. xvi. 7). Christ could hardly have sat down with his disciples before nine or ten o'clock. During the supper much discourse took place, and various incidents occurred (St. Matt. xxvi.; St. Mark, xiv.; St. Luke, xxii.; St. John, xiii.). 'Supper being ended,' there came the washing of the disciples' feet, with its attendant circumstances (St. John, xiii.). Finally, 'after supper he took the cup,' etc., etc. (St. Luke, xxii. 19, 20). All this could hardly be before midnight." [7]

There remains the objection that the disciples received the Blessed Sacrament immediately, or shortly, after taking food, which was certainly the case. But what *was* this food? Not an ordinary meal to satisfy the appetite, but a religious and sacrificial feast, prepared for by a day of fasting. And we should bear in mind, also, the peculiar time at which the sacrament was instituted. One dispensation was about to fade into another, and it pleased our Blessed Lord to consecrate the closing hour of the one by eating the last Passover with his disciples before ordaining that which was to be the distinctive characteristic of the other—the great Unbloody Sacrifice, the Christian Passover, the perpetual memorial before God and men of his passion and death. To attempt, then, to continue the connexion between a "supper," in imitation of this Jewish feast, and the sacrament of the

---

[7] *Catechism of Worship*, p. 26, note; quoting from *Lecture Notes on the Sacramental Articles*, by Rev. J. S. Boucher (Mowbray).

Holy Eucharist were manifestly wrong; and the efforts of men to do this, from motives of mistaken reverence, only led, as we shall see, to the most unhappy results. Our Blessed Lord undoubtedly never meant, when he said " Do " or " Offer this," that every detail of his action in that upper chamber should be exactly copied by us, for, as says St. Gregory Nazianzen (A. D. 381), " Every action of Christ is not necessary to be imitated by us, for he celebrated the mystery of the passion with his disciples in an ·upper room, and after supper; but we do it in the church, and before supper." [8] This principle is also clearly brought out by Canon Bright, who says, " In contemplating our Lord's life, the Early Church saw plainly that while, in some respects, his actions were to be imitated closely, literally and forever, in others they were peculiar. to, and a part of, his redemptive and in-communicable relations to the human race." [9] For a clear and concise treatment of the celebrations of the Holy Eucharist mentioned in the Acts of the Apostles, the reader is referred to Canon Liddon's pamphlet, *Evening Communions contrary to the Teaching and Practice of the Church in all Ages.* In speaking of the attempt of Dean Stanley and other rationalistic writers of modern times to identify the Agape with the Eucharist, he says, " It is certain that from the first they were entirely distinct; and it is observable that in no one of the celebrations recorded in the Acts of the Apostles is there any trace of the Agape as linked to the eucharistic service. The question of priority is difficult to decide upon. If the actual traditions of the Catholic Church be held to settle the question, we must infer that the

[8] *Orat. 40 de Bapt. Vide* Bingham. *Ant. Christian Church,* xv. vii. 8. [9] *Evening Communions,* p. 4.

Eucharist preceded the Agape. If, with *Lightfoot* and *Schöttgen* in our hands, we examine the question as illustrated by Jewish antecedents, and our Lord's actual form of procedure, we must rule that the Agape preceded the Eucharist. And to this latter conclusion we decidedly incline." [10] The custom of holding this "feast of charity" undoubtedly grew up in the Early Church, not only through a mistaken feeling of reverence, which sought to reproduce in every detail the original Eucharist, but also from practical reasons. Part of the oblations brought by the faithful to Christ, and not required for the Holy Sacrament, "went," as Bingham tells us, "towards the maintenance of the clergy. Out of the rest a common entertainment was usually made, which, from the nature and circumstances of it, was usually called Agape, or feast of charity; because it was a liberal collection of the rich to feed the poor." St. Chrysostom gives this account of it, deriving it from apostolic practice; he says, "The first Christians had all things in common, as we read in the Acts of the Apostles; and when that ceased, as it did in the apostles' time, this came in its room, as an efflux or imitation of it." [11]

Without doubt, many of these poorer Christians came from a distance to the services of the church, and such a feast became a practical necessity. But, even in those early days, this feast of love began to be abused. St. Jude speaks of evil men who were as spots in this feast of charity [12] . . . "feeding themselves without fear." And the condition of things in the Corinthian Church, as described by St. Paul, was shocking in the extreme.

---

[10] *Evening Communions*, pp. 7, 8.   [11] Bingham, xv. vii. 6. St. Jude, 12.

Each one strove before the other to take his own supper [13]—some were famished, others feasted to repletion,
and many went drunken to receive the body and blood
of Christ. The apostle reproves them in the strongest
terms. He tells them what the sacrament is in the very
words of Christ; he reminds them of what their preparation should be, and he closes with the significant
words, " The rest will I set in order when I come."

That St. Paul did (under the guidance of God the
Holy Ghost), upon his subsequent visit to Corinth, set
this abuse in order, once and for all time, there is left no
room for us to doubt, from the fact that fasting communion became at once the general practice of the Universal
Church. In confirmation of this, Scudamore points out
that a year or two later, when the apostle came to Troas,
he "broke bread" [14] *before* the subsequent meal; and the
words of St. Augustine (395–430 A. D.), are most conclusive. He writes, " It is clear that when the disciples
first received the body and blood of the Lord they had
not been fasting. Must we then censure the Universal
Church because *the sacrament is everywhere partaken of
by persons fasting?* Nay, verily; for from that time it
pleased the Holy Spirit to appoint, for the honour of so
great a sacrament, that the body of the Lord should
take the precedence of all other food entering the mouth
of a Christian; and it is for this reason that *the custom
referred to is universally observed.* For the fact that the
Lord instituted the sacrament after other food had been
partaken of does not prove that brethren should come
together to partake of that sacrament after having dined
or supped, or imitate those whom the apostle reproved

I. Cor. xi. 20–22.   *Notitia Eucharistica*, p. 31.

and corrected for not distinguishing between the Lord's Supper and an ordinary meal. The Saviour, indeed, in order to commend the depths of that mystery more affectingly to his disciples, was pleased to impress it on their hearts and memories by making its institution his last act before going from them to his passion. And, therefore, he did not prescribe the order in which it was to be observed, reserving this to be done by the apostles, through whom he intended to arrange all things pertaining to the churches. Had he appointed that the sacrament should be always partaken of after other food, I believe that no one would have departed from that practice. But when the apostle, speaking of this sacrament, says, 'Wherefore, my brethren, when ye come together to eat, tarry one for another, and if any man hunger let him eat at home, that ye come not together unto condemnation,' he immediately adds, 'And the rest will I set in order when I come.' Whence we are given to understand that, since it was too much for him to prescribe completely in an epistle *the method observed by the Universal Church throughout the world*, it was one of the things set in order by him in person; for we find *its observance uniform amid all the variety of other customs.*" [15]

If we wish to see what was the practice of the Early Church in this matter, immediately after apostolic days, we have the celebrated letter of Pliny, the Roman governor of Bithynia, to the Emperor Trajan, giving him an account of the customs of the Christians in his pro-consulate. This letter was probably written in the year A.D. 140, at a time, as has been said, "when as yet

---

[15] *Letters to Januarius*, Letter iv. Clark's Library, vi. 8.

the voice of the Beloved Disciple had hardly died away in the churches of the Lesser Asia. It exhibits the Bride of Christ as she had grown up under that apostle's eye, and had received his parting blessing. The words are too precious to be forgotten." [16] He writes: "They affirmed the whole of their guilt, or their error, was that they had met on a certain stated day *before it was light*, and addressed themselves in a form of prayer to Christ as to some God, binding themselves by a solemn oath (*sacramento*), not for the purpose of any wicked design, but never to commit any fraud, theft, or adultery, never to falsify their word, nor deny a trust when they should be called upon to deliver it up, *after which* it was their custom to separate, and then reassemble to eat in common a harmless meal." [17] The Church has always believed that this "sacramentum" was nothing less than a celebration of the Holy Eucharist. "From this time," says Father Hall, "we never hear of the Eucharist and the Agape together; the former is celebrated in the morning, the love-feast in the evening." [18]

The relative positions of the love-feast and the Holy Eucharist, before and after the ruling of St. Paul at Corinth, are ably defined by Father Puller, in a paper read before the Confraternity of the Blessed Sacrament, in May, 1891. To this valuable essay the reader is referred.[19]

For Patristic testimony upon the practice of fasting communion, we have first, in point of time, Tertullian (who was probably converted about the year A. D. 196).

---

[16] Liddon's *Evening Communions*, p. 9.   [17] Melmoth's *Letters of Pliny*, ii. 667.   [18] *Fasting Communion*, A. C. A. Hall, p. 6.   [19] *Concerning the Fast Before Communion*, F. W. Puller, pp. 27-30.

In his letter to his wife, in speaking of the difficulties which she, as a Christian woman, would have to encounter when married to a heathen husband, after his own death, he refers to the Holy Communion and says: " Will not thy husband know what thou art tasting secretly before all (other) food ?"[20] In another treatise he says, " The sacrament of the Eucharist, commanded by the Lord at the time of supper, and to all, we receive even at our meetings before daybreak."[21]

Next in order is St. Cyprian (A. D. 250), who writes, "It may be said that it was not in the morning, but after supper that the Lord offered the mingled cup. Ought we then to celebrate the Lord's cup after supper ? . . . It behoved Christ to offer about the evening of the day that the very hour of sacrifice might shew the setting and the evening of the world, as it is written in Exodus, 'and all the people of the synagogue of the children of Israel shall kill it in the evening;' and again in the Psalms, ' Let the lifting up of my hands be an evening sacrifice.' But we celebrate the resurrection of the Lord in the morning."[22]

St. Basil (who died in A. D. 380), in a discourse upon fasting in general, uses these words with regard to a priest's fasting before his celebration : " It hallows the Nazarene, it perfects the priest. For without fasting, it is impossible to venture upon the sacred function."[23]

St. Ambrose (A. D. 374), bears the testimony that, in his time, " they prepared themselves by fasting to approach the Holy Table."[24]

---

[20] *Ad. Ux.* lii. c. v. tom. iii. p. 74.   [21] *De. Cor. Mil.* Lib. Fathers, x. 164.   [22] *To Cœcilius.* Ep. lxii. 16, Clark's Edition.   [23] *Hom.* i. *de Jejun,* tom. ii. p. 5.   [24] *Book of Elias and of Fasting,* c. x.

The feeling of St. Chrysostom upon this subject is best given in substance in the following quotation from the Rev. H. R. Percival: "St. Chrysostom (who died in A.D. 407), says, 'but thou before thou hast partaken *fastest*, that in a certain way thou mayest appear worthy of the Communion;' he then goes on to recommend that they should likewise fast afterwards. But, lest they should think this *after*-fast of obligation he adds, 'what then? Ought we to fast after receiving? I do not say this, nor do I use any compulsion. This indeed were well, but I do not enforce this.' The one was enforced, the other recommended. (*Hom. xxvii. in I. Cor. xi.*) In his ninth homily to the people of Antioch he argues that if they eat their breakfast and therefore cannot receive the Holy Communion, yet that there is no reason they should not come and assist at the mass and hear the sermon. Once more, Chrysostom, when charged with having given to some persons not fasting the Holy Sacrament, answers with great violence, 'if I have done any such thing, let my name be stricken from the roll of bishops, and let it not be written in the book of the Orthodox Faith, for, if I have done any such thing Christ will reject me also from his kingdom.' (*Ep. 125 ad Cyr.*)" [25]

Next in order would come St. Augustine, whom we have already quoted.

An exception, which only proves the rule that the Sacrament was always celebrated in the early hours of the day, we find in the African Church where, on one day of the year, Maundy Thursday, the day of the institution, the Holy Sacrifice was offered in the evening—but

---

[25] H. R. Percival—Article on *Fasting Communion* in *American Ch. Review*, Mar. 1884; *cf.* on *IX. Hom. to People of Antioch*, Bona, *De Reb. Lit.* lib. i. cap. xxi.

even so, the faithful continued their fast until they had received. There were, it is true, as Sozomen the historian (third century) tells us, "several cities and villages in Egypt where, contrary to the usages established elsewhere, the people meet together on Sabbath evenings, and, although they have dined previously, partake of the mysteries."[26] These are severely censured by Socrates, his brother historian, who observes, "But they do not partake of the mysteries, as is the custom for Christians; for after feasting, and being filled with every description of eatable, when they come to eventide they partake of the mysteries."[27]

To check these men, who had certainly returned to Corinthian licence and irreverence, the Third Council of Carthage (A. D. 397) passed a canon (canon 29), "That the Sacrament of the Altar shall be celebrated only by those who are fasting, except on the one anniversary when the Supper of the Lord is commemorated." And soon this exception was removed by the Council of Trullo (A. D. 692) in its XXIX. Canon, where, in referring to this African custom, it says, "Although for some local reasons profitable to the Church those divine fathers made such a regulation, yet since there is no inducement for us to abandon the strict line, we determine, *in accordance with the apostolical traditions of our fathers*, that, in the last week of Lent, the fifth day must not be broken; for it is a dishonouring of the whole Lent."

It may be objected that these councils, and the few others to which reference is made in this paper, were only of local authority; but nevertheless they serve to

---

[26] *Eccles. Hist.* 6, vii. chap. 19, Bohn's Ed. p. 344.   [27] *Eccles. Hist.* v. 22, Ed. Hussey, vol. ii. p. 632.

shew clearly what was the mind of the Church in different lands. And with regard to the Council of Trullo
just mentioned, we should bear in mind that its decrees
were accepted as part of our own English code, by a
synod held at Chelsea, A. D. 785.[28]

The history of the other councils, in this matter, is
simply the record of their legislation to check the sacri-
legious practice which sprang up, from time to time,
among the clergy, of breaking their fast before they had
celebrated. In Spain, the Council of Braga (A. D. 572)
enacted that : " If any presbyter shall be found after our
edict any longer so mad as to consecrate the oblation not
fasting, but after having taken any food, let him be immediately deprived of his office and deposed by his
bishop."[29] France had to deal with the same abuse at
Auxerre in A. D. 578. This council decreed that, " No
presbyter, deacon, or sub-deacon, shall touch the mass
after touching meat or drink."[30] The Second Council
of Macon (A. D. 585) also forbids priests to celebrate
mass after they have eat and drunk.[31] And Toledo
adds (A. D. 646), " Lest what has been advised by reason
of the langour of nature should be turned into a dangerous presumption, let it be understood that no one shall
celebrate mass after taking any, even the least, meat and
drink."[32]

Our consideration of the subject has now brought us
down to the days when our own part of the great
Church Catholic began to come more into prominence
in the eyes of men; to the time when the various

---

[28] See Frederick Hall, *Fasting Communion*, p. 19, note. [29] *Conc.
L. et C.* tom. v. 898, or Blunt's *Dict. of Theology*, Art. *Fasting*.
[30] *Ibid*. [31] Dupin's *Hist. of Eccles. Writers*, 1. 716. [32] Blunt's *Dict.
of Theology*, Art. *Fasting*.

churches of the Saxon Heptarchy were fused into one united, national church, chiefly through the efforts of Archbishop Theodore. And here, before entering into the practice of the medieval, the Anglo-Saxon, the modern Roman, or the Anglican Church, with respect to fasting communion, let us pause for a few moments and look back.

How can we possibly account for this universal custom in the Church of God, unless we believe that it was ordained by God himself, speaking by the mouth of his apostles; unless this were one of the things that "seemed good" to the Holy Ghost and to them? If antiquity be unanimous in anything, it is in the necessity of receiving the Holy Sacrament fasting. Surely, as old Jeremy Taylor says, "it is a *Catholic* custom," and "he that despises this custom gives nothing but the testimony of an evil mind."

It will only be necessary to glance at medieval and modern Roman usage. Four centuries after St. Augustine, quoted above, we have Paschasius Radbertus, who writes, "This is the sacrament, which the Lord after supper delivered to his apostles. . . . But *universally* in the Church *all fasting* with the highest devotion are wont to communicate." [33]

Four hundred years more, and we come to St. Thomas Aquinas, who says, "Anything prevents the worthy reception of this sacrament in one of two ways. Either, first, by its own nature, *e. g.*, deadly sin, which is contrary to the signification of the sacrament; or else, secondly, on account of the prohibition of the Church; and thus anyone is shut out from receiving this sacrament

---

[33] *Lib. De Sang. et Corp. Dei*, cap. 20.

worthily if he have already received food and drink, and
this for three reasons: first, out of honour to this sacrament, that the mouth which it enters should be clean
from all food or drink; second, for symbolism, to set
forth that Christ, who is the inward part of this sacrament, ought first to be poured into our hearts (before
our bodies are fed), according to that saying, 'seek ye
first the kingdom of God;' thirdly, out of fear of vomit-
ing or drunkenness, which sometimes happen because
men have inordinately feasted, as the apostle says, I. Cor.
xi. 21." [34]

In the years 1415 and 1549, we have respectively the
Councils of Constance and Mayence, at the former of
which the English Church was represented. Constance
rules (sess. 13) that, " The praiseworthy authority of the
sacred canons, and *the approved custom of the Church
has held and still holds* that a sacrament of this kind
ought not to be celebrated after supper, nor received by
the faithful who are not fasting; except in cases of infirmity, or other necessity, on a right either granted or
admitted by the Church." [35] And Mayence adds, "We
seriously enjoin all parish priests and ministers of
churches not to give the Eucharist to any except those
who are fasting, and have made confession, unless it be
in cases of infirmity or necessity." [36]

The Catechism of the Council of Trent, published by
command of Pope Pius the Fifth, contains these words,
" The name of The Supper has also sometimes been given
to this sacrament by the most ancient fathers, in imitation of the apostles, because it was instituted by our Lord

---

[34] *Summa Pars* III. Q. lxxx. A. viii. [35] *The Fast before Communion*, by Rev. N. Poyntz, p. 9. [36] Blunt's *Dict. of Theol.* Art.
Fasting.

at the saving mystery of the last supper. This circumstance, which regards the time of its institution, does not, however, justify the inference that the Eucharist is to be consecrated or received by persons not fasting; the salutary practice of consecrating, and receiving it fasting, introduced, as ancient writers record, by the apostles, *has always been observed in the Church.*" And again, when speaking of the preparation of the body, " We are to approach the Holy Eucharist fasting, having neither eaten nor drunk, at least from the previous midnight." [37]

The Rituale Romanum says: " The Viaticum can be given to persons likely to die in a short time, though not fasting. . . . But, to other sick persons who communicate in illness out of devotion, the Eucharist must be given before any meat or drink; just as to the other faithful to whom it is not permitted to take anything before, even by way of medicine." Scudamore, who quotes the above, adds, " The *'short time'* of the Rituale is interpreted to mean *before the next morning;* that is, the patient may communicate after eating, if it is thought that he will not outlive the day." [38] We might go on adding passage to passage to shew that the usage of the medieval and modern Roman Church was entirely in accord with the practice of the Church in her primitive days; but such a thing would be unnecessary. Extracts from the writings of fathers, schoolmen, and doctors could be found for every century; Bellarmine and Gury might be quoted, but we would simply close this portion of our subject with the words of Cardinal Bona: " It is, therefore, an ancient and apostolic tradition that no one

---

[37] Part II. Sec. on Sacrament of the Eucharist.   [38] *Notitia Eucharistica*, p. 1037.

should dare to approach the Divine Mysteries unless he be fasting. The contrary abuse the councils and fathers treat as the gravest crime against the Church, and inflict for it the most weighty punishment of anathema and deposition." [39]

To refer briefly to the custom of the Greek Church, before considering the practice of our own, we learn from Scudamore that, "In the East the rule of fasting communion is relaxed, as by the Latins, in favour of the sick. Thus, Nicephorus, Patriarch of Constantinople (A. D. 806), 'It is right to impart of the Divine Communion to the sick in danger of death, even after they have taken food.'" [40] But in the case of the well, "the rule we are considering is," as Father Hall says, "*as strictly enforced* in all the Eastern Churches, orthodox and schismatical, as in the Roman." [41] Liddon, in quoting Timothy, Patriarch of Alexandria, says, "This prelate (A. D. 380–385) gave certain 'regulative answers' to certain questions proposed to him. The sixteenth question is, 'If one who is fasting in order to communicate has, while washing his mouth, or while in the bath, involuntarily swallowed water ought he to communicate?' The answer is, 'Since Satan has found an occasion for hindering him from communion, he will do this the oftener."

See this in Mansi, *Conc.* iii. 1253, Beveridge, *Pand.* ii. 169. Timothy's answer probably means, (especially when compared with a previous answer of his), "Let him communicate, and so foil Satan." But the question points to a general usage." [42] A passage from the Arme-

---

[39] *Rerum Liturg.* Lib. I. c. 21; also article in *Am. Ch. Review*, Mar. 1884. [40] *Notitia Eucharistica*, p. 1037. [41] *Fasting Communion*, p. 10. [42] *Evening Communions*, Note ix.

nian Canons quoted by Scudamore, says: " If .any presbyter shall be found to have taken food before mass, let
him not dare to approach the bread of the mass, else let
him be separated from his colleagues. Similarly, the
' principes' who are invited to Agape, must take part in
the divine office and the mass; before mass, let them not
dare to take food and drink in their own houses. Anyone who does so must not dare to go to the bread of the
mass, lest he bring judgment on himself, and disgrace
the holy feast—for this is self-indulgence. If anyone
dares to do so, let the archpresbyters drive him out, for
the Church abhors this impiety." [43]

H. C. Romanoff, in treating of Lenten customs in his
work, *The Rites and Customs of the Greco-Russian
Church*, says: "On Tuesdays and Fridays after vespers,
a deacon, or priest, reads aloud on the Amvon, for those
who intend to communicate the following day, an address
or exhortation, interspersed with psalms, ejaculations,
and reflections; it is called 'The Rules,' and is im-
mensely long. After the hearing of these rules, no food
whatever ought to be taken until receiving the Holy
Eucharist." [44] A fast even longer than our own.

Turning now to the practice of our own branch of the
Catholic Church, we learn from Lingard, that, even in
Anglo-Saxon days, "The conditions required of the
communicant were that he *should come fasting*, a practice
which remounts to the first ages of Christianity;" [45] and
in Rock's *Church of our Fathers* it is also affirmed as the
unmistakable custom of that period, that, "Then, too, as
now, the Sacrament was taken fasting, except in cases of

---

[43] *Evening Communions*, Note x. [44] *Rites and Customs*, p. 132.
[45] *Hist. and Antiq. of the Anglo-Saxon Church*, i. 328.

extreme illness." [46]   Theodore, archbishop of Canterbury
(A. D. 673), and Egbert, archbishop of York (A. D.
740), both rule that if a man eat "before he go to
housel," he shall do penance for seven days. [47]   In the
Capitula of Theodulf (A. D. 794), which were much used
as an Episcopal charge in France and England (being
translated into Saxon by Elfric in the tenth century), we
have, as a rule for Lent: " It is requisite that after noon-
song (Nones, at the ninth hour, 3 P. M), a man hear
mass, and after mass his even-song at the season   . . .
and afterwards take meat." [48]   The venerable Bede (A. D.
734), also bears testimony by several incidental allusions,
that the custom in his day was always to receive the sacrament fasting. [49]   In the reign of King Edgar (A. D.
960), it was by canon enacted that " No man take the
housel after he hath broke his fast, except it be on account of extreme sickness." [50]   St. Anselm, archbishop
of Canterbury (A. D. 1093), says: "If a man puts off
taking food because he has not yet that day been to the
celebration of the Holy Eucharist, when he has accomplished what he had made up his mind to do first, it is
not improperly said to him, Take your food now, because you have now done that for which you put off
taking it." [51]   St. Osmund, bishop of Salisbury (A. D.
1078–1099), to whom we owe the use of Sarum, and
Hubert Fitzwalter (A. D. 1200), and Stephen Langton
(A. D. 1222), archbishops of Canterbury, all forbid a
priest, having two celebrations in succession, to receive
the ablutions of the first until after the second, lest he

---

[46] *Church of our Fathers*, i. 130.   [47] Baron's *Anglo-Saxon Witness*, p. 28.   [48] *Notitia Eucharistica.*   [49] *Eccles. Hist.* b. iv. c. 23,
24.   [50] Johnson, *Laws and Canons of the Ch. of Eng.* Lib. Cath.
Theol. i. 419.   [51] *Cur Deus Homo*, c. ix.

should break his fast.[52]   And Simon Langham, also an
archbishop of Canterbury (A. D. 1367), ruled: " Let
none presume to celebrate mass twice a day, unless on
the day of Nativity or Resurrection of our Lord, or when
one has a corpse to bury, and that in his own church
only; and then let not the celebrator drink the washings
of his fingers and of the cup."[53]   Malcolm MacColl, in his
work, *Lawlessness, Sacerdotalism and Ritualism* (3d ed.
p. 209), says that " Fasting communion was the rule of
the Church of England in the days of Queen Elizabeth."
Richard Cosin (who died A. D. 1597) "speaks of the
Primitive Church having altered 'the time of the receiving of the Sacrament of the Eucharist, being according
to the institution usually received after supper, to have
it received, *as it is* in the morning, fasting.'"[54]   " Dean
Hook accounts for the early hour at which the consecra-
tors of Archbishop Parker (A. D. 1559) began the service
—between five and six on a December morning—by the
fact that 'the Holy Communion was received fasting.'"[55]
Dr. Lake, who was chaplain to Lady Mary, afterward the
wife of William of Orange, gives, among his instructions
for Sunday mornings, " Having finished your closet de-
votions, go forth to church fasting, that so a portion
from God's table may be the first morsel."[56]   Bishop
Jeremy Taylor (died A. D. 1677), who, as has been said,
" laboured with all his power to revive the lost Catholic
customs which had been universal before the great rebellion," writes in his *Worthy Communicant : " It is the
custom of the Church of great antiquity and proportionable*

Frederick Hall, *Fasting Reception of the Blessed Sacrament*,
pp. 21, 22.   [53] *Ibid.* p. 22.   [54] Frederick Hall, pp. 22, 23.   [55] Liddon,
Evening Communions, Note xv.   [56] *Fasting Communion*, A. C.
Hall, p. 9.

regard that every Christian that is in health should receive the Blessed Sacrament fasting." [57]   Again, in his
Life of Christ he says: " Fasting before the Holy Sacrament *is a custom of the Christian Church*, and derived to
us from great antiquity; and the use of it is that we
might express honour to the mystery by suffering
nothing to enter into our mouths before the symbols." [58]
And once more, in an extract from his *Ductor Dubitantium*, to which reference has already been made, he says,
" he that despises this custom gives nothing but the testimony of an evil mind." [59]

Dr. Sparrow (died A. D. 1688), bishop of Norwich, in
speaking of the usual hour for celebrating the Holy Communion—9 A. M.—says : " Till the service was ended
men were persuaded to be fasting, and, therefore, it was
thought fit to end all the service before noon, that people
might be free to eat."   And he also adds, " This sacrament should be received fasting.   And so was the practice of the Universal Church, says St. Augustine, *which
is authority enough to satisfy any that do not love con-
tention.*" [60]

Bingham in his *Christian Antiquities*, already referred
to more than once, tells us that, "*The general custom of
the Church* was to receive the Eucharist fasting." [61]

Bishop Wilberforce, in charging his clergy, in 1860,
against the practice of evening communion, says : " that
it is *contrary to the usage of the whole Church*," and,
referring to Pliny's letter, he tells them that, from that
time downward, we have an " unbroken chain of proof"
as to what was the "*practice of the Church.*"

---

[57] *Worthy Communicant*, vii. 1.   [58] *Life of Christ*, ii. xii. 13.
[59] *Ductor Dubitantium*, iii. iv. 15.   [60] *Rationale upon Book of Common Prayer*, Oxford ed. p. 196 and p. 219.   [61] *Antiq.* xv. vii. 8.

Christopher Wordsworth, bishop of Lincoln, writes that " In sub-apostolic times, it became usual to receive the Holy Communion very early in the morning."[62] The Rev. J. H. Blunt says: " Fasting before communion has been practised from the time of the apostles in all countries."[63] Canon Bright, professor of Ecclesiastical History in the University of Oxford, gives it as his opinion that " Nothing less than the authority of the apostles will adequately account for the *universality of morning celebrations in all the widely-separated branches of the Church*."[64] Some, we know, are wont to quote the revered name of John Keble, as of one who disregarded the obligation of fasting from midnight before communion; but, in Coleridge's *Life of Keble* (p. 539) it is clearly stated that " For many years it had been his custom, whenever he was to celebrate in the course of the day, to eat nothing before."

The custom of John Wesley is well known; and in the *Life of Selina, Countess of Huntington*, Whitfield's practice is thus shewn to us: " He and some of his brethren seemed only to aim at restoring the practice of the primitive Christians as to daily sacraments. In one or other of the London churches he was found every day before day-break in the morning; the streets being on these occasions as thickly studded with lanthorns as at any time when people leave the opera. In 1750, he was with the Countess of Huntington at Ashby, where the Sacrament was administered every morning." At these early meetings were also Venn, Wesley, Fletcher, Berridge and many others.

---

[62] *Twelve addresses* (1873), p. 74. [63] *Dict. of Doct. and Hist. Theol.* Art. *Fasting.* [64] *Evening Communions*, p. 7.

In the journal of Charles Wesley we have ever-recurring notices of the early sacrament "before breakfast," "at six," "at five," "at four," "before it was dawn." And in one of his hymns he writes:

> " Before the rising morn
> He comes his flock to feed ;
> His flock with hungry hearts return
> And seek their daily bread."

In the Scotch Kirk, a reference to the practice of fasting communion seems to remain in the appointment of one day in the week before Communion Sunday as a solemn fast day. Blunt mentions the fact that in England, as late as the year 1869, many could remember that their mothers always rose early on " Sacrament Sunday " and went to the church to receive fasting. And the writer, in his own parish, has found among persons from England and Ireland more than one case where this ancient and godly practice has never been relinquished. It would seem as if there lingered in minds, otherwise clouded by "Orange" prejudice, this fragment of Catholic usage, as the knowledge of the One True God often remains in the breast of the heathen.

Even upon those who do not practise, or who write against, this reverent custom, there seems to be laid the necessity of bearing their testimony to its worth, and of confessing that it was universal in the Church. "Dr. George W. Sprott" (I am quoting Dr. Percival), "at the present time minister of North Berwick, and one of the Lecturers on Pastoral Theology appointed by the General Assembly of the Kirk of Scotland .. . . says, ' there is no authority for fast days before the observance of the Lord's Supper, in the legislation of the Church (*i. e.*, Scottish establishment), though the practice of receiving the communion fasting is almost as old as Christianity, and was common in some parts of Scotland till a generation ago.' (*The Worship and Offices of the Church of Scotland*, Lecture III.) "[65]   The Rev. W. H. Barlow in a paper upon " Evening Communions " read at Southport in 1888, is forced to confess that " In the time of St. Augustine it was clear that early communions, and fasting communions *were universal.*" [66]   And Bp. Kingdon, in his most singular and erratic book against fasting communion, is good enough to admit that " The custom is in no way despised ; " adding that " If persons wish to shew their deepening love," or " to offer their self-denial or devotion," " let this be one of their rules."   And who is there, among devout and loyal Churchmen, who would not wish to shew this " deepening love " for Christ, and for his Church, when he considers the nature of this sacrament, and the overwhelming weight of authority with which this practice of fasting communion comes down to us ?   The Christian duty *cannot* be escaped unless one is willing to assume the untenable position of Dean Goulburn in his *Lectures upon the Communion Office.* He says : First, " That not a vestige of any warrant for it is to be found in the Holy Scripture," and second, " That the Church of England, as a distinct communion, the Church from which we received our baptism and grafting into Christ, is absolutely silent upon the subject." [67].   But, with regard to the first, does he wish us to believe that the voice of God the Holy Ghost speaks only from the pages of the Scripture ? Will he limit the promise of Christ, " He shall guide you into all truth," to the work

---

[65] *Amer. Ch. Review*, Mar. 1884.   [66] *Church Eclectic.* Aug. 1886, p. 432.   [67] Chapter II. of the Appendix.

alone of inspiring the canonical books of what we call
the Bible? Is the voice of the Undivided Church to go
for naught? Not only does he ignore the patristic interpretation of St. Paul's words "The rest will I set in order
when I come," but he gives to his other words "If a
man hunger let him eat at' home," an interpretation exactly opposite to the traditional one, which is, that "If
any man be hungry and is not willing with patience to
wait for the others, let him eat at home his food, that is,
let him be fed with the bread of earth, but let him *not*
afterward receive the Eucharist."

And, with regard to his second point, that the Church
of England, as a distinct communion, is silent upon the
subject, this is simply to degrade the Church to the position of any Protestant sect, which had its birth two or
three hundred years ago, and which is cut off from all
Catholic antiquity. It also contradicts the distinct teaching of Canon XXX., of the Canons of 1603, which says,
"So far was it from the purpose of the Church of England to forsake and reject the churches of Italy, France,
Spain, Germany, or any such like churches, in all things
which they held and practised that it doth with reverence
retain those ceremonies which do neither endanger the
Church of God, nor offend the minds of sober men ; and
only departed from them in those particular points
wherein they have fallen both from themselves in their
ancient' integrity, and from the Apostolic Churches which
were their first founders." Far be it from us to doubt
the honesty of this writer in the attack which he makes
upon a universal custom of God's Church; but we cannot help wishing that the feeling which he expresses at
the beginning of this chapter—a shrinking from putting
forward his own opinions—had been just a little stronger.

Before leaving this portion of our subject, I would like to quote the strong words of Father Puller upon the lasting character of the rule of fasting communion, as binding upon the entire Church; "The rule of receiving the Holy Eucharist before other food may almost certainly be traced to the legislative action of the apostles. The object of that rule is to give due honour to our Lord in the sacrament of his love, and to protect and guard, as far as such rules can, the most sacred institution of the Gospel covenant. Such an object has nothing of a transitory nature in it. It is a most holy object, and it is a lasting object. It is an object which must be most dear to the heart of the Church so long as she holds fast to the teaching of the apostles concerning the presence of our Lord's body and blood in the Mysteries of the Altar. The Church dare not give up the rule—she cannot give it up. The law, coming as it does from the apostles, and guarding as it does such a central institution of Christianity, is far more sacred than if it had been enacted at an ecumenical council. The Church has realised this all along. Disciplinary canons of ecumenical councils have been abrogated, or have passed into desuetude; but the rule of the fast before communion remains, and will remain. It is impossible to conceive a church, which had not fallen into heresy, formally abrogating the rule. It is also impossible to conceive Church-people, duly instructed in the apostolic doctrine about the Holy Eucharist, and realising that the rule of the eucharistic fast comes down to us from apostolic times, attempting to get rid of the rule by setting up a contrary custom." [68]

May we not now leave the argument from authority and custom to the devout consideration of all who love

---

[68] *The Fast Before Communion*, pp. 30, 31.

the Church and her ancient ways and who long to honour our Blessed Lord present in this sacrament of his deepest love. It remains to consider very briefly the argument from reverence, and a few practical points and objections.

If we believe at all in the presence of our Lord's body and blood in this sacrament, it surely behooves us to do all in our power to make ourselves fit for their reception. "There are three acts," says Frederick Hall, " of special reverence to our Lord's body which have been embedded in the pages of the Bible by God the Holy Ghost, and which seem especially to bear on this subject before us. 1. We are told that, when the Saviour of the world was born, the Virgin brought forth her '*firstborn* Son.' 2. When our Lord rode into Jerusalem on Palm Sunday, the entry was made upon an ass' colt 'whereon never man sat.' 3. After our Lord's death, Joseph of Arimathea laid the sacred body 'in his own new tomb,' 'wherein never man before was laid.' And the Catholic Church 'discerning the Lord's body' in the Sacrament of the Altar, has observed the custom of preparing for him, who deigns to come under our roof, a lodging in which nothing has that day been previously laid." [69] The fitness and propriety of this reverent custom need hardly be argued with any devout Christian. Rather will he be ready to say with St. Chrysostom, " Purer than the sunbeam should not that hand be which is to sever the flesh, the mouth that is filled with spiritual fire, the tongue that is reddened by that most awful blood." [70] These words were spoken, indeed, of priests; but do they not refer as well to the laymen in that bodily purity which should go before a devout reception ?

[69] *Fasting Reception of the Blessed Sacrament.* Frederick Hall, pp. 31, 32. [70] *Hom.* lxxxii. 5.

On the other hand, to lie in bed through the early hours of the Lord's Day, and then to come and receive at a late celebration, joining in spirit in the prayer, "And here we offer and present unto thee, O Lord, ourselves, our souls and bodies, to be a reasonable, holy, and living sacrifice unto thee"—after having eaten a hearty breakfast—is surely the veriest parody upon the meaning of the Prayer Book, and the intention of the Church.

It has been well said that "The Blessed Sacrament is not only a manner of communion with Christ, but it is also a memorial of his passion and death. That death, preceded as it was by a long and painful fast, was the crowning act of his self-denial. When we, therefore, desire to represent his sacrifice, it is plain that, unless we come to do so in some way which requires self-denial on our part, we so far fail to shew forth his death, because we are not 'bearing about in the body' (and, therefore, most likely not in our souls), 'the dying of the Lord Jesus' (II. Cor. iv. 10)."[71]

The practical advantage, also (to descend for a moment to a lower plane), the helpfulness and the added zest, which come from early and fasting communion, will appeal to anyone who has ever given it an honest trial. The spiritual nature, like the mental, is sluggish when the body has received food, and hardly, under such circumstances, can the soul rise to such heights of devotion as may be obtained when the body is fasting. "If it were but a matter of apostolical injunction," says Bishop Wilberforce, "it was, I doubt not, a deep and wise instinct of the Church which so early associated this great mystery . . . with the first services of the Lord's

---

[71] *The Christian Passover*, by the Editors of *The Priest's Prayer Book*, p. 44.

day, that he"[72] (the faithful Christian) "may give to it the freshness of his spirit and the stillness of his soul." Where do we find Christians who are manifestly growing in a deeper apprehension of the meaning of this sacrament, and in á firmer belief in the reality of that wondrous presence? Is it not, almost always, in the ranks of the early and fasting communicants? Another proof, it seems, of the truth of those words of Christ, "If any man will do his will, he shall know of the doctrine." [73]

It is sometimes objected by priests, that, if fasting communion be strongly taught and insisted upon as of absolute obligation upon every Christian, it will greatly lessen the number of those who draw near the altar. It may do this, it is true, for a time (even where pains are taken to instruct the people, and where numerous celebrations are provided); but, it will be found that this state of things will not continue. On the contrary, it will not be long before the priest sees, with thankfulness, that the spiritual life of his communicants is being deepened, and that the number of those who shew their devotion by coming to the early service is steadily growing. And even if this should not be the case, it must be remembered, as has well been said, "That the Holy Eucharist was not ordained for the purpose of displaying the strength of the parish, but for pleading the sacrifice of Christ and imparting to the faithful his body and blood." [74] "Depend upon it," says Bishop Wilberforce, in writing against evening communions, "that if you have a host of evening communicants to shew" (and this applies just as well to a mid-day communion), "you have not done anything like so much for the Christian-

---

[72] *Charge of 1860*, p. 17.   [73] St. John, 7 : 17.   [74] Rev. S. J. French in *Church Eclectic* for Oct. 1889, p. 625.

ising of your parish, as if you had but a fraction of that number of early communicants. . . . It is not every short cut that brings you safe to your journey's end." [75]

The objection is also often raised by the laity, that, for many of them, the custom of receiving fasting is a practical impossibility; but, as Father Hall well says, "It may be confidently affirmed that, in a great number of cases where impossibility is alleged or feared, the difficulty could be overcome with a little effort and determination, and by degrees would vanish." [76] The experience of many other priests confirms this statement. The writer himself has seen persons otherwise unable to bear great physical strains of any kind, as in the case of delicate women, grow accustomed to the practice of fasting communion, and regularly receive, at early celebrations, both with profit and devotion. Would it not seem as if God gave them special strength to perform this duty?

In conclusion, we ask again, what further arguments are necessary for those who love the Church, and who seek to follow in her reverent ways? Behind this godly practice lie the custom and the authority of the entire Catholic Church; and the obligation to fast is surely *unavoidable*. Reverence suggests it, the practical advantages are manifest, and obedience always has a rich reward. And, on the other hand, what are the arguments against it? Simply those which spring from a lack of devotion, from sloth, ignorance, or from a preference for one's own will.

> " By many deeds of shame
> We learn that love grows cold."

---

[75] Bp. Wilberforce, i. c. p. 13, quoted by Liddon in *Evening Communions*. Note xiv. [76] *Fasting Communion*, A. C. Hall, p. 12.

The Indissolubility of Marriage.

SO much has been written on this subject that it cannot be entered upon with the idea of affording
new matter or fresh argument. Nor is there any
need of presenting again the mass of much used and elo-
quent statistics which shew how rapidly we are going
down hill and losing all hold upon God's holy ordinance
of Marriage.

It seems at least doubtful whether the State govern-
ments or the government of the United States will or can
do anything substantial in the way of reform. The institution of marriage has never been rightfully committed
to the charge of civil governors, so that they have any
power to make definitions of it, to bind or to loose. It
is God's ordinance; and it has been committed to his
Church; not to change it, or to take any liberties with
it, but to preserve it; and by her unswerving testimony
to hold it up before the eyes of all the world as the sacred
thing which is absolutely necessary to keep mankind
from the vileness of sensual sin.

The sacred character of marriage is so well argued by
a distinguished Presbyterian divine[1] that it may be well
here to give his words at some length:

---

[1] Dr. Chas. Hodge, Prof. Theological Seminary, Princeton, N. J.
Systematic Theology, Part iii. chap. xix. § 11.

"Marriage is a divine institution: 1. Because founded on the nature of man as constituted by God. He made man male and female and ordained marriage as the indispensable condition of the continuance of the race. 2. Marriage was instituted before the existence of civil society, and therefore, cannot, in its essential nature, be a civil institution. As Adam and Eve were married not in virtue of any civil law, or by the intervention of a civil magistrate; so any man and woman cast together on a desert island could lawfully take each other as husband and wife. It is a degradation of the institution to make it a mere civil contract. 3. God commanded men to marry when he commanded them to increase and multiply and replenish the earth. 4. God, in his Word, prescribed the duties belonging to the marriage relation; he has made known his will as to the parties who may lawfully be united in marriage; he has determined the continuance of the relation and the causes which alone justify its dissolution. These matters are not subject to the will of the parties or to the authority of the State. 5. The vow of mutual fidelity made by husband and wife is not made exclusively by each one to the other, but by each to God. . . . Any violation of the compact is, therefore, a violation of a vow made to God.

"Marriage is . . . a sacred institution. Its solemnisation is an office of religion. It should, therefore, be entered upon with due solemnity and in the fear of God; and should be celebrated, i. e., the ceremony should be performed by a minister of Christ. He alone is authorised to see to it that the law of God is adhered to; and he alone can receive and register the marriage vows as made to God. The civil magistrate can only witness it as a civil contract, and it is, consequently, to ignore its religious character and sanction to have it celebrated by a civil officer. As the essence of the marriage contract is the mutual compact of the parties in the sight of God and in the presence of witnesses, it is not absolutely necessary that it should be celebrated by a minister of religion or even by a civil magistrate. It may be lawfully solemnised, as among the Quakers, without the intervention of either. Nevertheless, as it is of the greatest importance that the religious nature of the institution should be kept in view, it is incumbent on Christians, so far as they themselves are concerned, to insist that it should be solemnised as a religious service."

After a paragraph shewing that the State must make certain regulations about marriage, property rights, etc., Dr. Hodge goes on to say :

" The legitimate power of the State in these matters is limited by the revealed will of God. It can make nothing an impediment to marriage which the Scriptures do not declare to be a bar to that union. It can make nothing a ground of dissolving the marriage contract which the Bible does not make a valid ground of divorce. . . . It is a violation of the principles of civil and religious liberty for the State to make its will paramount to the will of God. Plain as this principle seems to be, it is nevertheless, constantly disregarded in almost all Christian nations, whether Catholic or Protestant. . . . Because marriage is in some respects a civil institution, to be regulated within certain limits by the civil law, men have treated it as though it were a mere business engagement. They ignore its character as a divine institution regulated and controlled by divine laws. Civil legislatures should remember that they can no more annul the laws of God than the laws of nature. If they pronounce those not to be married who, by the divine law are married; or if they separate those whom God hath joined together, their laws are absolute nullities at the bar of conscience and in the sight of God."

This general position is unassailable. Dr. Hodge unfortunately implied, as he believed, that there are Scriptural grounds for dissolving a marriage. In that and in some other points we cannot go with him. But very few amendments would make his words here quoted a perfectly clear and satisfactory setting forth of sound doctrine. The weighty responsibility lies with the Church, and with her pastors, not of making or changing the law of marriage, but of keeping it as the Lord distinctly gave it to her, and of teaching men so, both by word and act. It is the duty of every member of the Church, in his degree, to try to know what God's law is, and to see to it that his part of the Church shall not fail in maintaining it. For, as in other matters, so especially in this, not all parts of the Church have been equally faithful; although there is clear testimony to shew exactly what that law was which our Lord delivered. It is expressed by himself in the wonderful phrase "*one flesh.*" To dissolve a marriage is to kill both of the souls that were no more twain after God had joined them together. Marriage cannot be dissolved by man, or by separation, or by sin. Only the act of God, in taking one of the souls out of the flesh can make one unmarried who has been married.

It is proposed to confine this paper to this single point; to bring together the proofs that this is the law of God, and to consider how they ought to affect the practice and legislation of the Church.

Some Christians prefer to depend upon the words of Holy Scripture not interpreted by the Unwritten Word. Others believe that we must depend upon traditional interpretations if we would arrive at the true meaning of the Bible. Both of these " schools," honestly following their several methods, will come to one conclusion about the question before us. May it be a bond of union !

I.

THE SCRIPTURES ALONE.

It will not be questioned that in the New Testament we have the final, and, therefore, the controlling revelation. And there are not many subjects upon which it is possible definitely and surely to put together *all* that the New Testament says, as it is in this case. Almost every Protestant writer has put most of the texts together, and many have then proceeded to explain them away, each by a different method of criticism; all of them equally amazing when applied to such plain words. The texts are, strictly speaking, seven in number. An eighth is generally added by Protestant teachers in order to argue that "malicious desertion" is a lawful ground for or cause of divorce *a vinculo*.

The seven are :

1. "It hath been said, Whosoever shall put away his wife let him give her a writing of divorcement : but I say unto you, That whosoever shall put away his wife, saving for the cause of fornication, causeth her to commit adultery : and whosoever shall marry her that is divorced committeth adultery." St. Matt. v. 31, 32.

2. " The Pharisees came unto him, tempting him, and saying unto him, Is it lawful for a man to put away his

wife for every cause ? And he answered and said unto them, Have ye not read that he which made them at the beginning made them male and female, and said, For this cause shall a man leave father and mother and shall cleave unto his wife; and they twain shall be one flesh ? Wherefore they are no more twain, but one flesh. What therefore God hath joined together let not man put asunder. They say unto him, Why did Moses then command to give her a writing of divorcement and to put her away ? He saith unto them, Moses because of the hardness of your hearts suffered you to put away your wives: but from the beginning it was not so. Whosoever shall put away his wife except *it be* for fornication, and shall marry another, committeth adultery: and whoso marrieth her which is put away doth commit adultery. His disciples say unto him, If the case of the man be so with *his* wife it is not good to marry. But he said unto them, All men cannot receive this saying, save *they* to whom it is given. . . . He that is able to receive it, let him receive it." St. Matt. xix. 3–12.

3. " The Pharisees came to him and asked him, Is it lawful for a man to put away his wife ? tempting him. And he answered and said unto them, What did Moses command you ? And they said, Moses, suffered to write her a bill of divorcement and to put her away. And Jesus answered and said unto them, For the hardness of your heart he wrote you this precept. But from the beginning of the creation God made them male and female. For this cause shall a man leave his father and mother and cleave to his wife ; and they twain shall be one flesh : so then they are no more twain, but one flesh. What therefore God hath joined together let not man put asunder. And in the house his disciples asked him

again of the same *matter*. And he said unto them, Whosoever shall put away his wife and marry another committeth adultery against her. And if a woman shall put away her husband, and be married to another, she committeth adultery." St. Mark, x. 2–12.

4. "Whosoever putteth away his wife and marrieth another committeth adultery: and whoso marrieth her that is put away from her husband committeth adultery." St. Luke, xvi. 18.

5. "The woman which hath a husband is bound by the law to *her* husband so long as he liveth, but if her husband be dead she is loosed from the law of her husband. So then if, while her husband liveth, she be married to another man she shall be called an adulteress: but if her husband be dead she is freed from that law; so that she is no adulteress though she be married to another man." Rom. vii. 2–4.

6. "Unto the married I command *yet* not I, but the Lord, let not the wife depart from *her* husband: but and if she depart let her remain unmarried, or be reconciled to her husband: and let not the husband put away his wife." I. Cor. vii. 10, 11.

7. "The wife is bound by the law as long as her husband liveth; but if her husband be dead she is at liberty to be married to whom she will; only in the Lord." I. Cor. vii. 39.

In this last passage, which is really identical with the fifth, and almost identical in terms, we have an answer to those who say we must not depend on the fifth, because it only speaks of the law of marriage by way of illustration of the new union between Christ and his Church, made possible only by his death. There might well be exceptions, they say, in the actual law of marriage, which would not be noticed in a mere allegorical mention of it. Our answer is, that if in writing to the Corinthians of the literal and actual law of marriage, St. Paul uses almost the very words that he used in writing to the Romans by way of illustration, it is clear that his figure was drawn from an absolute law that had been given to all the churches, and was well understood by them all.

The eighth passage, of which Protestant writers make much use (or misuse), occurs between the sixth and the seventh, following immediately upon the sixth. It would be placed in order, as the seventh, if it really taught anything on the subject of divorce.

8. " If any brother hath a wife that believeth not and she be pleased to dwell with him let him not put her away. And the woman which hath a husband that believeth not, and if he be pleased to dwell with her, let her not leave him. For the unbelieving husband is sanctified by the wife, and the unbelieving wife is sanctified by the husband : else were your children unclean ; but now are they holy. But if the unbelieving depart, let him depart. A brother or a sister is not under bondage in such *cases :* but God hath called us to peace. For what knowest thou, O wife, whether thou shalt save thy husband ? Or how knowest thou, O man, whether thou shalt save thy wife ? But as God hath distributed to every man, as the Lord hath called every one, so let him walk. And so ordain I in all churches." I. Cor. vii. 12–17.

On this they found their argument in favour of divorce and marrying again for " malicious desertion " (which means wilful or persistent desertion), in the face of the passages which go before and follow after—passages in which St. Paul seems carefully to guard against such an inference, by first going back to the express direction of our Lord (v. 10), and then recalling the well-known law (v. 39) which must have been ordained in all churches from the beginning.

They argue that wilful desertion is such a wicked violation of the marriage vow as to prove the offender no better than an infidel, and that therefore, as in the Early Church, if an unbelieving spouse insisted on departing, a brother or a sister was not under bondage, so also the deserted in these days is under no law whatever, but is absolutely unmarried.

From the Scriptures alone it is impossible to shew that in this place St. Paul allowed the deserted brother or sister to marry again. " Let him depart" seems really to be the sum of the whole matter. " Not under bondage" is not synonymous with "free to marry again." But if they refer us back to the teaching and practice of the Early Church, and claim that in those days it was understood that the brother or sister could marry again, it must be remembered that the very Fathers who may be so quoted also hold most distinctly that every true and real marriage is indissoluble except by death. Therefore, in every case in which remarriage was lawful, they must have held that the previous heathen or Jewish union had never taken the character of true marriage according to God's ordinance.

St. Paul had been asked, as it seems (see v. 1), to decide several questions about marriage. They were: Is it better for Christians to remain unmarried? What are the duties of married persons towards each other? What is God's law as to divorce or separation? Must one who was married before becoming a Christian separate from the still unbelieving spouse? Now the question about

divorce he answers in our sixth passage, and, lest that
which follows should be misunderstood, goes back to it
again in the seventh. But the next question, which he
answers in the eighth passage, does not relate to divorce
at all, but to difference of religion as constituting a bar
to the true marriage relation. For what was called marriage in those days, whether among the heathen or the
Jews, was often not true marriage. The essence of marriage lies in the consent of the parties to that union
which was instituted by God at the beginning. A consent to any other kind of union is not marriage. A consent to a polygamous union, even though one were the
first wife, would not be marriage. Neither would a consent to a union terminable by the will or the fault of
either party. But yet any union could be made to be
really marriage by the actual keeping of the primal law,
as for example, the marriage of Isaac and Rebecca.
Now when one of a heathen or Jewish couple was converted the question would arise, *for the unbelieving to
decide*, shall this union be continued according to Christian and primitive principles, or shall it be now dissolved
as having arisen only in a consent to some such union as
Jews and heathen ignorantly practised? St. Paul commands the converted spouse to try in each case to con-
vert the union into true marriage; and he states the practical advantages of doing so. But if it cannot be done,
then, he says, they are not to be held under the bondage
of any other sort of union.[2]

---

[2] When it was afterwards ruled in the Church that non-Chris-
tianity should be an absolute bar to a marriage with a Christian,
the case was different. Such a marriage was declared null and
void from the first because a Christian was forbidden to marry
except "in the Lord."

The eighth passage must be ruled out of the array of Scriptural evidence, because it refers not to the dissolution of a true marriage, but to the conversion of an unsanctified union into a holy one if possible, with the alternative of separation. It cannot be applied to the case of a Christian couple who have once contracted true marriage, and of whom one afterwards become wicked and deserts the other. Its legitimate application occurs in the conduct of missions to the heathen or unbelievers.

Confining ourselves, therefore, to the seven passages of the New Testament which are all that speak of divorce, what do they say?

1. They repeal the Mosaic temporary legislation.

2. They do not give a new law, but go back to the original institution.

3. They deny the possibility of divorce *a vinculo*.

4. They permit separation for some causes.

5. They imply that the law is equal for the man and the woman under the Gospel.

Let us take these five points up in order.

1. Our Lord clearly told the Jews that the law of Moses about divorce was only a temporary provision for the hardness of their hearts. It was precisely like the permission of polygamy. Both were contrary to the original institution. Neither of them was consistent with the fact of "twain" being "one flesh." Because of the fallen nature of men these great measures of relaxation were allowed before our Lord's coming, the law only providing such restrictions as could be enforced, that the Israelites might not adopt all the abominable and unclean ways of the heathen. Considering marriage as a divine institution it may be said that it only existed among the Jews in those singular instances in which God's grace

wrought a better morality than the law of the time demanded. No doubt there were many such. But there
were also many faithful Israelites who lived in what
would now be sinful unions. With the coming of new
grace and holiness by the Gospel, the standard of marriage was to be raised up again.

2. It was to be raised only to the original condition
and endowed with supernatural graces. The union
of our first parents had God's full blessing and was
most holy. There can never be any better marriage.
In many things the redeemed can go on to a higher
state than that of the first creation; but not in marriage. There is no better marriage except our Lord's
own union with his Church of which human marriage
was ordained to be a type. There could be no question
of divorce in that first union. And as *they* could not be
put asunder, so can no couple of their children who are
married be put asunder, except by the act of God. But
if marriage were dissoluble, God would have told our
first parents that they were married, and were condition-
ally "one flesh;" that is to say, that if either of them
should eat of the forbidden fruit, the other would be entitled to a divorce *a vinculo matrimonii*, and that he would
create another partner with whom the holy one might
become one flesh while the sinful one that was cast off
still lived.[3] It will not be held that Adam had any such
conception of the marriage relation.

Nor can it be contended that we are held at this present time by a somewhat lower rule of marriage than that
of the first creation, because of the hardness of men's
hearts, and that when our Lord republished the original

[3] See St. Chrysostom, Hom. xxii. *on St. Matt.* xix. 3-11, quoted
in Keble's *Sequel to Argument*, &c., p. 74.

law he only did-so by way of prophecy of its going into force at some period still future; for the institution of marriage is to have no such future.   His express declaration is that it ends with this earthly life; "When they shall rise from the dead they neither marry nor are given in marriage, but are as the angels which are in heaven."[4] And although in this present life we are not pure and holy as our first parents were created, yet the power of sin is counterbalanced by the great out-pouring of grace; "Where sin abounded, grace did much more abound."[5] And, therefore, we are able to keep the primitive and divine law of marriage.

3. Our Lord was not content to send us back to the first law only in general terms.   He has also, by his own words and St. Paul's, particularly declared that in no case of separation can either party contract another union. This is disputed, because, it is said, he was answering the question of the Jews, and referred only to their loose customs of divorce without trial and judgment given, and at the caprice of the husband.   But he gave this law *in his private conference with his disciples.*   And St. Paul repeats it to the Romans and Corinthians.   And the Sermon on the Mount, in which the first of our texts occurs, gives everywhere the true principles of morals that are to prevail in the kingdom of heaven, which were indeed the basis of the law of Moses, but which that law was never able to enforce, or even to make fully known.   Nowhere does our Lord concern himself simply to correct a looseness in the observance of the law as it should have been practised before his coming.   His words are for all time.   He does the same thing about the seventh commandment that he does about the sixth

---

[4] St. Mark, xii. 25.   [5] Rom. v. 20.

and the third and the eighth and others. He sends us back to the original principles of holiness which are shadowed forth in the law of Moses, which alone can fulfil that law, and of which not one jot or tittle can pass.

The only seeming exception to the rule of indissolubility is found in one, or, as some think, in both of the texts from St. Matthew. ᐧ In the first there is no mention of the husband's marrying again, and she who is put away is expressly declared *incapable of it*. And if she is so bound why is not he? In the second, the Lord said, " Whosoever shall put away his wife except it be for fornication, and shall marry another, committeth adultery." But St. Mark and St. Luke record that he absolutely declared it adultery to marry another, without any mention of the cause of divorce. Therefore, if the words in St. Matthew establish an exception, there is a contradiction. Not a discrepancy or a difficulty in harmonising, but an irreconcilable contradiction. For if at one time it be said that whoever puts away his wife for any other cause than fornication, and marries another, commits adultery; but that if he puts her away for fornication and marries another he does not commit adultery; and then at another time it be said that every man who puts away his wife and marries another commits adultery— the contradiction is irreconcilable. First he does not, and then he does.

It has been said that to suppose an exception does not involve a contradiction, because it may well occur in lawgiving that a general law forbidding a certain act in one place may be supplemented by exceptions given at other times. For instance, the commandment " Thou shalt not kill" has numerous exceptions. While this is true of some laws, it is not true of all. Especially is it untrue of the first and seventh commandments, between which Scripture everywhere shews a mystical connexion. It is impossible to think of an exception to either of them. Marriage under Moses was a different thing from marriage under Christ, and therefore the limits of adultery were different. But while there are many exceptions to the sixth commandment, both under the Law and under the Gospel, there are none to the seventh under either. One may kill in self-defence, but must not commit adultery in self-defence. Therefore, because our Lord's general law of indissolubility given in St. Mark, in part defines the new limits of adultery, if we suppose that at a previous time, perhaps in the same day, he gave a law of divorce containing a weighty exception to indissolubility, we suppose him to have contradicted himself.

Now, we cannot suppose a contradiction. Neither can we take anything away from the absolute rule given in St. Mark and St. Luke. For they are Holy Gospels. They were delivered to large parts of the Church, and read by them years before St. Matthew came to their knowledge. St. Mark (St. Peter's Gospel) was given to the Romans; St. Luke (St. Paul's Gospel) to the Greeks. These were very large parts of the Church. Did they first learn the rule of no divorce whatever both from their Gospels and from St. Paul's Epistles to the Romans and Corinthians, and then have to correct it by such an important exception when at last they got St. Matthew's Gospel also? Surely there would have been discussion and difficulty if St. Matthew had been so understood. But there is no historical trace of any such trouble.

There is, therefore, no way left open to us but by the enquiry, Does St. Matthew really establish an exception? He does not. Whenever our Lord says " except for fornication," he is speaking to Jews. St. Matthew wrote his Gospel expressly for Jews. Now, according to the law of the Jews an adulteress was to be put to death. After her death, of course, her husband could marry again. To the captious Pharisees, eager to catch at any word spoken against the Law, our Lord is careful to reply in an unanswerable way. When, as St. John records, they tried to make him a party to the legal punishment of a woman whom he knew to be penitent, he did not deny the Law, although as to its temporal severity it was to pass away; but he shamed them by their own consciences, and then, as himself the lawgiver, absolved the adulteress. This punctilious regard for the Law was a good thing also to keep before the minds of the Jewish Christians and unconverted Jews for whom, especially, St. Matthew wrote the Gospel.

Moreover, it is probable that St. Mark had a copy of St. Matthew before him when he wrote. In many places he almost repeats St. Matthew's words. We may reasonably suppose that when he came to the nineteenth chapter and the words, "And I say unto you, whosoever shall put [6] away his wife, except it be for fornication, and shall marry another, committeth adultery," etc., St. Peter, who overlooked him, said, by the Spirit, " Leave those words out. They were intended for the Jews, because, by the Law, adulteresses were put to death. But afterwards, in the house, we asked him again of the same matter, and he then gave us the rule that we were to give to the whole Church. Record that rule for these people, who are to learn to seek the repentance and restoration of adulteresses, lest they should think that they can marry again if they have put away their wives

---

[6] Observe the special direction of the saying, "Unto *you*."

for adultery, *while those wives are still living.*"   St. Mark, therefore, records no more of the words spoken to the Pharisees than those by which they were sent back to the first law of marriage together with the conclusion, "what God hath joined together let no man put asunder"; but then he goes on to give the most interesting and even conclusive fact of the private conference in which the law was given to the disciples for the Church that was to be: "*Whosoever* shall put away his wife and marry another committeth adultery against her.   And if a woman shall put away her husband and be married to another, she committeth adultery."   This was the Christian law, entirely new and strange to his hearers, as their sayings soon shew, in that it made the sexes equal in respect[7] of divorce.   The woman had no power of divorce under Moses, and there was no such offence as adultery in which a married woman was not a party.

The words in both passages from St. Matthew easily bear the sense required, as will be seen by simply putting them in parenthesis and supplying the expression "of course."   "Whosoever shall put away his wife (save, of course, for the cause of fornication) causeth her," etc. "Whosoever shall put away his wife (unless, of course, for fornication), and shall marry another, committeth adultery."   It seems perfectly clear that the Jews would understand the parenthesis to be nothing more nor less than a disclaimer of all intention to relax the first severity of the law against adultery.   And that law was not that the adulteress might be cast off and left free to go on sinning, but that she was to be cast off and be put to death, and that her partner in sin was to be put to death also.

---

[7] St. Matt. xix. 10.

This explanation is sanctioned by the Church in the Book of Homilies.[8] It justifies the canon law of the whole Western Church, and our Marriage Service. And it avoids all contradiction between different Scriptures.

It has been objected that the Jews had not the power at this time of inflicting the death-penalty, according to their saying to Pilate, St. John xviii. 31. Josephus also said that the Sanhedrim could not hold a court without the procurator's assent, and the Talmud asserts that forty years before the destruction of Jerusalem, Israel lost the power of life and death. Dr. Döllinger very fully answers this objection, shewing that the Sanhedrim still had this power, in Appendix II. to *The First Age of the Church*. It is sufficient here to point out that the things they did and threatened, as recorded[9] in St. John and in the Acts of the Apostles, and Pilate's saying to them twice, "Take ye him and crucify him," are ample proofs that the power existed. Pilate was trying to appease the people and the rulers, and would not have publicly insulted them by saying such words to them if they had no such power. The Jews must have meant, therefore, we can kill no one (1) on a charge of high treason; (2) now, during the feast. Josephus says nothing about the power of the court being limited when it had permission to sit. The Talmud is clearly wrong, having made a serious mistake as to dates.

On the other hand it has been objected that as adulteresses *were* punished with death, our Lord could not have meant to include adultery in the word "fornication," and that therefore some explanation of the text widely differing from the usual one must be sought. Döllinger

---

[8] *Sermon against Adultery*, 2d Part. [9] St. John v. 8: vii. 1, 25; Acts v. 33: vii. 57: xxvi. 10.

so reasons.[10] But it must be remembered that it was not our. Lord's manner to speak without reference to the future of the Church—at least in his words that are written in the Gospel. The golden age to come was always in his thoughts ; and all that he said was formed by his foresight of the questions and perplexities that should agitate his Church. Therefore, although his answers were complete as against the possible cavils of contemporary Jews, they also provided, secondly, for the time when adultery should no longer be punished with physical death, but rather with separation and spiritual death, or excommunication ; punishments devised not. for the avenging nor for the setting free of the injured husband or wife, but in order that the soul of the sinner may be saved by repentance. And this repentance will, in many cases, be sealed by the coming together again of the forgiving and forgiven spouses, who, though parted by sin, yet know that they are still husband and wife so long as they both shall live. A law which should allow the " innocent party " to marry another would make directly against the merciful design of the Gospel by cutting off the place of return.

It is often said that if a man's wife is unfaithful she becomes " dead to him ;" and that his life ought not to be " ruined." But such ought not to be the feeling of a Christian man. He should rather be willing to suffer whatever he may be called to suffer for the sinner in the hope that she may be cleansed ; or, at least, in order that the indissoluble sanctity of marriage may be illustrated by his patient endurance of the loss of his earthly happiness.

---

[10] *First Age of the Church*, vol. ii. p. 268.

4. It is unnecessary to argue at length that the Script-ures allow "the innocent party" to withdraw, for a time or for life, from the bed and board of a spouse guilty of certain offences. From St. Matthew, v. 32, it has been concluded that they must only be such offences as may be put under the general head of fornication. But this has been found a very general head. In the Scriptures the word is often used of apostasy. St. Augustine so under-stood it. And it seems certain that if one cannot abide with a spouse without forsaking God, there must be a separation. Such divorce is evidently contemplated by St. Paul, who at the same time requires either continence or reconciliation, and expects the latter to be constantly kept in view. Its lawfulness is necessarily inferred also from the fundamental canon which our Lord gave his disciples in the private conference recorded by St. Mark. That law is full of meaning and very clear in its few words, "Whosoever shall put away his wife *and marry another* committeth adultery against her. And if a woman shall put away her husband *and be married to another* she committeth adultery." Therefore, there may be cases in which either party may put the other away, and yet if they do not marry another they shall not com-mit adultery. And this means that they shall do no wrong; for *any* offence against marriage is adultery. But it cannot be concluded from the words of Holy Scripture what all the causes are for which separation may be lawful.

5. By the same fundamental canon our Lord makes it evident that the husband and wife are *equal* parties to their union. Whatever one may do, the other may do. Whatever one may not do, the other may not do. This is all the more evident from the fact that in so pronouncing

he was against the whole Jewish idea of the position of the woman. To speak of a woman putting away her husband in the same way as of a man putting away his wife was to be revolutionary in the eyes of the men of that time. They had heard of some half-heathen examples of women divorcing their husbands;[11] but it was an utterly strange and foreign idea that any such equality should be according to the law of God. Perhaps it was partly this, together with the indissolubility of marriage declared at the same time, that induced the disciples to say to our Lord, "If the case of the man be so with his wife it is not good to marry." For we are all disinclined to surrender exclusive powers.

It seems the more important to speak particularly of the equality of the sexes in the matter of the marriage bond, because so great a commentator as Bishop Wordsworth maintains that divorce *a vinculo* is allowed for adultery *if the wife is the offender*, but never to the wife if the husband is guilty. He defends this singular position by a too literal following of the words of our Lord, supposing that in St. Matthew, xix. 9, an exception to the law of indissolubility is created, and that because it applies literally only when the woman is guilty, therefore, it extends no further.

It only remains to consider briefly another interpretation of the passages in St. Matthew, which has found favour with some thoughtful and distinguished writers of late.[12] They maintain that the word "fornication" does not mean the sin of the wife after marriage, which would be called adultery, but sin before marriage, which, according to the law of Moses, was such an injury to the de-

---

[11] As in the case of Salome, Herod's sister. Josephus, *Antiq.* lib. xv. c. 7. [12] Among them Döllinger as referred to above.

ceived man as would justify him in putting away the woman that she might suffer the death penalty.[13] The objection to taking the word fornication in this sense is that it has never occurred to any writer before the present day to do so. In all the ancient writers who refer to these two places in St. Matthew, it is taken in its generic sense, of carnal sin, including adultery; and by some it is expressly said that fornication committed by a wife is adultery. Nevertheless, if any are careful to observe the law of God rather than to please themselves, it would seem that even if there were no other way of reconciling St. Matthew to the other evangelists, yet the fact that this limited meaning of fornication may be the true one (for it is by no means disproved), ought to be enough to make them unwilling to contract a second marriage unless freed by death.

But in this case, and in the case of every other divine commandment, too many are more eager to find out how far they can go than whether they are surely within the law. It may be asked why our Lord did not make his law of marriage perfectly clear; why he left an ambiguous rule. The answer is, that he did make it perfectly clear for all those who are very desirous to obey. For the others no law is clear or can be made clear. Obedience must come from a willing mind. We may well challenge the production of any more unmistakable statement of the law that there can be no divorce *a vinculo*. For if he had said nothing of any cause for putting away, then men would have declared that it was too monstrous that any should be compelled to live with an unchaste spouse, and that, therefore, he must have meant to speak only of unauthorized divorces, not de-

---

[13] Deut. xxii.

creed by any proper authority after examination. And if it be asked why he did not use the word "adultery" instead of "fornication," if that was his meaning, the answer is that the generic term includes very foul and urgent causes for separation, which cannot be more particularly spoken of, and which might be thought not to be included under "adultery." And if it be asked why our Lord did not distinctly place the essence of the offence in a divorced person's *marrying again*, the answer is that that is precisely what he did, most emphatically, in the law which he gave to the disciples in the private conference, and what St. Paul has also done in the Epistles.

II.

THE TESTIMONY OF THE CHURCH.

In speaking of the evidence of the Fathers, the canons and decrees on this subject, it is often said "There is no *consensus*." This is said because the testimony is not all equally clear and decided. There are some hesitating voices, some that are not always consistent with themselves. Some do not affirm all that others do. In later times, also the Eastern Church has clearly, by canon, allowed divorces contrary to Holy Scripture, and no less contrary to the early Church and to the whole Western Church. Therefore, it is said, "There is no *consensus*."

But we must not ask impossibilities. It would be a greater miracle than most if every writer, every council, every patriarch and metropolitan had with one equal voice proclaimed, "There is no divorce from the marriage bond." We can find no such *consensus* even for the doctrine of the Holy Trinity. The only question is, what does all the evidence at our command shew to have been the doctrine, and the interpretation of Holy Scripture received by the Church in the beginning? It will appear to have been the doctrine that marriage is indissoluble without exception, *because* the Mosaic allowance as to divorce is done away and the original law as given in Eden again promulgated; that, nevertheless, separation must take place in some cases, especially for unchastity ; and that the inferiority of the woman is taken away, making her an equal party to the marriage bond. This doctrine is at least in the position in which that of the Divinity of our Lord was before the Council of Nicea. And if it shall ever have its ecumenical triumph in the course of this world's history, it may be for years afterwards as unpopular and as fiercely hunted down as that great doctrine was after Nicea. For the secular power has always been violent against God's law. The hardness of heart for which divorce was allowed to the Jews was not peculiar to them. Liberty of divorce has been more fiercely demanded by carnal men, and more weakly yielded by Church authority, than any other ungodly licence. The early Christian empire seems to have made no pretence of following the law of God about marriage. The Byzantine court at last completely overcame the virtue of the Church in the eleventh century, when the patriarch, Alexius of Constantinople, gave the four decisions following, which have since been the law of the Eastern Church:[14]

" 1. No clergyman is to be condemned for giving the benediction at the marriage of a divorced woman when the man's conduct was the cause of the divorce.

" 2. Women divorced from men whose conduct has been the cause of the divorce are not to be blamed if

[14] Fulton, *Laws of Marriage.*

they choose to marry again; nor are the priests to be blamed who give them the benediction. So, too, with regard to men.

"3. Whoever marries a woman divorced for adultery is an adulterer, whether he himself has been married before or not; and he must undergo the penance of an adulterer.

"4. Any priest who gives the benediction at the second marriage of parties divorced by mutual consent (which is a thing forbidden by the laws) shall be deprived of his office."

In this position the Eastern Church has certainly not followed the prevailing voice of antiquity. The very early testimonies on the subject are most clear and unqualified. As we go on, we find here and there a wavering note; yet none earlier than the latter part of the fourth century. But no sounds that are *uncertain*, even if they were much more numerous, can countervail such witnesses as these that follow.

Hermas [15] (about A. D. 100–150) writes:

"Sir, if a man shall have a wife that is faithful in the Lord, and shall catch her in adultery, does a man sin that continues to live with her? And he said unto me, As long as he is ignorant of her sin he commits no fault in living with her; but if a man shall know his wife to have offended, and she shall not repent of her sin, but go on still in her fornication, and a man shall continue nevertheless to live with her, he shall become guilty of her sin, and partake with her in her adultery.

"And I said unto him, What therefore is to be done, if the woman continues on in her sin? He answered, Let her husband put her away, and let him continue by

---

[15] *Pastor Mand.* IV. § 1.

himself. But if he shall put away his wife and marry another, he also doth commit adultery.

"And I said, What if the woman that is so put away shall repent, and be willing to return to her husband, shall she not be received by him? He said unto me, Yes; and if her husband shall not receive her, he will sin, and commit a great offence against himself; but he ought to receive the offender if she repents; only not often; for to the servants of God there is but one repentance. And for this cause a man that puts away his wife ought not to take another, because she may repent. This act is alike both in the man and in the woman."

Athenagoras[16] (about A. D. 177) declares against all second marriages, even of the widowed, which of course is an error. But he supports it by an appeal to the *known law* that whoever puts away his wife commits adultery if he marries again.

Clement of Alexandria[17] (about A. D. 200), says:

"Now that the Scripture counsels marriage, and allows no release from the union is expressly contained in the law, 'Thou shalt not put away thy wife except for the cause of fornication'; and it regards as fornication the marriage of those separated while the other is yet alive. . . . He that taketh a woman that has been put away, it is said, committeth adultery; and if one puts away his wife he makes her an adulteress, that is, compels her to commit adultery. And not only is he who puts her away guilty of this, but he who takes her, by giving the woman the opportunity of sinning; for did he not take her she would return to her husband. What then is the law? In order to check the impetuosity of the passions it commands the adulteress to be put to

---

[16] *Apologia*, c. 33.   [17] *Stromata*, Bk. ii. c. xxiii.

death, on being convicted of this, and if of priestly family
to be committed to the flames.[18]   And the adulterer also
is stoned to death, but not in the same place, that not
even their death may be in common.   And the Law is
not at variance with the Gospel, but agrees with it. How
should it be otherwise, one Lord being the author of
both ?   She who has committed fornication liveth in sin
and is dead to the commandments ; but she who has re-
pented, being as it were born again by the change in her
life, has a regeneration of life, the old harlot being dead,
and she who has been regenerated by repentance having
come back again to life.   The spirit testifies to what has
been said by Ezekiel, declaring, ' I desire not the death
of a sinner but that he should turn.' " [19]

The Apostolic Canons : [20]

" If any layman put away his wife and take another, or
if he marries a woman divorced by another man let him
be suspended."

The Council of Elvira (A. D. 305):

" C. 9.   A Christian woman who shall abandon an
adulterous husband *who is a Christian*, shall be forbidden
to marry again ; and if she marry she shall not receive
the Communion until he whom she has married is dead,
unless the necessity of grievous sickness require it to be
given to her.

" C. 24. It is decreed that a man shall by all means be
prevented from dismissing his wife in order to take another in her place ; and whoever shall do so shall be cut
off from Catholic communion."

The Council of Arles (A. D. 314) :[21]

---

[18] Lev. xx. 10.   Deu. xxii. 22.   Lev. xxi. 19.   [19] Ezk. xxxiii.
11.   [20] Can. 48, according to Dr. Fulton.   [21] Can. 10, according to
Dr. Fulton, *Laws of Marriage.*

" Concerning those who detect their wives in adultery, and they themselves are Christian youths and are forbidden to marry again, it is decreed that, as far as may be, counsel be given them not to take other wives during the lives of their former wives, adulteresses though they be."

This council was of great importance, and is often called a General Council by St. Agustine. Its decree is, therefore, a strong testimony as to what doctrine was then received. Dr. Pusey[22] thinks that canon 9 (as he has the number) shews the coming in of a new strictness of opinion (" and are forbidden to marry," i. e., are by the notions now coming in prohibited), and that the counsel to be given them is the result of such influence. But it is just as easy, or even easier, to argue the other way. Why may not the canon rather shew that secular influences had begun to weaken the primitive soundness revealed to us by Hermas, Athenagoras, and Clement, expressed in the Apostolical Canon 48, and afterward zealously upheld by St. Augustine, who had so great respect for this " General " Council of Arles? Why should we not conclude that the bishops at Arles thought it best simply to affirm the evangelical rule (namely, that " they are forbidden to marry ") so unpopular in the world, and then leave it, as we sometimes think we must do, to conscientious sanctions alone to enforce it? Why should the council make a solemn decree to advise young Christians not to do a thing which the law of God allows?

Lactantius (about A. D. 320) says:[23]

---

[22] Note O, on Tertullian, lib. ii. *ad Uxorem*, Oxford Transl.
[23] *Inst.* vi. 23.

"The divine is not like the civil law, which holds that none but a married woman can commit adultery, while her husband, however many women he may take, does not commit adultery. The divine rule so joins the twain in marriage, that is to say, in one body, under an equal law, that he is an adulterer who rends apart the union of that body."

Smith's *Dictionary of Christian Antiquities* cites Lactantius as holding marriage permissible to the husband who has dismissed his wife for adultery, because, further on in the chapter just quoted from, he says that while the general rule of Christian chastity is that none should do to another what he would not that another should do to him, "yet lest anyone should think that he can evade the divine commandment, this is added that all pretext and occasion of fraud may be taken away, that he is *an adulterer* who shall marry a divorced woman and he also who shall put away his wife save for the crime of adultery, that he may marry another ; *for God will not have that body disjoined and rent apart.*" Lactantius is here simply quoting St. Matthew xix. 9, though not literally, yet in fact and according to his method. He means just what our Lord meant, no more, no less ; he is not interpreting the text ; he simply points out that it is an additional hedge to the general virtue of chastity. The passage, therefore, is not available for any purpose in this argument. But even granting its availability, what does it shew ? Above he said that the twain are joined in one body *under an equal law.* Then he says he is *an adulterer* who shall marry a divorced woman. Why therefore shall *she* not be an adulteress who shall marry a divorced man ? For God will not have the bond dissolved. On the whole we must claim Lactantius.

St. Ambrose (A. D. 333–397) says :

" [24] Let no man deceive himself with human laws which declare that adultery is not committed with a single woman but only with one who is a wife. Every unlawful sexual commerce is adultery; and what is unlawful in a woman is unlawful in a man. The same chastity is due by the husband as by the wife; and any sin committed with a woman who is not his lawful wife is condemned as the crime of adultery."

And in his exposition of the Gospel, according to St. Luke,[25] after speaking forcibly and at great length about the evils of divorce in general, St. Ambrose says :

" Thou puttest away thy wife as if of right, without cause, and thinkest that this is lawful to thee because the human law does not forbid it. Thou who art subject to men, fear God. Hear the law of God, to which they also are subject who make the law : 'What God hath joined together let not man put asunder.' (Matt. xix. 6.)

" And not only this heavenly commandment but also an institution of God is violated. Wilt thou suffer, I ask, thy children, while thou art living, to be under a step-father? Or while their mother is yet alive under a step-mother? Suppose the divorced wife does not marry again ; should she be displeasing to thee who keeps her faith to her adulterous husband? Suppose she marries ; thine is the guilt that compelled her; and what thou reckonest marriage is adultery. And what does it matter whether thou committest it with open confession of guilt or as an adulterer in the guise of a husband? Except that it is worse to have adopted a rule of wickedness than to commit a stolen crime.

---

[24] *De Abr. Patr.* I. 4.   [25] *Lib. viii. on St. Luke xvi. 18.*

"But perhaps someone will say, why did Moses command to give the wife a bill of divorcement and to put her away? Whoever says this, is a Jew. Whoever says this, is not a Christian. And therefore, because he makes this objection against the Lord, the Lord replies to him: Because of the hardness of your hearts, he says, Moses allowed you to give your wives a writing of divorcement and to put them away. He says Moses allowed; not God commanded; but the law of God is from the beginning. What is the law of God? A man shall leave his father and mother and cleave unto his wife, and they twain shall be one flesh. Therefore whosoever puts away his wife tears his own flesh, divides his own body."

Then, referring to what St. Paul wrote to the Corinthians, he says:

"The Apostle denied (1 Cor. vii. 10) that it is according to the divine law that any marriage whatsoever can be dissolved; nor did he direct it, nor give authority to the deserter (v. 15), but only declared the deserted blameless."

In all that he says, St. Ambrose gives no hint whatever that there is any cause for which a marriage can be dissolved. The above passage has been given at length because otherwise no clear idea of what St. Ambrose thought could be obtained. It will readily be seen that if he knew of any exception to the indissolubility he must have mentioned it.

St. Jerome (A. D. 340–420) says:

"So long as a man lives, though he be an adulterer or a sodomite, or swallowed up in every conceivable vice, and though his wife may have left him because of these crimes, he is yet held to be her husband, and it is unlawful for her to take another man. . . . He who marries a divorced woman is an adulterer." [26]

---

[26] *Epist. ad Amandum*, c. 3.

"Wheresoever, therefore, there is fornication or suspicion of fornication, the wife may be freely put away;
but because it might happen that someone should slan-
der an innocent woman, or even allege a crime against
her in order to clear the way for a second marriage,
therefore he is required to put away his first wife only
on this wise, that he shall have no other while the first
lives." [27]

St. Jerome also writes[28] of Fabiola, who had put away
a husband who was not only an adulterer, but stained
with all manner of crimes, and who, after the death of
her second husband, submitted to a public penance imposed by the Bishop of Rome. She only excused her
fault by the fact that she had been ignorant of the strictness of the Gospel in this matter. This interesting event
shews that the discipline of the Church in that day
regarded the remarriage of "the innocent party" as a
public scandal.

We now come to St. Chrysostom (A. D. 354–407),
whose testimony is important because of an impression
in some minds that the East received a different tradition
from the West (surprising thought!), and that Eastern
Fathers are as strong in allowing remarriage as Western
ones are in denying it. The passages that might be
quoted from St. Chrysostom are copious and very many;
and although he nowhere addresses himself directly to
the question of a new marriage after divorce, yet he
shews the same strong holding of the indissolubility of
marriage and of the wickedness of divorce which we find
in St. Ambrose; and of him also it may be said that if
he had believed that adultery dissolved a marriage he
could not have written all that he has on the general

---

[27] *Comm. in Matt. xix. 19.* [28] *Ad Oceanum.*

subject, and especially on St. Matthew xix., and never
have mentioned so important an exception. He states
very strongly the equality of the sexes in the matter of
the marriage bond, and gives a remarkable explanation
of the laxity allowed by Moses.

A few of his words only can be given as specimens.
In *Homily xviii. on St. Matt. v. 28*, after speaking of
women who deck themselves to draw looks of desire, he
says:

"Why doth he not discourse with them also? It may
be said, *Because the laws which he appoints are in every
case common*, although he seems to address himself to
men only. For in discoursing with the head, he makes
his admonition common to the whole body also. For
woman and man he knows as one living creature, and
nowhere distinguishes their kind."

And a little below, on verses 31 and 32:

"But these things (the provisions for divorce) were
done by reason of another, a far greater wickedness; I
mean had he made it necessary to keep in the house her
even that was hated, the husband hating would have
killed her. For such was the race of the Jews. For
they who did not spare children, who slew prophets,
and shed blood as water (Ps. lxxix. 3), much more would
they have shewed no mercy to women. For this
cause he allowed the less to remove the greater
evil. . . .

"Observe him everywhere addressing his discourse to
the man. Thus, he that putteth away his wife, saith he,
causeth her to commit adultery; and he that marrieth a
woman put away committeth adultery. That is, the former, though he take not another wife, by that act alone
hath made himself liable to blame, having made the first

an adulteress: the latter again is become an adulterer by taking her who is another's. . . .

"She who hath been made aware that she positively must either keep the husband who was allotted to her, or, being cast out of that house, not have any other refuge, she, even against her will, was compelled to make the best of her consort."

Evidently St. Chrysostom had the tradition of no possible marriage after divorce, and considered it the best safeguard against divorce.

Speaking of the case of a wife who has a brutal and wicked husband, or one who "constantly avoids her and persists continually in doing so," he says:[29]

"Endure, said he, all this slavery. For when he is dead then only shalt thou be free. But during his life thou must needs take one of two courses; either train him with great earnestness and make him better, or, if that be impossible, bear nobly the war which admits of no negotiation or truce. And, as before he said, ' Defraud not one another except it be with consent for a time;' so here, *when she is separated, he bids her abide in continence even against her will.*"

In his *Homily xxii. on St. Matthew xix. 3–11,* also quoted by Keble, St. Chrysostom says:

"Making it a fearful thing to find fault with this legislation and fixing the law, he said not, Therefore drag not asunder nor separate, but ' What God hath conjoined let no man separate.' And if thou allege Moses, I tell thee of Moses's Lord: and I enforce it by the time also. For God *from the beginning* made them male and female: and this is the elder law even though it appears now to

---

[29] *Treatise on Virginity,* p. 268, § 39, quoted by Keble.

be introduced by me; and it is laid down with much earnestness; for he did not merely bring the woman to the man, but bade him even forsake father and mother. Neither did he simply exact that one should come to his wife, but even to *cleave* unto her: by the turn of the phrase indicating inseparability. Nor was he satisfied even with this, but sought out likewise another and a completer union: for 'the two,' said he, 'shall be one flesh.'

"Then, having quoted the ancient law, authorised as it was both by words and deeds, and having recommended it to respect by the thought of the giver; with authority, after that, he himself, too, interprets and gives the law, saying, 'Wherefore they are no more twain, but one flesh.' *As, therefore, to mutilate the body is impious, so to divorce a wife is against all law.* And he stayed not at this, but brought in God also, in saying, 'What therefore God hath joined together, let not man put asunder:' shewing that such a thing is both against nature and against law; against nature because one flesh is dissevered; against law, because when God hath conjoined and forbidden separation, ye of yourselves *endeavour* to bring it about."

Mr. Keble,[30] who thinks that our Lord, in St. Matthew xix. 9, was simply giving the true meaning of the existing law of Moses, but yet, of course, holds strongly that there is no marriage after divorce, gives other passages

---

[30] When this paper was, as the writer supposed, nearly finished, he fortunately got access to Mr. Keble's very scarce and very valuable work, "An Argument against immediately repealing the laws which treat the Nuptial Bond as Indissoluble," with Sequel to the same, Parker, London, 1857. This work ought to be reprinted.

at great length from St. Chrysostom, and then sums up the result of his careful examination of this Father as follows :

" It is plain that St. Chrysostom, first, understood the Pharisees in their question to be covertly referring to some former expression of our Lord's mind on the subject of divorce. He specifies the text in his Sermon on the Mount. But surely the conversation recorded by St. Luke might also be in their recollection: especially as it was so very recent.

" 2. He regards our Lord's reference to the creation of the woman and to the original institution of marriage as equivalent to the saying, divorce is unlawful.

" 3. He considers our Lord's decision of this case as parallel to his decisions in the case of the Sabbath, and in that of outward and inward defilement.

" 4. His expressions when he speaks of the hardship of not being allowed to put away, convey the notion of *actual binding together*, not simply of *the bond of marriage continuing ;* as where he speaks of 'an untamed beast *shut up continually in the house with you.'* "

This last is the same as to say that St Chrysostom took it for granted, as a thing well understood among Christians, as did also the other Fathers generally, that the only divorce allowed by God's law, and that under severe restrictions, was the separation *a mensa et thoro.* This attitude of their minds must be remembered in interpreting all passages from the early Fathers.

Returning now from East to West, we find a clear statement from Pope Innocent I. (A. D. 402–417), who in his *Third Letter to Exuperius*, cap. 4, says :

"You have asked why men who are communicants will not consort with adulterous wives, while wives, on the contrary, continue to consort with adulterous husbands. The Christian religion condemns adultery equally in both sexes; but women do not readily accuse their husbands of adultery, and secret crimes pass without punishment. Men, however, are wont to accuse their wives who have sinned, and when the sin is revealed the women are punished. Thus adulterous husbands are not excommunicated because their sin is not known, but they are to be expelled if the crime is disclosed. The guilt in either case is the same, though justice fails for lack of evidence.

"[31] It is manifest that when persons who have been divorced marry again, both parties are adulterers. And moreover, although the former marriage is supposed (*videatur*) to be broken, yet if they marry again they themselves are adulterers; but the parties whom they marry are equally with them guilty of adultery: as we read in the Gospel, 'He who putteth away his wife and marrieth another committeth adultery; and likewise he who marrieth her that is put away from her husband committeth adultery.' Therefore all such are to be repelled from Communion."

Here is the principle which we found to pervade the words of St. Chrysostom. Divorce *a mensa et thoro* was a sort of dissolution of the marriage, but *never so that they could marry again*. This is the idea of all the. ancient writers, and must be borne in mind when we interpret them.

We may well crown our selections with a few words from St. Augustine (A. D. 354–430).

[32] "It may chance that a Christian who has put away his wife for the cause of fornication shall be tempted by

---

[31] Ibid. cap. 6.   [32] *De Conjug. Adult.* lib. I. c. 18.

a woman who has not yet embraced the faith, but who promises to become a Christian, not hypocritically but sincerely, if he will marry her. To such a man the tempter may make these suggestions: 'The Lord has said, Whosoever putteth away his wife save for the cause of fornication, and marrieth another, committeth adultery; but you who have put away your wife for that cause will not commit adultery if you marry another.' To such a suggestion let him answer out of a well instructed heart, that he is indeed guilty of a more heinous adultery who marries another after putting away a wife without the cause of fornication; but that he who puts away a wife for that cause cannot be acquitted of adultery if he marries again; just as he is certainly guilty of adultery who marries a woman who has been put away but not for the cause of adultery, while he is not to be acquitted of adultery who marries a woman who has been put away for that cause; and because the language in Matthew is somewhat obscure, it is more fully expressed in Mark: 'Whosoever putteth away his wife and marrieth another committeth adultery', and likewise in Luke it is not said that some commit adultery and others do not, but that 'whosoever putteth away his wife and marrieth another,' he, without exception, 'committeth adultery.'"

Commenting on Romans, vii. 2, 3, he says:

[33] " The words of the Apostle so often repeated and pressed home, are true and living, sound and plain. A woman cannot begin to be the wife of a second husband unless she has ceased to be the wife of the first. Now she ceases to be the wife of the first if he dies, not if he fornicates. The wife is, then, lawfully dismissed for

---

[33] Ibid. lib. II. c. 4.

the cause of fornication, but the bond of the former union endures, and *because of it* he becomes guilty who marries her that is put away even for the cause of fornication.

" For as the sacrament of regeneration remains in him who is excommunicated because guilty of some crime, and he lacks not that sacrament even though he never be reconciled to God, so the bond of the marriage contract remaining in the wife who is put away for the cause of fornication, she shall not be free of that bond even though she never be reconciled to her husband; but she shall be free if her husband dies.[34] But the excommunicated man shall not be without the sacrament of regeneration, though not reconciled, because God never dies.

" Furthermore, if we are willing to understand with the Apostle, we cannot say that an adulterous husband is to be reckoned dead, and that therefore his wife may marry another. For though adultery is death—not of the body, but of the soul, which is worse—yet the Apostle was not speaking of this death when he said, ' If her husband be dead let her marry whom she will;' but only of that by which we leave the body. For if by the adultery of a spouse the marriage bond is dissolved the absurdity follows . . . that the woman may be loosed from the bond by her unchastity; and if she is loosed she shall be free from the law of her husband; and so she shall not be an adulteress if she sin with another man, since by adultery she has been freed from her first husband—which is as foolish a thing as could be said, and so far from the truth that no mind that is human, not to

---

[34] This thoroughly disposes of those who say that the prohibition of marriage to the guilty party is *punitive* and not because of the bond, which they declare to be dissolved by adultery.

speak of Christian, can admit it. Really, therefore, a woman is bound as long as her husband liveth; or, to speak more clearly, as long as her husband is in the body. Therefore, in like manner, the husband also is bound as long as his wife is in the body. Hence, if he wishes to dismiss an adulteress let him not marry another, lest he himself commit the fault for which he blames another."

St. Augustine, in his *Retractations*,[35] modestly expresses a fear that he has not been clear enough in the books quoted above. There is certainly no ground for such feeling in the passages we have taken. Like St. Paul, he seems to try to press the truth home, and to make it plainer than plain by iteration.

Very much more might be quoted from his various writings, including his subscription to the Canon of the Council of Milevum (about A. D. 416), which decreed that:

"*According to the Evangelical and Apostolic discipline*, neither a man put away by his wife, nor a woman by her husband, may be married to another, but they shall so remain or be reconciled to each other. If they disregard this they must undergo penance. In which matter we must ask for an imperial law to be promulgated."

How it can ever have been thought that the advocates of divorce *a vinculo* can get any comfort from St. Augustine is a mystery. From the beginning to the end of the period in which he wrote, he has simply piled up statements of the same doctrine. He admits that one *not yet baptized* might pardonably fall into error on this point. He feels that there may be some difficulty arising from St. Matthew xix. 19. But yet, although he

---

[35] II. 57.

attempts no thorough clearing up of that difficulty, he is unswerving in his assertion of the Catholic doctrine always received in the Church. And he also argues[36] (and we have followed him) that the difficulty of supposing a contradiction between that text and the others is really insuperable. He says:

" Suppose that, not at all doubting the truth of what we read in Matthew, we were to ask whether it is then only adultery to take another wife when the first has been put away without cause of fornication, . . . shall we not be answered out of Mark, why ask whether this man be an adulterer and the other not ? ' Whosoever putteth away his wife and marrieth another committeth adultery.' "

St. Augustine pleads very earnestly for the Christian duty of restoring the sinner who has been put away for adultery, and strongly urges that although that, or (failing that) to continue unmarried and unrevengeful, may be very hard to the natural man, yet divine grace is sufficient for either.

Here, for brevity's sake only, let us pause in the consideration of the testimony of the early Church in favour of the indissolubility of marriage. It is strong and clear and overwhelming. There is no difference between the earlier and the later writers, none between East and West. Hermas, Athenagoras and Clement of Alexandria are at one with St. Chrysostom and St. Augustine. Egypt, Carthage, Rome and Constantinople heard the same doctrine from their greatest teachers, and had it enshrined in one of the apostolical canons (48). What is a *consensus*, if this is not ? And they had the greatest possible difficulties to contend with in enforcing this law.

---

[36] *De Adult. Conjug.* c. 12.

Before the conversion of Constantine they had to deal
with converts who had been accustomed either to the
Jewish or the Roman law of divorce, both of which were
scandalously lax. After Christianity became the religion
of the court they were obliged to face and oppose the
ungodly legislation of their own emperors, very much as
we are required to do in this day and country. ·The
Church never had any help in this matter except that
unseen life which is within her. And if the will of the
Holy Ghost had not been what St. Augustine and the
others believed it was, some part of her certainly would
have shewn a different doctrine before the first three
centuries had passed. Some bishops did yield; but we
only read of their action in order that the Church's condemnation of it may be recorded.[37]

All these great men of old who have spoken so clearly
have shewn a marvellous agreement on the main points
of the doctrine, although their reasoning, when they contend for it, follows various lines of thought. From many
different premises they converge to the same conclusions,
which they, no doubt, felt· bound to maintain, because
they knew them to be the doctrine originally delivered.

Of those writers who have been alleged by Bingham
and others to be against indissolubility, none that wrote
before the middle of the fourth century bear any such
testimony. Tertullian was earlier, but he is so obscure
on· this point that he cannot properly be considered as
giving testimony. Dr. Pusey, however, in his note O on
Book II. ad Uxorem (Oxford translation), thinks that
Tertullian is with him in holding remarriage admissible.
The passage is:

[37] See Origen, *Tract. 7 in Matt.*, quoted by Bingham.

" I have but just now, best beloved fellow-servant in the Lord, traced out for thee, as well as I was able, what course should be followed by an holy woman when her husband is, by whatever hap, taken away. Let us now turn to the next best counsel, out of regard to human infirmity, the example of certain women warning us, who, when by divorce or an husband's death, an occasion for continency is offered, have not only thrown away the opportunity of so great a good, but even in marrying have not chosen to remember the rule that first and chiefly they should marry *in the Lord*."

Now, with all reverence for Dr. Pusey, is he not requiring too much of this passage when he says that Tertullian in it " explicitly" (though "incidentally") allows of marriage to a woman who has on adequate grounds divorced her husband ?   For Tertullian speaks of certain known examples as *warnings*, that those who throw away an occasion of continency will not always be careful what sort of union they contract, but have been known to marry in a way *forbidden to Christians by the Scriptures.*

Other passages of Tertullian,[38] Mr. Keble thinks, sustain the doctrine of indissolubility.   They are also alleged on the other side.   They are intricate and confused in expression.   But as they were written after the author's fall into heresy, when he held that even death does not dissolve a marriage, it does not seem likely that he thought divorce could do it.   We need not consider Tertullian.

Of the few later writers that speak for the exception, or seem to speak for it, there are only four whose words may fairly give rise to a doubt.

---

[38] From *Contra Marcion* and *De Monogamia.*

St. Asterius of Amasa (about A. D. 370) says:[39]

" They are no more twain, but one flesh. What therefore God hath joined together let no man put asunder.
So he then spake to the Pharisees: Hear it now ye who
trade in wives; who change them as garments from time
to time; . . . who marry the dowry and the property, but count the persons matter of gain and traffic;
who on slight offence write a bill of divorce, and leave,
as it were, many widows living. Make up your minds,
be entirely convinced of it, that marriages are severed by
nothing save death and adultery."

Mr. Keble goes on to say of Asterius: " He dwells on
the subject long and earnestly, introducing a great variety
of topics, as one who was dealing with a present and
flagrant evil; allowing, however, in conclusion, that if
the husband justly plead adultery as his ground of
divorce, all our approbation and sympathy should go
along with him."

But this writer nowhere speaks of the injured husband
as having a right to *marry again*. His argument stands,
if we understand him, as others clearly did, to be speaking only of separation. And even if this is thought im-
probable in this case, yet it must be remembered that
he "seems to have been perfectly overwhelmed and
scared by the multitude of divorces under the imperial
law."

The second is St. Epiphanius (about A. D. 376), who
says:[40]

---

[39] This I have found only in Bingham and in Mr. Keble's *Argument*, who refers to St. Asterius's Homily, *An liceat dimittere
uxorem*, near the end of Homilies by St. Leo and others, edited
by Raynaud, Lyons, 1623. [40] From Keble's *Argument*. Epiph.
Hæres. lix. 4.

"It is lawful to bear with the weakness of the lay people; and if they cannot quiet themselves on the loss of a first wife, they may join themselves to another after her death. He, indeed, who has had but one wife is in greater praise and honour among all who come into our Churches; but he who cannot rest contented after the death of the first, (or) when separation hath ensued for whatever ground—fornication, adultery or other evil cause—him the Word of God censures not though he be joined to a second wife (or a wife to a second husband), neither doth it declare them cast out from the Church and from life, but bears with him by reason of his infirmity. *Not for him to have two wives at once, the first yet surviving:* but if he be cut off from the first, and if (so it chanced) he be lawfully married to a second, him the holy Word compassionates, and the holy Church of God; especially if such an one be in all things devout, and his conversation after the law of God."

Of this passage Mr. Keble observes that, although it is plainly corrupt, its general drift is clear. It would be interesting to know whether the clause from "(or)" to "evil cause" is a corruption—for that clause alone gives it any value as an argument for the exception; and the clause we have put in italics certainly makes the other one look like an interpolation. Mr. Keble also observes that Epiphanius "alleges no ground from Holy Scripture, but simply states an existing interpretation and custom, and implies his own acquiescence in it."

Acquiescence, in the worldly ways of the Christian empire, must have begun about this time, or soon after it. It would have been a miracle if human nature had everywhere withstood the pressure of the times. In all ages of the Church holy bishops, much taken up with some great need of the times, have been content, upon other points, rather to register the prevailing sentiment than to teach the exact truth. In the fourth century the Arian controversy was a dreadful present evil; and its paramount importance must often have driven many other subjects to the wall. Whereas, some doctors, like St. Gregory Nazianzen, were bold even to preach to the emperor himself against the impiety and inequality of the secular laws of divorce [41] (by which women were punished for adultery, but men were allowed to go free, and by which a man was allowed to put away an adulteress and marry another, but a woman was compelled to live with her sinful husband); yet even so great a bishop as St. Basil, after his consecration, was content to state what law was in actual use, only feebly expressing his dissent from it. But before he was exalted to the episcopate he most clearly stated the law of the Gospel. St. Basil the bishop almost seems to be rebuked beforehand by St. Basil the recluse and student.

About the year 361 he wrote his *Moralia*, a series of heads of Christian morals, each one supported by Scriptural texts alone. In his *Regula lxxiii.* we find:

" 1. The husband must not be separated from his wife nor the wife from her husband unless one of them is taken in adultery or is a hindrance to piety."

This he supports by St. Matt. v. 31, 32; St. Luke xiv. 26; St. Matt. xix. 9; I. Cor. vii. 10, 11.

" 2. It is not possible for one who divorces his wife to marry another, nor for her that is divorced from her husband to be married to another."

This he supports by St. Matt. xix. 9; the very text upon which the advocates of the exception depend.

---

[41] See Keble's *Sequel,* pp. 52–56.

After his ordination to the priesthood, A. D. 364, he writes: [42]

"Husbands love your wives, even though you were foreigners to each other before ye came together in the marriage union. Let this bond of nature, this yoke imposed by benediction, be the joining together of the separated. . . . The wife must needs endure her husband although he be rough, although he be even wild in temper, *and on no plea consent to tear asunder the union.*"

Up to this time St. Basil's recorded opinions seem all against any exception to the Indissolubility. But in the year 370 he was consecrated bishop of Cæsarea, and in 374 he wrote a *Canonical Epistle* to St. Amphilochius, bishop of Iconium; "in which, as he states at the commencement, he partly recites what he had heard from those before him, partly reasons things out of himself in harmony with those traditions." In other words he tries to make himself a mouthpiece of the accepted views of his day and people. His sentences were afterwards adopted as canons in the East, but were not given as such by him in the first place, as their very form will shew.

"Can. 9. It is true that *our Lord's decision* concerning the unlawfulness of withdrawing from marriage except for fornication doth, if its meaning be carried out, appertain *equally to husbands and wives. The custom however* is not so; for in respect of the wives we find great strictness: the Apostle saying, 'He that is joined to an harlot is one body;' [43] and Jeremiah, 'If a wife be married to another husband, she shall not return to her own husband, but she shall be altogether polluted;' [44] and again,

---

[42] *Hexæmeron*, viii. § 5, 6; t. 1, 68. [43] I. Cor. vi. 16. [44] Jere. iii. 1.

'He that retaineth an adulteress is foolish and impious.'
Whereas *custom enjoins* that husbands who are even
adulterers and living in fornication be retained by their
wives. So I know not whether she who cohabits with
a divorced man can be called an adulteress. For in that
case the blame attaches to her who has put him away,
for whatever cause she withdrew from the marriage. For
if being beaten she cannot endure the blows, she ought
rather to bear it than be separated from her husband; or
if she cannot bear pecuniary loss, neither is this a just
excuse. Or if it is because he lives in fornication we
have not this rule in our ecclesiastical custom; yea
neither is a woman commanded to be separated from an
unbelieving husband, but to remain because of the uncertainty of the event: 'For how knowest thou, O wife,
whether thou shalt save thy husband?' And so she that
forsaketh is an adulteress if she have gone to another
man, but the forsaken husband is worthy of pardon and
she that cohabits with him is not condemned. If however the husband depart from his wife and betake himself to another, both he is an adulterer because he makes
her to commit adultery, and she who cohabits with him
is an adulteress, because she transferred another woman's
husband to herself."

If these are St. Basil's own opinions he changed very
much in ten years. But surely he is rather giving an
account of the customs which he found established in
Cæsarea, customs which seemed strange indeed to him,
and for which he could not account. He was drawing
near the end of a life which, if not long, was full of
labour; and he was probably worn out by his severe
conflicts with the Arians and by his great austerities.
He may have felt himself unable to contend against the

prevailing state of things as to divorce. *After an illness* he went on and answered the other questions of Amphilochius in the following year.

"Can. 21. If a husband living with his wife but dissatisfied with the marriage fall into fornication we judge such an one a fornicator, and are more stringent towards him in our penalties. Yet have we no canon for bringing him under the charge of adultery, if the sin take place with one not bound in marriage. For while 'the adulteress,' saith he, 'shall be utterly defiled, and shall not return to her husband,' and 'he that retaineth an adulteress is senseless and profane,' the unchaste husband nevertheless is not to be debarred from intercourse with his wife. And so the wife must receive her husband coming home from his fornication, but the husband must send away her that is defiled from his house. *Of all this again it is not easy to give an account:* but custom has thus prevailed."

Does not St. Basil here speak *satirically* of the prevailing ecclesiastical law?

"Can. 48. She that is forsaken of her husband, in my judgment, ought to remain (as she is). For if our Lord said: 'Whoso leaveth his wife except for the cause of fornication causeth her to commit adultery', by calling her an adulteress, he hath excluded her from a union with another; it being impossible for the husband to be guilty, as causing adultery, and the wife to be without blame; denominated as she is an adulteress by the Lord on account of her connexion with another man."

Lastly St. Basil reports not the custom of Cæsarea, but the decree of our Lord, and the penalty that would be inflicted if the ancient laws still prevailed.

"As to the man who quits the wife lawfully joined to him and marries another: by the Lord's decree he incurs the sentence of adultery. And it was enacted by our fathers that such should be Mourners for a year, Hearers for two years, Prostrators three years, and in the seventh year should take their stand with the faithful: and so to be deemed worthy of the offering, if with tears they repent."

The one remaining ancient author in favour of the exception has been quoted as St. Ambrose. But as he is now universally believed to be another person, he is commonly known as Ambrosiaster. He says (about A. D. 384) on I. Cor. vii. 10, 11:

"The Apostle's advice is, that if a wife depart by reason of the ill life of her husband, she henceforth remain unmarried or be reconciled to her husband. But, saith he, if she cannot contain herself, because she is not minded to fight against the flesh, let her be reconciled to her husband. For it is not permitted to a woman to marry, if she have sent away her husband by reason of fornication or apostacy, . . . because the meaner party has not the same rule to abide by as the more dignified. However, should he have apostatised, as she may not marry another so neither may she return to him.

" Neither may the husband put away the wife. Understand, however, except for the cause of fornication. And there he did not go on and say, as concerning the woman, But if he depart let him so remain: because the husband may marry if he have put away an offending wife: the husband not being bound by the law as the wife is; for the head of the woman is the man." [45]

---

[45] In App. Op. St. Ambrose. Ed. Benedict, ii. 161,

This writer's argument is founded upon the untenable and unchristian idea of the inequality of the sexes. He thinks the greater honour of the man lies in greater indulgence to the flesh. He does not think that permission to a Christian to marry after divorce can be upheld except by this corrupt Jewish principle.

Then on verse 15 he says:

" If the infidel depart for hatred of God, the believer will not be guilty of dissolving the marriage. . . . The reverence of marriage is not due to him who abhors the author of marriage; that marriage, being invalid, which is without devotion to God: and therefore there is no sin in him who is divorced for God's sake if he unite himself to another."

This passage is certainly of no avail to those who would maintain divorce for desertion of one Christian spouse by another. On the contrary, it shews that verse 15 was taken to refer only to those unions which could not be made to be marriage according to " God's holy ordinance," and which therefore were pronounced "invalid " from the beginning.

Now, these four are absolutely all the ancient authors who can be cited in favour of the exception by any device: St. Asterius, " overwhelmed and scared," speaking not quite clearly; St. Epiphanius, if the passage is not corrupt as it looks; St. Basil, either contradicting himself or intending to give the words of men rather than of God; and the spurious St. Ambrose, with his truly Semitic licence to men as against women. There is not a council nor a canon.

On the other hand, in order to keep within our space, only a few selections have been given from the testimony which places the doctrine of indissolubility beyond all

doubt as that of the primitive Church. It is much to be
desired that a new edition of Mr. Keble's *Argument* may
render this mass of testimony accessible to the public.
It is of this work Dr. Pusey speaks in a letter referred
to by a correspondent of the *Church Times* of November
26, 1886. Dr. Pusey wrote in 1884 : " I always say, if
asked, my own opinion is that the innocent party in the
ancient Church was allowed to marry, but dearest J(ohn)
K(eble) thought the contrary, and wrote against my
statement in my note on Tertullian, which implied a very
strong conviction on his part." Further on Dr. Pusey
says a thing that is nothing less than surprising, as
coming from him, about the ground of his opinion :
" There are *three local councils*[46] (one of them Roman)
which I got out of Coteler, *Patres Ap.*, which I do not
think can be explained away. Dearest J. K. thought
otherwise."

And this brings us to the medieval Church. For Dr.
Pusey in his note, after citing some of the Fathers given
above on one side or other of the question, proceeds to
his canons of " local councils." Instead of only three
he gives eight, which seem to him to prove the exception. But they are simply local and temporary enact-
ments, and such as they are, it is not clear that they were
meant to establish the exception. All but one of these
councils are later than A. D. 750. The early one was
held at Vannes, in Brittany, A. D. 465, and does not seem
to have been important. Its canon is :

" Such as have left their wives (as is said in the Gospel
' Save for the cause of fornication '), and without proof
of adultery have married others, we declare to be excommunicated."

---

[46] The italics are ours.

This only treats of the exception in a negative way, and the canon may very well have been passed to meet a special case in which the exception did not exist, and to justify individual bishops in dealing with scandals. We know that in our own days some demand "a more explicit canon," not esteeming the Word of God to be law sufficient.

Of the force of this canon in the Latin Church we may judge from the fact that three centuries later (774) when Charlemagne entered Rome[47] "as the deliverer of the Church, which led soon after to his coronation as emperor of the West, the pope, Adrian I., laid before him the code of canons of the Roman Church containing the express words of the" Apostolical Canon 48 and of the Milevitan Canon quoted above. "In this Adrian was following the example of his predecessor Pope Zachary, A. D. 747, in a long answer to divers ecclesiastical questions, propounded by Pepin, Charlemagne's father, and the other nobles of France. Evidently it was a prime point in their discipline, but as yet imperfectly received in France."

Of the others of Dr. Pusey's eight councils, four may be regarded as practically only two.[48] The same canon which was passed by the Roman Council under Pope Eugenius II. (A. D. 826), was renewed under Leo IV. (A. D. 853).

" No man, but for the cause of fornication, may quit his wife, and give himself to another: with that one exception the right thing is, that the transgressor should be united again in the bond of the former marriage."

---

[47] Keble's *Sequel*, p. 183.   [48] Perhaps these, with Vannes, make the " three " referred to in Dr. Pusey's letter above.

To the same effect is a provincial canon of Bourges (A. D. 1031), adopted at Limoges the same year.

" That such as without guilt of fornication put away their wives, take no others as long as their first wives are living, but that there be mutual reconciliation."

Now of these two (or four) councils it may fairly be maintained that while the second pair speak of the question only by implication, the first probably put in the clause "except for fornication," because our Lord had done so in the Gospel, and meant the words to be taken as the text has been taken,[49] as if there were two members to it, thus: " Whoso putteth away his wife, except for fornication committeth adultery," and " whoso marrieth another committeth adultery." The following decision of the Council of Friuli (A. D. 791) fairly supports this idea :

" It was decreed that when the marriage bond was loosed because of fornication, the husband may not lawfully take another wife, so long as the adulteress lives ; nor may she take another husband, whether he whom she has shamelessly wronged be living or dead. For although we read in the holy Gospel that the Lord said, 'A man might put away his wife only for fornication,' we do not read that he permitted him to marry another in the lifetime of the first: nay, it is held as unquestionable that he forbade it altogether. For his words are, ' Whosoever shall marry her that is divorced committeth *adultery.*' . . . Now since a clause is interposed here of doubtful meaning, *i. e.,* 'except for fornication,' there is room of course for an enquiry whether that clause is referred to the permission only to put away a wife, or to the other point also, *i. e.,* to the

---

[49] See Corn. a Lapide *in loco.*

taking of another wife in her lifetime: *q. d.*, 'He who puts away his wife and marries another, except for fornication, is an adulterer.' And therefore we have caused diligent examination to be made of the commentary of the learned St. Jerome . . . whereby it became immediately evident that the clause relates solely to the permission to put away. . . . The husband ought not to imitate the crime of the adulterous wife; nor if she, by her whoredom hath divided into three the two, or rather the one flesh, ought he to divide it into four. So that one may clearly understand that as long as she lives, though in adultery, it is not lawful for the husband to contract a second marriage, nor can he do so with impunity."

Even taking Dr. Pusey's councils at their worst, they are only the equivalent of our General Convention canons. They tacitly provide that " the innocent party " shall be exempt from excommunication. The other three councils are Verberie (A. D. 752), Compiègne (757), and Tribur (895). These do *not* make an exception of ordinary adultery, but only allow remarriage in favour of the spouse sinned against by incestuous adultery or some other extraordinary, unnatural crime. They floundered a little in considering peculiarly shocking cases.

On the other hand, besides the great councils already quoted and shewn to have been generally accepted,[50] we have that of Nantes (A. D. 658) given by Dr. Pusey as forbidding remarriage; and the Second Council of Soissons (A. D. 744), which says:

---

[50] Mr. Keble thinks the Apostolic canon 48 and the 105th African canon (Milevit.) were accepted by the Ecumenical Councils of Ephesus and Chalcedon respectively.

"We enact that while the husband is alive no other take his wife, nor while the husband is alive let a woman take another; for a husband ought not to dismiss his wife save when the cause of fornication is detected."[51]

And the Council of Hertford, English (A. D. 673), enacted:

"That none quit his own wife except, as the holy Gospel teaches, on account of fornication.

"That supposing any to have expelled his own wife united to him in lawful matrimony, if he choose to be a Christian indeed, he must connect himself with no other woman, but must so abide or be reconciled to his own wife."

Dr. Pusey argues that this council could not have meant to deny the exception because Archbishop Theodore, who presided, permits divorce and remarriage in his *Penitential.* So he does; and that for many and light reasons, such as desertion, or captivity even, but only to the man. The fact is that Theodore, who came from the East, was filled with very lax Oriental notions on the subject of marriage before he learned the truth in the West. His *Penitential* was written some time before he went to England, and reflects the condition of the Eastern Church in his day. When he met his bishops at Hertford he had received better instruction and had profited by it.[52]

---

[51] Can. 9, Conc. ix. 292. [52] By comparing Eastern law as given by St. Basil, Theodore, and the Patriarch Alexius, it will be seen to have been very fluctuating and to have undergone marvellous changes. The present law is more strict than Theodore's and more just than St. Basil's. Contrast with these changes the permanency of the Catholic law.

Other English canons uphold the same doctrine of Indissolubility, without exception, up to the last, Canon CVII. of the Canons of 1603, according to which:

" In all sentences pronounced only for divorce and separation *a thoro et mensa*, there shall be a caution and restraint inserted in the act of the said sentence, That the parties so separated shall live chastely and continently; neither shall they, during each other's life, contract matrimony with any other person. And for the better observation of this last clause, the said sentence of divorce shall not be pronounced until the party or parties requiring the same have given good and sufficient caution and security into the court that they will not any way break or transgress the said restraint or prohibition."

Thus the law of indissolubility to which the British bishops subscribed at Arles, and which St. Augustine of Canterbury brought from Rome with him, is the law of the Church of England to-day. There is a curious superstition in some minds to the effect that acts of Parliament in some way affect the law of the Church. It is hard to understand why any should think so when it is known that the representative part of Parliament is from two other realms beside England, and consists of persons of all religions or of none, only the clergy of the Church of England being excluded: and when the Canon [83] law provides for the excommunication of any one who shall affirm that the sacred Synod of the nation is not the true Church of England by representation. The Parliament can no more change the law of the Church of England than the Congress of the United States can change the law of this Church.

---

[83] Can. CXXXIX. of 1603.

For the rest of the Western Church the same holy tradition and law has found its final expression in the VII. Canon of the Council of Trent, as follows:

" If any man shall say that the Church errs when she teaches, as she has taught in accordance with evangelical and apostolic doctrine, that the bond of marriage cannot be dissolved on account of the adultery of either party; or when she teaches that neither of them, even an innocent party who has not given cause by adultery, can contract another marriage while the other party lives; or when she teaches that the husband who puts away an adulterous wife and marries another, and also the wife who puts away an adulterous husband and marries another is guilty of adultery, let him be anathema.

" If any man shall say that the Church errs when she decrees that a separation of married persons from the bed of each other, that is to say, of their cohabitation for a time, certain or uncertain, may take place for many causes, let him be anathema."

The position of the Eastern Church has already been stated. The difference between the East and the West was distinctly defined at the Council of Florence, though it was not much dwelt upon.

And now, in final reply to those who say there is no *consensus* of the voice of Christendom on this question, it may justly be said, You are wrong. There is a *consensus*. The Church at first received and will ever hold the law that our Lord gave in private conference with his apostles, which he first gave in Genesis, which repeals and supersedes every other law, which allows neither party to marry so long as they both shall live, which makes the woman equal to the man. So the whole Church believed in the beginning—so a goodly part has believed ever since—so the majority of the Church teaches now.[54]

There is indeed no *consensus* among those who reject this doctrine, and there never has been, in ancient times or modern. They run from one cause for dissolution to twenty. They differ in every way. Some of them say the bond is broken by the sinful act itself. Others say it is broken only by the authority of the State. Others say it is broken by the will of the injured party, who may, if he chooses, condone the offence. It needs not much thinking to run out each of these theories into glaring absurdities, as St. Austin has done with the first of them. Nor have those who try to stay the destructive process, after they have begun it, any ground in reason. Dr. Woolsey of Yale College, for example, holds that only adultery can justify divorce, because it so injures the innocent party as to destroy the bond. But Dr. Hodge of Princeton thinks that wilful desertion works exactly the same destruction; because one who refuses to recognise his wife can no more be a husband to her than one in his grave or one who is joined to another woman. Yet he would end the matter here. What, however, is to prevent another doctor from teaching that such cruelty as makes love impossible, or such mental or physical incapacity as would render one incapable of contracting marriage, is also equivalent to death in destroying the existing bond?

[54] The writer of the above paper is very greatly indebted not only to Mr. Keble's *Argument and Sequel* but also to Article III. in the *Church Quarterly Review* for April, 1887, entitled, *Convocation, Divorce, and the Power of the Keys*, and to *The Laws of Marriage*, by John Fulton, D. D., LL. D.

There is no way of preserving marriage but by a strict holding to the terms in which the Church orders it to be contracted: "So long as ye both shall live;" "Till death us do part." Let those who say that divorces ought to be allowed among us think of one making that agreement solemnly before God while yet a former husband or wife is living with whom he first took the same vows. Let them think of the priest solemnly bidding them to have "the dreadful Day of Judgment" in mind, and then going on to dictate such perjury to them. Then let them try to get the service altered and see what God will let them do in that way. Our ancient Marriage Service is a witness of the Catholic "*consensus*" that we have the blessing to have inherited. Of itself it is law enough for us. The canon law also of our Mother Church is yet untouched. May her rulers be kept by God's grace from consenting to any change. There is no English Church-law later than the Canons of 1603. Would that there were no American Church-law later than that on the subject of divorce! or at least that the exception might be stricken out of our canon. That exception is a treasonable blot which we ought to pray and work to have removed. As long as it stands it will be taken as a canonical declaration by the Church, in direct contradiction to her Marriage Service, that remarriage is lawful, and that it is blessed of God. Because it is a contradiction of the law of Christ the clergy ought to contend against it in every way; not only by trying to have it repealed, but by refusing Confirmation and Holy Communion to those who are so "married." They ought to teach the people to separate from the company of those who are joined otherwise than as God's Word doth allow. Divorce is becoming too respectable of late years.

Charity to the souls of our acquaintance and of our posterity requires that it should be ostracised. To adopt a famous expression of some years since, DIVORCE MUST BE MADE ODIOUS.

❧The Anointing of the Sick.

The Church of England and the Protestant Episcopal Church in America have discussed and used six of the sacraments of the Church; but until recently the Sacrament of Extreme Unction has received little attention and less use.

Some difficulty is felt by members of our Church on account of the name *Extreme* Unction, thinking that by that name is implied that the anointing is only to be made when the sick person is *in extremis*. But the *Necessary Doctrine and Erudition for any Christian Man*, one of our first books set out by authority after our separation from the Roman obedience, explains the term thus: "For the truth is, that the holy fathers of the Church did neither call this sacrament the Extreme Unction (that is to say, the last unction) because it should be ministered last and after all other sacraments, neither yet did they ordain that the same should be ministered only when sick men should be brought unto the extreme pangs of death; but they did call it by the said name of Extreme Unction because it is the last in respect of the other inunctions which be ministered before in the other sacraments of Baptism and Confirmation (in both which sacraments Christian men be also anoiled and anointed)."

When the anointings in Baptism, Confirmation, and Holy Orders were dropped from our Book of Common

Prayer we only lost appropriate accessories; but in losing the anointing of the sick, the whole sacrament of Extreme Unction was lost, and nothing was left us but the unsacramental form of Visitation of the Sick.

In considering this subject, let us first see the scriptural authority for the sacrament, then find out what references are made to it by early writers; lastly, read the authorised declarations of the Greek, Roman, and Anglican Churches on the subject.

The two passages in the Holy Scriptures which bear on this sacrament are St. Mark vi. 13, " And they cast out many devils and anointed with oil many that were sick and healed them;" and St. James v. 14, 15, " Is any sick among you? let him call for the elders (*presbyterous*) of the Church; and let them pray over him, anointing him with oil in the name of the Lord. And the prayer of faith shall save the sick, and the Lord shall raise him up; and if he have committed sins, they shall be forgiven him."

The latter passage is absolutely plain and simple. None of the other sacraments are commanded in clearer language; and some which we hold have far less apparent commandment than this.

Our definition of a sacrament is fulfilled to the letter. There is the " outward and visible sign," anointing with oil and the prayer of faith; "the inward and spiritual grace given unto us," salvation, raising up, and pardon of sins; "ordained by Christ himself" either in the passage quoted from St. Mark or during the forty days between his Resurrection and Ascension; "as a means whereby we receive the same, and a pledge to assure us thereof." Some theologians hold the opinion that Christ ordained this sacrament when he sent his disciples two and two before his face; but more favour the theory that he did not institute it until after he rose again from the dead and spoke to the apostles whom he had chosen " of the things pertaining to the kingdom of God." No writer supposes for an instant that St. James did more than promulgate the doctrine which he had received from the Lord.

It is rather startling, after reading this most clear and unequivocal command of the apostle, to find in Dean Alford's Commentary this assertion, "Among the daring perversions of Scripture by which the Church of Rome has defended her superstitions, there is none more patent than that of the present passage. The apostle is treating of a matter totally distinct from the occasion and the object of Extreme Unction." Bishop Wordsworth seems to think the command was to exercise miraculous gifts of healing, which have since ceased; but he acknowledges that the Greek and Latin Churches have continued its use until this day. Bishop Browne on the Thirty-nine Articles devotes only three pages, in a volume of 870, to this subject, and concludes by this dogmatic assertion: " We admit the proper use of Confirmation, Confession, Orders, and Matrimony; but Extreme Unction we neither esteem to be a sacrament nor an ordinance of the Church at all."

The bishop in the little space he allows to this topic makes two serious mistakes as to matters of fact. He says: "In the modern Church of Rome it is administered where all hope of recovery is gone, and generally no food is permitted to be taken after it." It is true that Extreme Unction is usually given when the sick person is in danger of death; but the statement about the food is unfounded. On the contrary a foolish superstition on

the subject is condemned by the Synod of Exeter, A. D.
1287 (Wilkins' *Concilia* ii. 295). Again he says, "The
Greeks still practice unction, but do not esteem it a sacrament." He was corrected in this particular by Archbishop Lycurgus of Syria, in 1870 at their conference,
who assured him that the Greeks do hold Unction to be
a sacrament, although not necessary to salvation. The
most extreme writer in the Roman Catholic Church
would be of exactly the same opinion.

It is pleasant to turn to Bishop Forbes of Brechin on
the Articles and to find him frankly regretting the disuse
of Unction in our Church, and saying: "There is nothing to hinder the revival of the apostolic and Scriptural
custom of anointing the sick, whensoever any devout
person may desire it." "It is indeed difficult," he says,
"to say on what principle it could be refused."

He also says "the unction of the sick is the lost pleiad
of the Anglican firmament. One must at once confess
and deplore that a distinctly Scriptural practice has
ceased to be commanded in the Church of England.
Excuses may be made of 'corrupt following of the
apostles,' in that it was used, contrary to the mind of St.
James, when all hope of the restoration of bodily health
was gone; but it cannot be denied that there has been
practically lost an apostolic practice, whereby, in case of
grievous sickness, the faithful were anointed and prayed
over, for the forgiveness of their sins, and to restore
them, if God so willed, or to give them spiritual support
in their maladies."

The following letter from Canon Wilberforce appeared
in the *Birmingham Gazette* and was widely copied in
England and America.

"THE DEANERY, SOUTHAMPTON,
April 26, 1889.

"My dear Sir:

"I cannot reply to your letter as you ask me 'in one line.' I have no shadow of doubt that I was healed by the Lord's blessing upon his own word recorded in St. James v. 15, 16, but as in so many cases, there was sufficient margin of time and possibility of change of tissue between the anointing and the recovery to justify the sceptic in disconnecting the two, and therefore my experience has been of more value in strengthening my own faith than in the direction of public testimony. I can only say that my internal ailment was of such a nature that leading surgeons declared it to be incurable except at the cost of a severe operation, which leading physicians thought me unable at the time to endure with safety. While endeavouring at the seaside to gain strength for the operation, the passage (St. James v. 15, 16) was impressed with indescribable force upon my mind. I resisted it and reasoned with myself against it for two months. I again came up to London and settled in a house near the eminent surgeon that I might undergo the operation, but the spiritual pressure increased until at last I sent for elders, men of God, full of faith, by whom I was prayed over and anointed, and in a few weeks the internal ailment entirely passed away. This was the Lord's doing and it was marvellous in mine eyes!

"I am faithfully yours,

· "BASIL WILBERFORCE."

The foregoing letter is *only* cited as shewing the divine command, and not as approving of the writer's view of the matter nor of the manner in which the anointing was done, of which the present writer knows nothing.

To a mind unwarped by prejudice it must be clear that St. James was right, and consequently those who do not desire the use of unction are wrong.

The following shews that among the Lutherans some have considered this subject and decided to obey St. James's injunction. In the *Correspondenzblatt*, December 1857, Löhe published the plan of a liturgy for "Apostolical visitation of the sick" with anointing. A distinguished lady who was afflicted with an almost incurable malady desired on her sick bed to be treated in accordance with James v. 14, *et seq.* The anointing is to be performed with the following words: "In obedience to the holy command, I anoint thee herewith in the name of the Lord, of the Father+, of the Son+, of the Holy Ghost+. To Him, the Triune God, be thanks and honour; but to thee come healing and peace if it be his holy will." (*Vide Lutheran Quarterly Review.* "The Liturgical Question." January, 1890.)

Martin Luther called this portion of God's Word " an epistle of straw;" but as we are bound to " unfeignedly believe all the Canonical Scriptures of the Old and New Testaments," we cannot so easily dismiss this plain command.

The first undoubted reference to this sacrament by the early writers of the Church is in an Epistle of Innocent I. to Decentius in the year 416. Decentius wrote to ask if a bishop might anoint the sick, and Innocent replied that a bishop might do what presbyters were commanded by St. James to do. He says, " The bishops, being hindered by other occupations, cannot go to all sick persons. But if a bishop either can or thinks it meet to visit anyone, he to whom it appertaineth to make the chrism itself can unhesitatingly bless and touch with the chrism."

Observe, in passing, that the earliest passage extant distinctly reserves the blessing of the oil to the bishop. Innocent adds, "For on penitents it cannot be poured, because it is a *kind of sacrament.* For to whom the remaining sacraments are denied, how can it be thought that one kind is allowed."

Cæsarius of Arles, A. D. 502, says, " Let him who is sick receive the body and blood of Christ, and then let him anoint his poor body, that that which is written may be fulfilled in him, ' Is any sick among you ? ' " etc., etc.

There is some reason to suppose that devout persons were allowed to carry home the oil blessed by the bishop, to use in case of necessity ; just as the Blessed Sacrament was taken home by the faithful and received before all other food on subsequent days.

In the sacramentary of St. Gregory the Great, A. D. 590, there is a short office entitled *Orationes ad visitandum infirmorum,* in which there is a direction of which the following is a translation : "Anoint him with holy oil and say, . . . Almighty God . . . have mercy upon this thy servant, and grant him remission of all his sins, and recovery from his present sickness by this unction and by our deprecation." (*Vide* Crouch.)

This is about all which we have in the ancient writers on the subject; but Bishop Forbes wisely says: " The meagreness of tradition is replaced in some measure by the agreement of the Greeks, the Armenians, the Nestorians and all the Orientals, with the Latins on the subject; so that one cannot doubt that a sacramental use of anointing the sick has been from the beginning."

Now, let us see what the authoritative teaching of the Greek and Roman Church is.

First, *The Orthodox Confession of Faith of the Catholic and Apostolic Church of the East*, which was drawn up by Peter Mogilas, Metropolitan of Kieff, the father of Russian theology (d. 1647), or under his direction, and was revised and adopted by the Græco-Russian synod at Jassy, 1643, signed by the Eastern patriarchs, and approved again by the synod of Jerusalem, 1672." (Schaff.)

"Question 117. What is the seventh sacrament (*mysterion*) of the Church?

"Ans. Blessed oil (*to euchelaion*), which was instituted by Christ himself. For when he sent his disciples two and two (Mark vi. 13), 'they anointed with oil many that were sick and healed them,' which the universal Church afterwards received as a religious custom, as appears from the Epistle of St. James (v. 14) where he says, 'Is any sick among you?' etc.

"Question 118. What is to be observed by us in this mystery?

"Ans. First, that this mystery, with all its consequences, should be administered by priests and no others. Second, that the oil be pure and not mixed with anything (*choris tinos artumatos*), and that the sick person be devoted to the orthodox Catholic faith, and that he should shortly before have made confession of whatever he has done wrong, to his spiritual father. Third, that during the anointing that prayer be said, which sets forth the power and efficacy of this sacrament.

"Question 119. What are the fruits of this sacrament?

"Ans. The benefits and fruits of this sacrament St. James narrates (in the place quoted) undoubtedly the forgiveness of sins, the salvation of the soul and even health of body, which, however, is not always obtained, yet remission of sins to the penitent soul is always obtained."

The second quotation is from the *Confession of Dositheus*, or *The Eighteen Decrees of the Synod of Jerusalem*, which is a refutation of Cyril Lucar's heresies.

" We believe the evangelical sacraments of the Church to be seven. Neither a greater nor less number do we admit of the sacraments of the Church." . . . And the seventh, he says, is: " Holy oil or Extreme Unction spoken of in Mark and promulgated fully by James, the Lord's brother."

The third Greek authority to be quoted is *The Longer Catechism of the Orthodox, Catholic, Eastern Church*, which was written by Philaret and examined and approved by the Most Holy Governing Synod.

" Question 364. What is unction with oil ?

" Unction with oil is a sacrament, in which, while the body is anointed with oil, God's grace is invoked on the sick, to heal him of spiritual and bodily infirmities.

" Question 365. Whence is the origin of this sacrament ?

" From the apostles, who, having received power from Jesus Christ, anointed with oil many that were sick, and healed them (Mark vi. 13).

" The apostles left this sacrament to the priests of the Church, as is evident from the following words of the Apostle James: ' Is any sick ? ' " etc.

These quotations from undoubted Greek authorities shew that the Greek Church does regard Unction as a sacrament, and also that it puts healing of the body as a possible fruit of the anointing, while spiritual benefits are undoubted.

The Roman Catholic doctrine is found clearly and definitely set forth in the decrees of the Council of Trent. (Session xiv., held November 25, 1551.)

"It hath also seemed good to the holy synod to subjoin to the preceding doctrine on Penance, the following on the sacrament of Extreme Unction, which by the fathers was regarded as being the completion not only of penance but also of the whole Christian life, which ought to be a perpetual penance. First, therefore, as regards its institution it declares and teaches, that our most gracious Redeemer who would have his servants at all times provided with salutary remedies against all the weapons of all their enemies, as, in the other sacraments, he prepared the greatest aids, whereby, during life, Christians may preserve themselves whole from every more grievous spiritual evil, so did he guard the close of life by the sacrament of Extreme Unction, as with a most firm defence. For though our adversary seeks and seizes opportunities, all our life long, to be able in any way to devour our souls; yet is there no time wherein he strains more vehemently all the powers of his craft to ruin us utterly, and, if he can possibly, to make us fall even from trust in the mercy of God, than when he perceives the end of our life to be at hand.

"Chapter I. Of the Institutions of the Sacrament of Extreme Unction.

"Now this Sacred Unction of the sick was instituted by Christ our Lord, as truly and properly a sacrament of the new law, instituted indeed in Mark, but recommended and promulgated to the faithful by James the apostle and brother of our Lord. 'Is any man,' he saith, 'sick among you?' etc. In which words, as the Church hath learned from apostolic tradition received from hand to hand, he teaches the matter, the form, the proper minister, and the effect of the salutary sacrament. For the Church has understood the matter thereof to be oil blessed by a bishop. For the unction very aptly represents the grace of the Holy Ghost, with which the soul of the sick person is invisibly anointed, and furthermore that those words, ' By this unction,' etc., is the form.

" Chapter II. Of the Effect of this Sacrament.

" Moreover, the thing signified and the effect of this sacrament are explained in these words: ' And the prayer of faith shall save the sick man, and the Lord shall raise him up, and if he be in sins they shall be forgiven him.'

" For the thing here signified is the grace of the Holy Ghost; whose anointing cleanses away sins, if there be any still to be expiated, as also the remains of sins; and raises up and strengthens the soul of the sick person, by exciting in him a great confidence in the divine mercy; whereby the sick being supported, bears more easily the inconveniences and pains of his sickness; and more readily resists the temptations of the devil who lies in wait for the heel; and at times obtains bodily health when expedient for the soul.

" Chapter III. Of the Minister of this Sacrament and the Time when it ought to be Given.

" And now as to prescribing who ought to administer this sacrament, this also was not obscurely delivered in the words above cited. For it is there shewn that the proper ministers of this sacrament are the presbyters of the Church; by which name are to be understood, in that place, not the elders by age, or the foremost in dignity amongst the people, but either bishops or priests by bishops rightly ordained by the imposition of the hands of the priesthood. It is also declared that the unction is to be applied to the sick, but to those especially who lie in such danger as to seem to be about to depart this life; whence also it is called the sacrament of the departing.

"And if the sick should, after having received this unction, recover, they may again be aided by the succour of this sacrament when they fall into another like danger of death. Wherefore they are on no account to be hearkened to who, against so manifest and clear a sentence of the Apostle James, teach either that this unction is a human figment or is a rite received from the fathers, which neither has a command from God nor a promise of grace; nor those who assert that it has already ceased, as though it were only to be referred to the grace of healing in the primitive Church; nor those who say that the rite and usage which the holy Roman Church observes in the administration of this sacrament is repugnant to the sentiment of the Apostle James, and that it is therefore to be changed into some other; nor finally those who affirm that this Extreme Unction may without sin be contemned by the faithful; for all these things are most manifestly at variance with the perspicuous words of so great an apostle."

Then follow four canons, which simply repeat the above statements with an anathema to those who differ.

The Church of England has quite early laws on this subject. They may be found in Volume II. of Thorpe's *Anglo-Saxon Laws*. The four commonly quoted are as follows :

"Our Archbishop Theodore (A. D. 680) contrasts the customs of the Greeks and Latins: According to the Greeks a presbyter may make the chrism for the sick, if need be ; according to the Roman use it is not allowed, save to the bishop only."

Egbert, archbishop of York (A. D. 732), in his extract *de jure Sacerdotali* has the rule, "That according to the enactment of the holy fathers, if any is sick he be diligently anointed with sanctified oil, together with prayers."

Among the canons enacted in the reign of King Edgar (A. D. 967) it is enjoined that "every priest give unction to the sick if they desire it" and "have both baptismal oil and unction for the sick."

The unction of the sick, "*if the sick man desire it*," is enjoined in the Canons of Ælfric (about the end of the tenth century), and a separate portion of the consecrated chrism is directed to be kept for that use. (Crouch.)

In the face of these Anglo-Saxon canons and the rubric in the Visitation of the Sick in the English Prayer Book, which says, "After which confession the priest shall absolve him (if he humbly and heartily *desire it*)." Bishop Browne says, "The English reformers retained a form of anointing the sick in the first Service Book of Edward VI.; though it does not appear that they attributed any sacramental efficacy to it, but merely allowed it to be used ' if the sick person desired it,' with a prayer for pardon of sins and restoration of bodily health."

It is hardly to be supposed that any one of the sacraments would be administered to an adult unless he "desired it;" so it is plainly unfair to imply that unction was only given to sick people since the reformation to humour those who were not wholly free from the ancient customs of the Church.

As to the First Book of Edward VI., attributing "any sacramental efficacy" to Unction, let us refer to the book itself for evidence.

The Office for the Visitation of the Sick provided for the sick person's confession and absolution, then his anointing and then for the administration of the Holy Communion; thus following the ancient order, which was changed in the Roman Church, so that unction came last. The rubric is:

"*If the sick person desire to be anointed, then shall the priest anoint him upon the forehead or breast only, making the sign of the cross, saying thus:*

"As with this visible oil thy body outwardly is anointed, so our heavenly Father, Almighty God, grant of his infinite goodness that thy soul inwardly may be anointed with the Holy Spirit, who is the Spirit of all strength, comfort, relief and gladness."

What could be clearer than the words used in this "form" to express sacramental efficacy?

The prayer continues, "And vouchsafe for his great mercy (if it be his blessed will) to restore unto thee thy bodily health and strength, to serve him; and send thee release of all thy pains, troubles, and diseases, both in body and mind. And howsoever his goodness (by his divine and unsearchable Providence) shall dispose of thee, we, his unworthy ministers and servants, humbly beseech the eternal Majesty to do with thee according to the multitude of his innumerable mercies, and to pardon thee all thy sins and offences committed by all thy bodily senses, passions, and carnal affections; who also vouchsafe mercifully to grant unto thee ghostly strength, by his Holy Spirit to withstand and overcome all temptations and assaults of thine adversary, that in no wise he prevail against thee; but that thou mayest have perfect victory and triumph against the devil, sin, and death, through Christ our Lord, who, by his death, overcame the prince of death; and with the Father and the Holy Ghost evermore liveth and reigneth God, world without end. Amen."

In addition to the Office for Anointing the Sick in the first Reformed Prayer Book, let us see what is said by the Reformers in their book, *The Institution of a Christian Man*, issued by a commission in 1536.

"As touching the sacrament of Extreme Unction, we think it convenient that all bishops and preachers shall instruct and teach the people committed unto their spiritual charge . . . that it shall therefore be very necessary and expedient that all true Christian people do use and observe this manner of anointing of sick persons, with due reverence and honour, as it is prescribed by the holy Apostle St. James . . . how that the holy fathers of the Church . . . thought it convenient to institute and ordain that this manner of anointing of sick men, prescribed by St. James, should be observed continually in the Church of Christ as a very godly and wholesome medicine or remedy to alleviate and mitigate the diseases and maladies as well of the soul as of the body of Christian men. And to the intent the same should be had in more honour and veneration, the said holy fathers willed and taught that all Christian men should repute and account the said manner of anointing among the other sacraments of the Church, forasmuch as it is a visible sign of an invisible grace; whereof the visible sign is the anointing with oil in the Name of God, which oil (from the natural properties belonging unto the same) is a very convenient thing to signify and figure the great mercy and grace of God, and the spiritual light, joy, comfort, and gladness which God poureth out upon all faithful people calling upon him by the inward unction of the Holy Ghost. And the grace conferred in this sacrament is the relief and the recovery of the disease and sickness, wherewith the sick person is then diseased and troubled, and also the remission of his sins, if he be then in sin."

The revision of this book under the name of *A Necessary Doctrine and Erudition for Any Christian Man*, does not make any change in the teaching. It says: " The other two sacraments, Confirmation and Extreme Unction, although they be not of such necessity but that without them men may be saved, yet forasmuch as in the ministration of them, if they be worthily taken, men receive more abundantly ghostly strength, aid, and comfort, they be very wholesome and profitable, and to be desired and reverently received." •

The Prayer Book of 1552 did not have the Office for Anointing the Sick; nor has any subsequent revision replaced it.

Bishop Forbes, however, says that as the Visitation of the Sick is a private office, Unction may be given without any change in the Prayer Book.

The Bishop of Pittsburgh has written a letter on this subject, which he allowed to be printed, and which is well worth repeating in this connexion:

" BISHOP'S HOUSE, SHADY SIDE,
" PITTSBURGH, Feb. 19, 1891.
" Rev. and Dear Sir :

" Concerning Anointing of the Sick, I said this: That, appealing to the Scripture, we seemed to stultify ourselves if we paid no regard whatever to the definite injunction of St. James, especially since there were not wanting those among the Methodists and Baptists (as I know) who observe the practice, and particularly since the modern mind cures and science cures and faith cures (to our mind caricatures of the apostolic method) are bringing the matter very prominently to the front. To my personal knowledge some of our people are becoming infected, and many are enquiring, 'What about St. James?'

"I said there was much to be said in favour of the position taken by a recent writer in the *Church Eclectic* that St. James v. 15, 16, is 'an unrepealed, inspired rubric,' and that if any sick person desired it, I did not see how any priest with the New Testament in his hand could *refuse* the unction. It certainly could do no harm, and the prayer of faith could be none the less the prayer of faith because the oil was used.

"Used as an unction for *recovery* it was a protest against Rome's *Extreme* Unction, and was no longer a 'corrupt following of the apostles.'

"There is no such direct precept concerning Episcopacy, or the Lord's day, or Confirmation, and yet our argument is that the widespread observance of these in the Church gives us the mind of the Church concerning them. The Anglican Church alone has disused it, and that for only a few generations, and *silently*, not by edict.

"With footwashing the case is different, so with the kiss of peace; neither of these has prevailed anywhere for any length of time.

"Nevertheless, there can be nothing compulsory about it, only if the sick *desire it*, only if he 'send for the elders of the Church.'

"And if the answer is made that oil was a remedial agent only, it must be *as much so now* as then. It is the *prayer of faith* which is to be emphasized.

"The *necessarily Episcopal* consecration of the oil is, I should say, not proven, and is more Roman than primitive. I read in the *Dict. Christ. Antiq.* that in early times others than the clergy consecrated the oil, sometimes lay people, male or female, of peculiar sanctity, and that the Gallican Church knew no such restriction as that only bishops should bless it. Such a custom is unknown in the East, where seven presbyters consecrate it.

"Therefore, I decline to consider it an Episcopal prerogative, and I said to my clergy, 'Surely, one who is bidden to say, sanctify this water to the mystical washing away of sin, is competent to ask God's blessing on the anointing oil.'

"This, in brief, is what I believe to be a temperate, scriptural view of the matter. No one has a right to insist upon anointing any man—indeed, here the devout layman, and not at all the clergy, must lead the way.

"Faithfully yours,

"CORTLANDT WHITEHEAD."

The bishop has certainly done good service in allowing this letter to be printed; but neither he nor the retired Bishop of Winchester need apprehend that the clergy will go about forcibly anointing sick people, any more than they will administer any of the other sacraments by force either physical or moral.

It may be thought that Article XXV. forbids Unction of the sick, but if it does it also forbids all "those five commonly called sacraments; that is to say, Confirmation, Penance, Orders, Matrimony and Extreme Unction," and we are not yet, let us hope, sufficiently "broad" to throw away all of these means of grace.

Anyone who wishes to read more fully on this subject should consult Morinus on *Extreme Unction*, Catalani's *Commentary on the Pontificale Romanum*, Chardon's *Histoire des Sacrements*, Vol. III., Baruffaldas's *Commentary on the Rituale Romanum*, Perrone's *Prælectiones Theologicæ*, Vol. VIII., Bellarmine, Martene, St. Thomas Aquinas, Gury's *Compendium Theologiæ Moralis*, and Billuart's *De Extrema Unctione*.

The "matter" of this sacrament is olive oil, pure and unmixed with anything else. The Western Church requires it to be blessed by a bishop, not necessarily by the bishop of the diocese where it is to be used.[1]

It is to be blessed every year on Maundy Thursday, and is then distributed to the priests, and the old oil is destroyed or burned in the lamp before the Blessed Sacrament. Should the oil of the sick become nearly exhausted it may be mixed with unblessed oil.

The Eastern Church allows the oil to be blessed by seven priests, and sometimes by as few as three or even two.

---

[1] A Roman Catholic Archbishop is the authority for this statement. In a letter to the writer he says:

" . . . February 8, 1889.
" Rev. and Dear Sir:

"A bishop can consecrate oil for use in a diocese other than his own. It is not unfrequently done in case of sickness or absence of the ordinary.

"A priest can use the oil of unction in any diocese in which he is permitted to administer the sacraments, without regard to the place in which the oil was blessed.

" Yours sincerely in Dno,
" + . . . Apb."

The " form " is the anointing with oil and prayer over the sick person.

The Roman *Rituale* requires the priest to anoint the sick person upon the eye-lids, ears, nose, lower lip, hands and feet.   Men are also sometimes anointed on their loins, but not women.   Lay people are anointed in the palm of the hand ; but priests on the back of the hand, because they were anointed at their ordination on their palms.   The oil is to be applied by the priest with the right thumb, marking each member with the sign of the cross. The First Prayer Book of Edward VI. provided for anointing, with the sign of the cross, on the forehead or breast only.   It was customary in ancient times to anoint also the seat of the disease ; but this is not now done.

The " minister " of the sacrament is the priest only. The Greeks have several priests at the anointing in *exact* conformity to the words of St. James, " Let him call for the *elders* of the Church."

The persons who receive this sacrament must be sick, and, in the Roman Church, dangerously sick.   For this reason a person condemned to capital punishment is not to be anointed.

Confession and absolution should precede its adminis-tration when possible.

In ancient times the Viaticum was given after Unction ; but now, in the Roman Church, Unction is given last of all.

Anointing may be repeated whenever a person is seri-ously ill.

The benefits of this sacrament are remission of venial sins, and if necessary even mortal sins; the healing of the body,. when God so wills, and the removal of the remains of sin, *i. e.*, "the proneness to evil, torpor and weakness left by past and forgiven sin."

No part of the Church teaches that Unction is necessary for salvation. But we must needs suffer loss if we neglect a means of grace which God has given us in his Church.

There are some practical difficulties in the way of the general use of the anointing of the sick in the American Church.

Many of our bishops would be unwilling to consecrate the oil of the sick. Some do bless the oil ; but most do not. Now the question naturally arises whether it would be better to follow the Eastern method and have seven priests consecrate the oil, or whether one should use the oil blessed by a bishop who is not his own diocesan; if his own bishop decline to provide the oil. The bishop of Pittsburgh thinks a priest may consecrate the oil, as we have seen; but the writer would advocate conformity to the Western use, since the earliest reference to the Anointing of the Sick, in Innocent I.'s letter to Decentius, plainly restricts the making of the chrism to a bishop. As we are Western Christians, why not follow Western traditions in this as in other sacraments ? Would any priest venture to administer Confirmation himself, because the Greek Church allows it, in such a case as that some years ago when Bishop Eastburn refused for years to administer that sacrament in the Church of the Advent, Boston ? The rector, who in that case was a bishop himself (Dr. Southgate), did not even give Confirmation because it would have been an intrusion into the bishop of Massachusetts' jurisdiction.

Many of us, the writer among the number, would scruple to administer Unction without authority, either in the Book of Common Prayer or from the bishop in whose diocese he was working; but since it is a part of our priestly trust received at our ordination, ought we not to pray for its restoration in the Anglican Church, and to do our best to have permission expressly given us to anoint with oil those who earnestly desire it?

"O Blessed Lord, who didst send forth thy disciples to anoint with oil such as were sick; Of thy loving kindness restore to us in this portion of thy Church the comfortable Sacrament of Holy Unction, that not only the sicknesses of our bodies but the diseases of our souls may be driven out by virtue of this holy anointing, and the merits of thy saving Cross; who livest and reignest with the Father and the Holy Ghost, one God, world without end. Amen."

www.ingramcontent.com/pod-product-compliance
Lightning Source LLC
Chambersburg PA
CBHW020847020726
47497CB00005B/1286